FRAGILE BRILLIANCE

ALSO BY ELIOT PARKER

Snapshots: Stories

Breakdown at Clear River

Stacy Tavitt Thrillers

Code for Murder

FRAGILE BRILLIANCE

A RONAN MCCULLOUGH NOVEL
BOOK 1

ELIOT PARKER

ROUGH
EDGES
PRESS

Fragile Brilliance
Paperback Edition
Copyright © 2024 (As Revised) Eliot Parker

Rough Edges Press
An Imprint of Wolfpack Publishing
1707 E. Diana Street
Tampa, Florida 33610

roughedgespress.com

Paperback ISBN 978-1-68549-417-9
eBook ISBN 978-1-68549-416-2

"We sleep safely at night because rough men stand ready to visit violence on those that would harm us."

WINSTON CHURCHILL

FRAGILE BRILLIANCE

CHAPTER 1

The bell-and-hammer alarm clock went off like a firehouse bell.

Ronan McCullough slapped the switch, pulled his arms over his head and then stretched out his body as the slatted sunrays coming through the window tickled his skin. The warmth of it made him feel oddly at peace. It was a weird and rare feeling, and he knew moments like this never lasted for long.

Lying on one side, pressed against Ronan, Ty took long, soft breaths and exhaled slowly.

Ronan turned over and spooned with him, his body melding perfectly with his lover's. Sliding closer, Ronan threw his arm over Ty and for some time just watched him sleep. Then he nuzzled Ty's neck and shoulder, delighting in his wonderful scent. It was faint and pleasant, not too striking or too overwhelming—just fresh and clean. The scent beckoned, and Ronan answered, pressing his lips into Ty's neck and kissing it softly.

"Did the alarm go off yet?" Ty mumbled as Ronan kissed his shoulder.

"It did."

Ty leaned up from the bed. "What time is it? Are we going to be late?"

Ronan sighed and rolled away. The late-afternoon sun now cast a faint yellow hue over the bedroom, which made it warmer. "It's only five p.m. We both have an hour until we have to report in."

Ty yawned and then coughed. He lurched forward but was held still by Ronan. "Sergeant, you can release me. I'm only going to take a shower and get dressed." He laughed and sprang out of bed.

Ty turned around and leaned over the bed, slapping Ronan on the stomach. "I know how you like to sleep, but let's go; you need to get up too." His rich, smooth voice even made commands seem less demanding.

Ronan sat up and lazily ran a hand through his hair. Then he scratched the base of his neck, stretched, eased out of bed, and shuffled into the bathroom. He was stopped in midstride when he found Ty standing naked in front of the mirror. Ronan stepped closer, awed by the hard, lean frame. He tried to tear his gaze away from the magnificent form, but it was no use.

Ty's devilishly handsome features shifted into a knowing grin as he caught Ronan's appreciative gaze. "Quit gawking at me," he bashfully demanded.

Ronan extended outward, open palms and feigned innocence. "I wasn't gawking; I was just admiring the view."

"You're something else, you know that?" Ty smiled. His lips were slightly full—the kind that end in a cute little smirk around the corners. He opened the glass shower door, stepped inside and turned on the water.

"I'm working as the charge nurse in the ER tonight," he added as he emptied shampoo onto both hands and rubbed them together until a foamy lather appeared. "I'll probably put in a little overtime since there's a full moon tonight."

Ronan chuckled and looked at Ty through the frosted glass. "I think we're the only two people who still believe in that old wives' tale."

"That's because we're the ones who have to deal with it when people do stupid things."

Ronan nodded to himself. "That's true."

"What we both need to do is get off of night shift and work during the day like normal people," Ty suggested.

"I like working nights. I make extra money, and I really don't sleep much anyway."

"Except when you're snoring."

Ronan rolled his eyes. He turned on the water, and Ty hissed. "Shit! Thanks a lot! Now the water is freaking cold!"

Ronan winced. "Sorry." He splashed a handful of cold water onto his face and then turned on the towel warmer. The high-end finishes in the bathroom, including the heated towel warmer, slate tile floors and the cream-colored marble countertop, always made Ronan afraid to touch anything. *It's just a bathroom* is what Ty would say as Ronan got ready each evening.

Patting his face dry, Ronan briefly regarded himself in the mirror. That always humbled him, and he often wondered why a young man like Ty would want to be with an older, haggard cop. Ronan's brown hair was closely cropped and youthful, but the weight of his job clearly showed on his taut, weathered face the same time each day. Both arms and sections of his thickset torso and legs were covered with scars and cuts from twenty years of working undercover in the Charleston, West Virginia Police Department.

Ronan exited the bathroom and walked across the bedroom to the closet. The plush white carpet felt good under his feet. He reached into the closet and grabbed the dark slacks, cobalt shirt and red tie checked with blue diamonds. After dressing, he secured his P226 pistol into its holster and clipped his shield onto his belt.

Ty emerged from the shower, water glistening from his body. His flawless olive, Polynesian skin accentuated his dark, pecan-shaped eyes, and those eyes brought out the natural beauty of his oval-shaped face. The dimples on his skin and chin flexed as he looked at Ronan.

"Are you the only sergeant on duty tonight?" Ty asked as he pulled on his blue scrubs.

Ronan struggled to button the cuffs on his dress shirt.

"No. Eric Bonamico is working with me. We're fully staffed tonight, which is rare during the summer. It seems like someone is always on vacation."

"Tell me about it," Ty replied as he tightened the noose-like tie hanging around Ronan's neck. "Now you're ready, Sergeant McCullough." He blushed and kissed Ronan. "I better go. I need to meet with my team before shift starts. I love you. I'll call you later."

Ronan grazed a hand over Ty as he scurried out of the room and then took one final look at himself in the wall mirror. He'd already managed to rumple his shirt and loosen the knot in his tie. *Perfect,* he thought.

As Ronan stepped outside, the relentless August heat started to give way. Kanawha State Forest lay over the hill from their townhouse, and the sun stared at the world through the crystal, clear sky. The glare of the fiery orb withered the trees on the mountains—many of them sagging as if exhausted from the unforgiving heat and humidity. Ronan got inside his Ford F-150 pickup truck, and a burst of stale, warm air hit him forcefully. The sweat immediately began to run down his forehead as he quickly revved the engine and turned on the air-conditioner.

As he turned from Oakwood Road onto Route 119, most of the traffic was leaving downtown Charleston. Cars streamed by in an orderly fashion as most passengers watched the road with meek but direct expressions.

Ronan veered to the right, taking the ramp across the remaining section of Route 119 and merged momentarily onto Interstate 64, traveling east. West Virginia was always a pretty place in the summertime, even the larger cities. He looked to his right for a moment at downtown Charleston. Bathed in golden strands of ethereal light, the city always looked spectacular and regal in the evening as the sun bounced light from Laidley Tower and other downtown office buildings down onto the Kanawha River. The river twinkled like diamonds, disturbed only by the churning water, created by boats and barges traveling up and down the river.

Ronan liked going on patrol. The long drives through the flat, open downtown streets and the winding, clustered neighborhoods in places like the West Side and Kanawha City sections of the city always made him feel more connected to what was going on. It also set a strong example to the younger officers that achieving a certain rank in the department did not exclude anyone from participating in the normal routines of patrol and investigation.

Ronan exited onto the Lee Street off ramp. He slowed, crossed the Elk River Bridge and then drove past various downtown Charleston intersections. Passing by the Marriott and the Embassy Suites Hotels, along with Laidley Tower, he made his way to Capitol Street. Realizing where he was, he slapped the dashboard in disgust. Despite having lived in Charleston for over fifteen years, Ronan still had trouble remembering that Capitol Street was a one-way thorough-fare, and he was about to turn the wrong way.

Just beyond Taylor Books, he slammed on his brakes to avoid hitting a crowd of people that stood circling in the street. Some were screaming while others waved at the traffic and pointed toward the Two Minute Warning Sports Bar. In front of the bar, three bodies stood huddled together just outside the swinging glass doors. Several shrieks and gasping pleas for help echoed around the street as cars, now blocked by Ronan's truck, screeched to a halt.

Capitol Street had suddenly lost its charm and seemed grubby and craggy.

Ronan charged into the huddled group and shoved them aside. A burly white man with short hair held a fair-haired young man stationary while a black man punched and kicked him. The kid gasped and heaved as his body became limp. When the burly man and his partner saw the globs of blood streaming from their helpless victim's nose and mouth, they ceased the relentless attack.

Ronan inched closer.

Finally, the burly man loosened his grip, and the youth took full advantage of the respite. Spitting a wad of blood onto the street, he reared back and stuffed an elbow into the gut of his heavyset captor. In response, the man's partner swung at him but missed. The young man countered, clawing at his second assailant. The black man shrieked in pain, and a grotesque squelching noise erupted from his throat as his eyeball exploded; blood oozed down his face.

"Stop! Police!" Ronan demanded in a deep, even tone.

One of the men turned to face Ronan who was now a few feet away. Sensing a chance to escape, the kid lunged forward. But the burly man collected himself and grabbed an arm, jerking him backwards. The bone made a horrendous cracking noise, and the young man toppled to the ground and vomited.

The black man pulled a revolver from his pants and pulled the trigger, sending a few shots into the air.

Ronan pointed his weapon toward the sky and yelled, "Everybody get down!"

The spectators screamed and tried to escape. Many of them ran into and over each other. Some folks squatted close to the street, collapsing together in clusters, in an attempt to shield themselves from any stray bullets.

Ronan lunged for the shooter, but a fleeing woman tripped him, and he fell forward—mere inches from the shooter. With his arms grazed in blood and vomit, Ronan called out again, "Police! Drop the weapon. Now!"

The man cast a vicious look down at Ronan. With a cop's instinct and lightening reflexes, Ronan steadied his service weapon at the exact same time the black man pulled his own weapon from its hiding place, settled it on the young man and pulled the trigger. A loud crack followed by the tight whine of the gun echoed through the crowd as the bullet discharged. Michael Warner dropped to one knee and rolled onto his side.

"Police! Drop the weapon. Now!"

The man cut a sharp look at Ronan from the corner of one eye and pointed the gun down at Michael.

"I said, drop the gun. If you don't, I'll shoot."

In a fit of rage, the man stepped toward Ronan, grabbed

his jaw, and shoved his face to the side. From behind, he felt a powerful roundhouse kick to the ribs. He howled in pain but managed to hold his position over the shooter.

What should I do? Ronan thought. *I'm stuck. That's what.* Several additional kicks to the ribs followed, and the black man squirmed away. As Ronan rolled over, the burly man slammed the end of his boot into him, this time knocking all the air from his body. Moments after Ronan rolled over, he saw a thin flash of silver. Then he felt something cold and sharp slice into his side. He gasped for breath; the intense pain making him forget all about the throbbing in his ribs.

The two men hurriedly fled the scene, and despite all the screaming around him, Ronan could hear their light, uneven footsteps quicken and then fade away.

A man and a woman soaked in sweat and looking disheveled knelt in front of Ronan and the injured young man.

"Call 911! Now! This kid needs help," Ronan commanded. His tongue felt thick and heavy as he spoke, but the couple understood the words. He nodded in gratitude and then grabbed the cell phone from his pocket and called in the incident.

"It's going to be okay, son. Hang in there."

The young man whimpered and sobbed heavily; the pain from the gaping wound in his shoulder was almost too much for him to bear.

The woman moved behind Ronan and tenderly lifted him up. From a seated position, the street and sidewalk outside the sports bar looked like a war zone.

He looked the boy over. "What's your name?"

"Michael," he stammered, in between heaving and crying.

"You got a last name, Michael?"

"Warner."

Ronan smiled, attempting to be reassuring. "My name is Ronan, and I'm a police officer. You're going to be okay."

In that moment, Ronan felt something slam against the

back of his head. He blinked—his eyes suddenly blurry. Unable to balance himself, Ronan collapsed onto the sidewalk before everything went dark.

CHAPTER 2

Ronan slowly lifted his heavy eyelids. His mouth was dry, and he smacked his lips a few times in hopes of creating some moisture. Apparently, he was in bed. The room was bright, and the light from the window reflected off the equally bright, white walls, making him desperate to close his eyes.

He felt like he'd slept for years but somehow was still tired. He heard the beeping noise of a machine and slowly turned his head toward the source of the noise.

A woman with a round, full face and chestnut hair pulled into a ponytail stood in front of a podium, typing onto a small computer. Ronan lurched up. The muscles in his neck and stomach were sore, and he let out a full-throated moan.

The noise startled the nurse. She stepped forward and placed her hands on his shoulders.

"Mr. McCullough, you need to rest."

Ronan swallowed twice, trying to find his voice. "What's going on? Where's Michael? Two men hurt him. You've got to find them."

"Mr. McCullough—"

Ronan's strong hand snared the nurse's wrist "Who are

you? I won't talk. I won't tell you who I'm working for," he shouted deliriously.

Another nurse stepped into the doorway. "Everything okay here?"

Ronan grimaced. "I won't talk! No matter what you do, I won't tell you who I'm working for."

Wide-eyed, the nurse called over her shoulder. "Go back to the station and call extension 10."

Suddenly, all the energy from Ronan's body was gone, and he felt weak, limp and helpless. He loosened his grasp on the nurse and settled back into the bed. He closed his eyes for a moment, only to open them again to discover that he was alone.

He flailed his head from side to side, squinting through eyes that seemed to weigh a ton. All he could hear was a cacophony of sounds—buzzing, clicking, air whistling. He pulled back the bed sheet to discover his stomach and abdomen wrapped tightly in bandages; splotches of dried blood pooled under the material.

Ronan closed both eyes again but sensed someone entering the room. He took a deep breath and tightened every muscle he could. The punishing pain made his eyes water.

A soft stroke grazed his cheek. Ronan flung open one eye as Ty slid a stool next to the bed and sat down.

"Now I know where I am," Ronan huffed. "I'm dead, and I made it to heaven."

"Not quite. You're at the Charleston Area Mercy Hospital, Ronan. Charleston Mercy. Do you know where that is?"

"Of course, I do, damn it! Don't talk to me like I'm senile."

Ty turned away and checked the monitors. "Your vital signs are good, and your blood pressure has come down, which is also good. We've been waiting to see that."

Ronan groaned as the stomach pain flared once more. "Waiting? How long have I been out?"

Ty pulled a chair next to the bed and leaned closer to Ronan. "Two days."

"Shit!"

"I've got to go," Ronan growled as he tried to haul his beaten body out of bed. "Two men stabbed a kid over on Capitol Street. I have to catch the bastards before they have time to make up alibis or get away."

Ty bolted to his feet and imitated the same posture the nurse had earlier. "Ronan, you're not going anywhere right now. You need to rest."

"I need outta here is what I need."

"Ronan—"

"Don't play with me, Ty! Let me go."

Ty refused, and pinched the morphine tube and silently counted to ten. Ronan continued to squirm. "Are you in pain?"

"No," Ronan replied defiantly.

"If you don't settle down, it's going to get worse without this morphine drip."

Ronan glared at Ty as he followed the tube sticking out from the top of his hand to the pinched portion of the IV bag. The pain in his side intensified, and he felt like his ribs were on fire.

"Hurting yet?"

"Yes! Yes, I am!" Ronan responded breathlessly and settled back into the bed.

Ty released the tube. "By the way, you do know that you intimidate the hell out of the charge nurse? So take it easy on the old girl. OK?"

Letting out a long sigh, Ronan responded. "What are you talking about?"

"Apparently, you told Megan to go find two men and do it immediately."

Ronan nodded. "Those are the men I just told you about, but I don't remember telling a nurse anything. I don't even remember a nurse being here."

Ty studied the monitor again. "That's because you're on some pretty powerful pain meds."

The comment hung in the air for a moment. "What's wrong with me?"

Ty stepped back and studied Ronan. "Paramedics found you bleeding and unconscious in front of the Two Minute Warning and brought you to the ER."

Ronan cut him off. "There was a kid at the bar being attacked, a kid named Michael Warner. One of his attackers had a gun. I was on my way to the station when I saw them pile out of the bar."

"Like I said—"

"How's Michael?"

Ty crossed his arms. "Mr. Warner was released yesterday. He had a small caliber gunshot wound to the shoulder, a fractured cheekbone and some contusions, but luckily no internal injuries. Eric Bonamico from your unit questioned him while he was in recovery."

Ronan let out another sigh, this one of relief. "That's good. Did they catch the perps?"

"I don't know, Ronan. Like I was saying, you have three bruised ribs, and…" Ty paused as a look of worry crossed his face.

Ronan reached out for Ty, and Ty stepped to the side of the bed and grabbed the outstretched hand. "And what?"

"You were stabbed in the side just above your ribs. The knife came within a few inches of reaching your spine."

Ronan remembered the sharp pain in his side as he tried to check on a fallen Michael Warner. Amidst the blood and chaos, he stupidly ignored it. He looked at Ty again who was now shifting his weight nervously from one foot to the other.

"It's okay. I'm fine."

"It was touch and go for you in surgery. There was so much blood." His lips began to tremble. "I thought I'd lose you."

Ronan pulled Ty close to him and kissed his hand. "I'm too stubborn to buy the farm that easily."

Ty rubbed his nose and sniffed. "You're so cheesy."

The tender moment was interrupted when Sergeant Eric Bonamico knocked on the door and then sauntered into the room.

The detective looked right at Ty, ignoring Ronan. "How's he doing?"

"He'll be fine, I think. But you need to ask his actual doctor."

The detective stepped around Ty and stood at the foot of the bed and patted Ronan on the leg. "How ya feeling? The captain sent me over to check on you."

Ty filled the space between Bonamico and the bed. "Visiting hours just ended, and our patient needs to rest. I'm giving you both ten minutes—tops." He cut a look at Bonamico and then back at Ronan. "I'll be down the hall if you need anything."

Bonamico dragged the stool to the end of the bed and sat down. Ronan squinted, struggling to focus on his partner. The solidly built, full-blooded Italian with a swoop of disheveled black hair and a rumpled gray suit filled up the stool and smiled at Ronan; his teeth blindingly white.

"You look like hell."

"That's rich coming from the man lying in a hospital bed."

Ronan relaxed a bit as the coursing pain subsided. "Who's working the investigation?"

Bonamico laughed softly. "I just came to see you, not talk shop."

"Please," Ronan replied. "That's exactly why you're here. Who's handling the investigation?"

"Actually, I am. Captain Ashby's overseeing it though."

"I'm told you questioned Michael Warner?"

"We did," Bonamico replied, wondering how Ronan knew this information. "Yesterday morning. Warner said he didn't know the men who attacked him. He claims he was sitting at the bar, watching the Reds on TV and having a few beers. Those two guys sat down next to him, ordered some beers and tried hustling him for money. Things escalated, and the manager threw them out. That's when the fun started. We spoke to the manager and some patrons too; they all said Warner is a regular, but they've never seen the other two."

Ronan blinked several times, trying to piece together the details. A burst of pain rocketed through him. Through gritted teeth, he looked hard at Bonamico. "So, this is just basically an assault with a deadly weapon?"

"Not quite. The paramedics found a dime bag of weed on Warner. We took him in after he was released from here. He's free on bail, awaiting a bench hearing."

Ronan shook his head. "I don't remember any of that."

"You wouldn't. You were out cold when paramedics arrived. Warner pleaded for them to help you first."

"That was nice of him," Ronan grumbled. "Who knocked me out?"

Bonamico folded his arms. "Eyewitnesses said the big dude came back after you chased him away and got in one more lick."

"Yeah, that's right. There was a couple, a man and woman. They tried to help me with Michael. I don't know; maybe the kid did know those two thugs after all. Hustling somebody for beer money is one thing, but hustling somebody with a weapon who you think has drugs is something else."

"What are you thinking?"

"Most crimes involve money, drugs or sex. Perhaps Warner owed those guys some drug money, or maybe they were enforcers sent to collect for someone else."

"Could be, but we can't explore that angle because we can't find the other men."

Ronan pulled himself up from a reclined position and glared. "What do you mean?"

"All Warner could tell us was their first names: Ben and Lo. We checked the surveillance cameras from the bar, and we got some physical descriptions and clothing, but that's about it. We've got a BOLO out now."

Ronan let out a short breath as he drummed his fingers on the mattress. "What's Ashby say about it?"

"He's concerned about you, and he wants to get those bastards big time, especially since they wounded a cop." Bonamico watched the small droplets of morphine slip from the bag into the opaque tube that ran into Ronan. "He'd have my shield if he knew I was telling you this, so as far as you can remember from your morphine-induced stupor, we never had a chat."

Ronan lapsed silent, and the beeping and humming of machines filled the room.

"I need to get out of here. I want to get them. There has to be more to this case than just drugs. Once they knew I was a cop, they wanted to kill me, and that doesn't happen over drugs alone."

Bonamico checked his watch. "It's nearly eight, and I don't think you're going anywhere tonight."

Ty rapped on the door behind them. "Ten minutes is up." The dark silhouette next to Bonamico changed as Ty stood in between them again.

"I'm sure your nurse will give you something to help you sleep, Ronan, so don't be a pain in the ass. Just take the pill and get some sleep," Bonamico directed with a wink as he looked at his partner and then at Ty.

Ty nodded, smiled and stepped back to face the detective. "Good night, Sergeant."

The detective smiled back. He began to leave the room but stopped near the doorway before turning around. "I'm glad you're okay. I'll tell Captain Ashby how you're doing. With those injuries, I bet he'll take you off this case."

Before Ronan could respond, Bonamico was out the door.

CHAPTER 3

Ronan spent two more days in the hospital before being discharged. Since he'd be finished with the Thursday night shift before Ronan was released in the morning, Ty called Sergeant Bonamico and asked him to take Ronan home.

Bonamico pulled off from Oakwood Road, found the townhouse on Autumn Road and drove slowly up the driveway. Ronan, still chafed over Bonamico telling Captain Ashby the status of his recovery—which would lead to his removal from the investigation—didn't say much.

The white, three-window frame garage door opened, and Ty emerged dressed in a gray pullover and navy polyester pants that snapped down the length of each leg.

"Nice to see you again," Bonamico said.

"And you as well," Ty replied politely.

The detective bent down to gather Ronan from the car, but Ronan brushed him back and steadied two hands on the door frame and then pulled himself out of the car. As Ty came over, Ronan stumbled and fell into his partner, muttering an inaudible expletive.

"Ronan will need this," Bonamico said, holding out an adjustable, black quad cane. "At least that's what the discharge nurse said."

"Let's get you inside."

"I'll get him. Grab Ronan's stuff in that hospital bag. Be careful, his gun is packed somewhere in there. Find him a comfortable spot inside, and I'll bring him in."

Ronan groaned again. "For Christ sake, I'm standing right here. Don't talk about me like I'm helpless."

"Be nice, or I'll squeeze those sore ribs," Ty warned.

Ronan rolled his eyes.

After a few awkward moments, Ty thanked Bonamico for helping Ronan into the house and then left to go prepare the living room.

"Thanks for bringing me home and for coming alone."

Bonamico held up an open hand. "Don't worry about it —now or ever."

Relieved, Ronan exhaled. "I appreciate it, but I still can't believe you told Ashby about me. You realize I'm going to be taken off the case now, don't you?"

Bonamico ignored the question. "The discharge nurse told me you'll have some weakness in the right leg for a few weeks until the muscles heal. Does Ty know?"

"I'm sure it's in the paperwork."

"Okay. We'll, I'm done here. I'll check on you tomorrow."

"You off this weekend?" Ronan asked.

"Yep. My son's baseball game is tonight. Midwestern is taking on Kanawha City. Big rivalry."

"Go K.C."

"You're such an ass, McCullough. City is weak this year, so my boy ought to get on base and score some runs."

To that, Ronan nodded, and Bonamico returned to his car and departed.

Ronan looked around the townhouse. Home never looked so good even though the décor still made him feel a bit uncomfortable. The travertine floors, custom stone mantel, and beautiful oak built-ins surrounded by a vaulted ceiling with vintage beams effused elegance, but the townhouse wasn't his. It belonged to Ty.

Ty could afford the luxury. Akamu Andino, Ty's grandfather, worked as a second-generation pineapple farmer in Wahiawa on the island of Oahu. During the 1950s, James Drummond Dole set out to expand his pineapple empire, and Akamu sold his thirty-five acres of farmland and became an instant millionaire. Yet Ty seldom mentioned the money that belonged to the Andino family.

Ty would be labeled "old money" by many on the Charleston police force, especially the uniforms and forensic techs who spent time combing through houses looking for evidence. But the money allowed Ty to complete college and nursing school at Marshall University with no student-loan debt and plenty of money to purchase a luxury townhome in the posh South Hills District of Charleston. None of that could ever be affordable on a nurse's salary alone.

Ronan staggered through the foyer and greeted Ty who was standing near the entryway. Stopping, he leaned against the archway and tried to catch his breath. As his breathing evened, he looked around the townhouse.

"I've got the couch ready for you with some blankets and pillows. We'll go when you're ready."

Ronan adored the kindness in Ty, which was equaled only by his stunning looks and tight physique.

"I've had pain before, Ty, but nothing like this."

He gave Ronan the once-over. "Those muscles in your leg are torn. It will take some time for you to heal and regain your strength."

Leaning against the cane, Ronan draped an arm over Ty as they shuffled into the living room. Ty carefully helped Ronan down on the couch and then placed both legs over the cushions, tucking pillows under him and covering him with a blanket.

He smiled sweetly at Ronan. "There. Much better than the hospital, I bet."

Ronan reached out a hand and stroked Ty on the arm. The smoothness of the skin against his fingertips aroused Ronan.

"Want something to eat? Betsy made some wonderful chicken salad after she cleaned the house today, and I can make you a sandwich if you'd like. I bet you're starving. Hospital food sucks."

"Actually, I'm not hungry. Just a drink is fine."

Ty disappeared into the kitchen, which was directly off the living room. While he began rummaging through the stainless-steel refrigerator, Ronan looked onto the loveseat next to the couch. Papers and folders were strewn all over it and across the floor, and a laptop computer sat on the edge of the end table.

"That's quite a mess you have here," Ronan called out to Ty.

"I'm working on sponsors and sponsorship donation levels for the hospital. CMH wants to break ground on the new children's pediatric ward in the spring, and my task force is responsible for fundraising. The Charleston State College has promised us an endowment, but we'll have to name something in the new wing after them for it. The college is presenting us a check at halftime during the first football game against Southern Virginia."

"Sounds exciting," Ronan said as he wiggled on the couch, trying to find a comfortable position.

"Open your hand."

Ronan did as instructed, and Ty dropped several small pills into the deep, calloused ridges.

"Take those."

Ronan stared at the pills, and then looked up at Ty for an explanation.

"Pain meds and something to help you relax."

"I'd rather have a beer," Ronan replied, handing the pills back to Ty.

Reluctantly, Ty went back into the kitchen and got Ronan his beer.

CHAPTER 4

As Ronan drove down Capitol Street near police headquarters, a young man resembling Michael Warner suddenly stepped into the middle of the road. Ronan swerved, but it was too late. The kid's body sailed through the air like a ragdoll, ending up a good twenty feet from where he'd been hit.

As the pickup truck rolled over and over, the seat belt snapped across Ronan's throat, choking him until he could barely breathe. Helpless and tethered, he stared out the driver's-side window. A bruised and bloodied Michael Warner stood near the curb looking back. Michael said nothing as he watched a burly man approach Ronan, a knife in one hand and a gun in the other. The man laughed maniacally and began stabbing Ronan as his partner, a black man, watched with satisfaction.

The searing pain dulled Ronan's movements as he desperately tried to start the truck, but the engine was dead. He looked to Michael for help, but no one was there. When Ronan looked at the burly man again, all he could see was the gun. Bam!

Ronan woke with a gasp, his mind reeling and his heart racing. Desperately, he tried to regain his bearings.

Ty appeared from the darkness and hugged Ronan. "It's all right. It was just a dream."

Had it only been a dream? The attack had been so vivid, so real, and his chest still ached deep inside. Sucking in a few choppy breaths, Ronan looked wide-eyed around the room, making sure he was really back home. "What day is it? Why—"

"The medicine can cause crazy dreams; it's perfectly normal and nothing to worry about."

Rolling to one side, Ronan slung both legs onto the floor and then stumbled to the bay window on the other side of the living room. The effort was exhausting, and sweat ran down his face and trickled into his collar. Resting for a moment, he looked out the window. The mountains that stood close watch on the neighborhood eased his spirit and brought a sense of tranquility to him. He watched the sun melt into the sky as a thin strip of gray slowly turned the horizon black beneath the waning colors of orange and gold.

"I'm sorry," Ronan said as Ty approached.

"Don't be. Go sit down, and I'll make you something to drink."

Ronan hobbled back to the couch and curled up with a blanket; the blanket was still damp with his sweat, but somehow it smelled like Ty.

Ty returned with a glass of iced tea.

Ronan grimaced.

"No more beer for a while. Beer and medicine are a lethal combination."

Ronan stared through the glass and reluctantly took it, tipping it back and swallowing a generous gulp of cold tea. As the ice settled into the bottom of the glass, the doorbell rang.

"Expecting company?" Ty asked.

"No. It might be Eric again. Maybe he left something here."

Ty disappeared into the hallway. A few beats passed

before he came back into the living room. Dark, soulful eyes lacked luster as he stared straight ahead.

"Who is it?"

Ty groped for words, but none came forth. When he did speak, it sounded like an unpleasant breeze—harsh and hollow.

"There's a kid at the door. Says he's your nephew."

CHAPTER 5

"Nick's here?" Ronan didn't understand.

Ty walked straight to Ronan and looked down at him with an air of authority that was almost palpable. "Deal with it."

Ronan tried to stand up, but he stumbled and fell into a painful heap. Ty made no effort to help his lover off the floor. Ronan secured the cane and collected himself, leaning on it for support and balance as Ty looked away.

"Shit!" Ronan exclaimed as he painfully dragged his injured leg behind him, and shuffled to the front door.

The shadow framing the doorway came into focus. Nick stood looking down at the doormat. "Hi, Uncle Ronan," he mumbled.

Ronan was confused, as if his brain had suddenly stopped processing information and needed rebooting. Looking around, everything seemed to be in fast-forward, while he remained motionless in the middle of it all.

Nick still didn't look up. "I guess I should've called or something."

"Jesus, Nick! What are you doing here?"

The question took away the kid's last bit of self-confidence. He swayed back and forth looking like he would burst into tears at any moment.

"Mom and I had a fight…about Bruce."

"Look at me, Nick."

Ronan angrily pressed the heels of his hands into his eyes until he saw nothing but stars. "So, you decided to travel all the way to West Virginia because you had an argument with your mom about your stepdad?"

"It wasn't the first time we've argued about him," Nick said, his voice higher than Ronan remembered.

"This is ridiculous. I can't believe it." Ronan leaned into the doorframe and spoke to the empty street. "Why didn't Melissa call and tell me you were missing? No, never mind. I know why. Well, I'm sorry, Nick, but you can't stay here. This isn't my house."

Nick absorbed the stinging words and replied, "I know it's been a long time—"

"Ten years."

"Please don't make me go back home! Bruce hates me! He and Mom fight all the time, and he's always telling me what a worthless piece of shit I am."

Now Ronan felt the sharp, resonating words spoken by his nephew.

"Stop mumbling, Nick. Look up at me!"

Nick looked nothing like Melissa. He had a rectangular face with a defined, slightly pointed chin and slack jaw line. His gray eyes were small and spaced evenly apart, sitting below trim eyebrows that seemed to curve into his sharply pointed nose. Nick had a bony face, and those features were a mere reflection of his entire body structure, and everything—from his skeletal arms to his paper-thin waist—screamed of unnatural thinness.

"How'd you get here? No bullshit either."

He nodded. "Bruce was drunk last night. Mom had fixed dinner, his favorite, meatloaf and mashed potatoes. Bruce started screaming at Mom over a bunch of things I couldn't hear upstairs. When I came down, Bruce grabbed a knife from the kitchen and told me to get back upstairs where I belonged. He said things were between him and Mom, and if I came any closer, he'd make sure I felt it."

Furious, Ronan swallowed hard. Then took a deep breath and tried to remain calm when all he really wanted to do was punch a wall.

"Did he harm you?"

"No."

"Did he harm your mother?"

Nick finally locked eyes with Ronan; the color drained from Nick's face.

"He's drunk a lot, Uncle Ronan."

"That's not what I asked you. Has he hurt your mother?"

Nick paused for a moment, working the question over in his mind. "I...I don't know. Mom's never said anything about to it me."

Ronan clenched a fist and rapped it into the door. "Damn it! I told your mother marrying Bruce would be the worst decision of her life. But she fell for the money and the Miami-beach lifestyle." He swiped the open space between them with an open hand. "I'm sorry. I shouldn't have said that. None of this is your fault. How old are you now?"

"Eighteen."

"You doing well in school?"

Nick nodded again. "Yep. I graduated in June."

"How'd you get here?"

Nick let the tattered book bag slide over his shoulder and down his arm and onto the front step. "After Bruce and Mom got done fighting last night, I snuck downstairs to get some water. Bruce left his wallet on the kitchen counter, so I opened it and grabbed the cash."

"You shouldn't have done that, no matter how big an ass Bruce might be."

"I know, Uncle Ronan, but I'd had enough. I took the money and left Mom a note. I went down to the Greyhound station and took the first bus I could find here."

Ronan furrowed his brow. "How long did that bus ride take? Fourteen hours?"

"Sixteen," Nick answered. "I changed buses in Atlanta and Charlotte."

Ronan let out a long breath. "I'm sorry Bruce is causing trouble for your Mom, but running away isn't the answer."

Nick blinked, and his face hardened. "I'm eighteen now. I can do whatever I want and live wherever I want."

"Legally you can, but I'm not sure if you should."

Nick stepped back, squinted and looked around Ronan. "What happened to you, Uncle Ronan? Are you hurt?"

Ronan didn't want to explain the incident again, but since Nick had been honest and forthcoming, he felt obligated to do the same.

"I was on patrol earlier this week, and I got jumped by a couple of thugs. Don't change the subject."

Nick eyed the cane. "Did the police catch 'em?"

"Not yet." The thought made Ronan roil with anger. "But we're working on it."

As Nick stared down at the ground again, Ronan cupped a hand on his shoulder. "Come on. I'm sure you could use a hot shower and something to eat. Maybe I'll order pizza. You haven't lived until you've had pizza from Husson's."

Nick appeared relieved. "Thanks. Who was that man at the door? Is he the butler? We don't have a butler, but we have a housekeeper. Her name's Fredericka."

Ronan let out a tense laugh. "No! We don't have a butler either, and the housekeeper's named Betsy. That was Ty. I'll introduce you to him."

Nick ambled past Ronan and headed to the living room. Ronan followed closely behind, catching a glimpse of Ty in the kitchen as he passed by.

Nick flopped onto the couch and removed the long-sleeved, blue and gray checked dress shirt, still damp with sweat. His white tee shirt was also damp, and he pinched the end of it and fluffed the material to generate some cool air onto his sticky skin.

"Let's get some pizza. What do you like on it?"

"Anything but anchovies is fine. And I like Coke, not Pepsi," Nick replied as he looked around the room, first at the glass that divided the living room and the foyer, and then at the 60-inch flat screen television that hung on the wall a few feet above the manila-colored fireplace.

Ronan heard the familiar pinging of his cell phone and followed it to the kitchen. As he grabbed the phone, Ty caught his hand.

"Do you mind? I need to check that."

Ty huffed. "We need to talk, or rather, you need to explain what's going on."

Ronan peered up at Ty to see pain-filled eyes looking back. The smooth, angular features of his face remained handsome even in this moment of confusion and resentment. "We've been together for over two years, and this is the first I hear about Nick?" Ty abruptly stopped speaking and cleared his throat, cautious of his voice level. "What's going on here, Ronan?"

"Nothing. My sister's a bitch, and she married a pretentious prick."

"I know the two of you aren't close, but I didn't know she had a kid."

Ronan ignored Ty's statement and scoured the text message. It was from Eric Bonamico.

We're in pursuit of the perps...thought you'd want to know.

"Are you listening to me at all?" Ty demanded.

"I'm getting kind of hungry," Nick called from the living room.

"I'm sorry I didn't tell you anything about Nick, but I haven't even seen the kid in over ten years. And before you say anything, I'm not proud of that fact, but I just can't stand to be in the same room with my sister anymore, especially since she married that bastard, Bruce Copeland. I know we need to talk about this, but I need to go now."

"Go where?"

"To the station. Eric's got a lead on those two men who attacked the Warner kid and me."

"I don't think so. You're in no condition to go anywhere except back to the living room."

"I've got to be there, Ty. I've seen these bastards close-up and *very* personal, and that's the kind of information needed in a manhunt."

"A manhunt?"

Ronan decided to be straight with Ty.

"I got a text message from Eric. They're in pursuit now, and I need to be there."

"No! You don't! I was in the ER the night you were brought in. I don't think you realize just how injured you really are."

Ronan cocked his head. "Seriously? I feel it every time I take a step or move a muscle."

"Exactly! That's why going to work is out of the question."

Ronan grabbed his duty belt from the closet near the front door. "I'll be home as soon as it's over."

"Ronan, stop it! Stop doing this!"

Nick interrupted again. "Is everything okay?"

Ronan hollered back. "Everything's fine."

"Just checking."

"Stop doing what?" Ronan asked as he snapped on his duty belt and secured his gun.

"Pushing yourself and putting me second."

Ronan froze and gazed up at the cathedral ceiling. Ty had never mentioned anything about feeling like a second-place finisher in their relationship, and the statement made Ronan's heart twinge. He flecked his tongue at the corners of his mouth and replied, "I'll be home later tonight."

"What am I supposed to do with Nick?"

Ronan clenched his jaw as he closed the door. "Order pizza."

CHAPTER 6

onan sped off Interstate 64, crossing the bridge by the Charleston Civic Center before swerving onto Capitol Street from Virginia. When he reached The Two Minute Warning, he slowed the truck and peered through the large plate-glass window. Everything seemed normal. Patrons ate and talked and stared up at televisions across the bar while outside two men stood smoking and fiddling with their cell phones.

As he approached the police station, a flurry of activity caught his attention. A squad of uniformed officers stood in the parking lot, checking their gear one last time before they deployed on their mission. Just ahead of him, a SWAT truck rolled into the parking lot and then slowly eased up to the squad and waited for the officers to embark. Ronan's heart quickened with a combination of anxiety and excitement. He parked his truck near the back of the building, and jumped out, forgetting entirely about his condition. His full weight landed squarely on his injured leg, and the excruciating pain instantly halted him in his tracks. Leaning back into the side of the truck, he muffled a scream and angrily grabbed his cane.

Stumbling, Ronan hobbled up the loading dock ramp and mingled with his fellow officers. A couple of them nodded at him, but most of them focused on the task at hand.

Inside the station, rows of tables lined the middle of the room. The constant ringing of phones and the tattoo of booted feet gave the space a purposeful, yet chaotic feel. Ronan headed to the back corner office, looking for Captain Ashby.

With some effort, Ronan opened the heavy wooden door of the captain's office and was greeted by a disaster; papers littered the mahogany desk, and empty Styrofoam cups spilled over the edge of a trashcan, falling into a pile upon the floor. A bulletin board that had been overloaded with tacks and documents hung crookedly on the wall. Captain Ashby stood to the side of the desk, clenching the telephone receiver and angrily tapping his foot. When he saw Ronan, he shot him a look that could have frozen the Kanawha River in the middle of August.

Captain Ashby was tall and broad-shouldered with dark, wiry hair and heavy, solemn brows that were offset by a stern chin, and his long nose was slightly crooked like it had been broken several times and then left to its imperfections. A pair of eyes, the color of sea glass, gleamed behind square-framed glasses. There was always an odd lightness about his eyes, as if there were something important to which only he was privy.

Ashby was a lifelong Charleston resident. After serving in Vietnam, he came home and exchanged his army uniform for a patrol officer's. Sharp and stern, but fair, he rose quickly through the ranks and had held the position of captain for over ten years. Ronan didn't always agree with Ashby, but he respected him for allowing all sides of an issue to be heard before rendering a decision.

"Yes, sir. We're prepared to move in and take the suspect. Right. I'll send you a full report as soon as possible."

Ashby slammed down the receiver and ran two fingers over the corners of his mouth. "That was Chief Toler. He wants a complete briefing as soon as the action is concluded."

Ronan leaned on the cane for a moment and steadied himself. "What are dealing with, Captain?"

Ashby brushed a stack of papers aside and sat down on the edge of his desk. "Earlier today, a Kanawha County sheriff's deputy pulled over a car with busted taillights. When he ran the plates, the vehicle came up stolen. He called for backup and then asked the two men in the car to step out and assume the position."

"Seems pretty routine."

Ashby nodded. "It was until the heavyset suspect shoved the deputy to the ground and then hightailed it back to the car and took off."

That's the bastard who beat me senseless, Ronan thought. "He fits the profile of the man who held me like a tackling dummy. I take it he's still at large?"

"It would appear so. When the other suspect tried to flee, the deputy managed to get a shot off and clip him in the leg. That subdued him until backup arrived."

"Where's the other one?"

"Right now, he's holed up in an empty warehouse next to Pugh Furniture."

"Warehouse? You mean old man Summers' property?"

Ashby nodded again. "Colony Realty bought the property last year, and it's been vacant since then. The suspect has a security guard hostage in there."

"I want in."

Ashby waved away the comment. "Not a chance. Go home and rest. Bonamico's handling this one."

"Captain," Ronan pleaded. "I've seen what this guy can do, and I'm telling you, he won't think twice about killing that hostage or killing your men. He would've killed me if he'd had the chance."

"I appreciate your willingness, McCullough, but..." Ashby paused and pointed at the cane. "You're no good if you can't walk."

"Then let me at least go along and help set up the perimeter and do what else I can to help the team."

Ashby drummed his fingers on the desk and considered Ronan's proposition. Ronan

heard the rumbling of the SWAT van preparing to depart and shot his boss an anxious glance.

"Fine. Go ahead."

As Ronan turned to leave, Ashby spoke. "Wait a second."

Ronan spun around to find the captain standing right behind him.

"Bonamico's in charge. Got that? What he says goes. I don't want any horseshit going down on this one. I want you to help set the perimeter, help with the briefing, and then get the hell out of the way. Do you understand?" The captain set his jaw and waited for an answer.

"Got it, Captain."

"Good. I'll tell Bonamico you're tagging along."

Ronan left Ashby's office and crossed the hall to the locker room. Inside, the smell of stale air made him sneeze. He trudged through the musty room and into the uniform room where his tactical gear was stored. As Ronan pulled on his heavy BDU trousers, the pain exploded through every inch of his battered leg. He fell down on the wooden bench in front of his locker and waited for the agony to subside. When it had reached a bearable level, Ronan finished dressing and then made his way out to the parking lot.

An officer reached out and hoisted Ronan into the SWAT van while a baby-faced officer secured the door behind him. Then the steel-plated van slowly rocked and bobbed its way from the loading dock.

Inside the dimly lit van everyone looked the same, and Ronan couldn't tell where Bonamico was sitting until a husky voice called out from the far corner. "What are you doing here, McCullough? I thought you were out on medical leave."

"I'm just here to offer some support. I cleared it with Ashby," Ronan replied, his breath clouding the helmet's face guard as he spoke.

A terse laugh followed and then silence.

Minutes later the van stopped, and the same baby-faced officer reappeared at the opened back door. It was now dark, but Ronan could tell they were on Morris Street. Once out on the street, he automatically ran a hand over his uniform, making sure everything was strapped down tightly and all weapons were secure. Clenching his jaw and flexing his hands, Ronan anxiously waited with the others for the order to move out. The order would most likely be "apprehend the suspect alive," but he thought "*dead* or alive" was a much better option.

Half a dozen squad cars with flashing blue lights lit the night as streams of color splashed against the dark brick façade of the warehouse. Bonamico and his men scurried from the light and into the shadows behind the van where they huddled in a loose, oblong-shaped circle. Ronan counted ten men, including him, waiting for instructions.

"All right. Listen up. The guy inside is Lorenzo White, and he's taken a security guard hostage." Bonamico stopped for a moment and peered through the plastic facemasks, silently demanding his colleagues' attention. "We don't know the condition of the hostage, but we have to assume White is armed and dangerous."

Ronan waited for Bonamico to find him, which he did a few moments after scanning the circle.

Bonamico held his gaze on Ronan and continued. "This warehouse is currently under construction, so we're likely to find all kinds of tools and equipment scattered about the place, especially near entryways and stairwells. This gives White plenty of places to hide." Bonamico looked away from Ronan. "There are two stairwells at each end of the building: the east side, facing the street, and the west side near the railroad tracks. Except for the solid brick exterior walls, the building's mainly made of wood. The ceiling is pretty high, around fourteen feet, so any noise you make will be amplified tenfold. We've got both exits covered, but I'm sending five of you in the front, and the other four will go in the back."

The team nodded almost in unison.

Bonamico gripped the M4 carbine rifle tightly in both hands and nodded at Ronan. "Sergeant McCullough is here with us tonight. He's seen this prick up close. Sergeant."

Ronan swallowed hard as all eyes locked on him. "I can guarantee you White is armed, and this isn't his first rodeo. Be careful." He let the comment hang in the air for a moment and then cut a sharp look at Bonamico. "Do we have the order to take him out?"

The muscles in Bonamico's neck tightened as his voice rose above the group. "We've been given orders to take White in alive, but if he fires then take him out. Understood?"

Everyone replied with a thumbs up.

"All right. The radio's on, and I want voice checks every five minutes. Tell us where you are and what you see."

The baby-faced team member re-emerged.

"Francisco, take Collins, Mendez, Woods, and Harrison in through the back. Chandler, Simmons and Gaffney, come with me," Bonamico ordered.

Ronan blinked and the men dispersed.

Eric lagged behind for a moment. "Follow O'Neill to the back and make sure the perimeter is secure. Daniels is back there with his unit. Their lazy asses don't like getting dirty, so I want to make sure nobody's getting out while we're coming in."

Ronan sucked in a breath. "Okay."

"How ya feeling?"

"Awful."

"Well, you look like shit. I can't believe you're out here." Bonamico turned away and then pivoted back. "But I'm glad you are." He slapped Ronan on the shoulder then dropped low to the ground and scurried after his men.

Unlike Bonamico, Ronan preferred the Beretta 92 semi-automatic pistol to the conventional SWAT rifle. A rifle required two hands to carry and operate, and Ronan liked the flexibility that a pistol allowed. He removed his weapon and held it under a streetlight, cocked the slide, and then examined the exposed ejection port and barrel mechanism.

To the left of him, Charleston police had set up a road-block near the Capitol Market. The sleek lines of the squad cars were illuminated under the streetlights, and the flashing blue lights ricocheted off the chipped red brick encasing the market.

Ronan looked to the right. Another roadblock had been set up at the opposite end of Smith Street to prevent any fleeing person or vehicle from approaching either the Inter-state 64 or 77 on-ramp near Appalachian Power Park.

As instructed, Ronan headed for the west side of the warehouse. Bonamico squatted on the sidewalk near the front entrance as the rest of the team pressed themselves flatly against the wall, weapons held in a vertical position.

"Unit 1 in position," Bonamico said over the radio's light static.

A moment passed. "Unit 2 in position."

Ronan assumed that the voice belonged to O'Neill, but it was difficult to tell.

"Unit 1 inside and setting up a perimeter."

"Copy that, Unit 1. We're prying off the door handle now, and we'll be inside any minute."

"Copy that, Unit 2."

In the semi-darkness, with only the moon and a few streetlights providing some faint light, Ronan could see the warehouse was long and narrow. Rows of small, square glass panes dappled the building, and the glass in some windows was cracked or missing completely. Ronan grazed his hand along the rough brick wall as he passed between the ware-houses, slowing his pace and giving his battered body a brief but needed rest.

When Ronan finally emerged from the shadowy crease, he found Corporal Tim Daniels standing before him with his weapon drawn and locked. As Ronan inched closer and into the light, Daniels withdrew and holstered his weapon.

"Sergeant McCullough."

The irritating, reedy voice of his subordinate exacer-bated Ronan's pain. "Corporal Daniels."

"I didn't think you'd be back to work this soon."

"Neither did I."

Ronan glanced at Daniels. Short and stout with a balding pate and beady eyes, he resembled a bowling ball. Ronan looked ahead and then watched as O'Neill led the second group through a long, narrow doorway.

"Unit 2 inside and moving up the west stairwell."

"Copy that," Bonamico responded in a hushed tone.

Daniels interrupted the transmission. "I'm glad you're doing okay. We all are."

"Thanks, corporal."

Ronan knew that Daniels always looked out for himself, and any sort of compliment was tinged with a bit of insincerity. Daniels remembered small details like an elephant, and he would often recall those moments of kindness when he needed a favor at some future date. Ronan wondered how much that compliment would cost him later.

Two officers, standing some feet away from Daniels and Ronan, clicked on their flashlights and shined the narrow beams of white light over the warehouse windows.

"Turn off those damn lights!" Ronan hissed. He broke away from Daniels and moved toward the men. His eyes briefly scanned the names Mack and Smith on their respective nameplates as he reached out and swatted the flashlight away from Smith. "You'll tip White off that we're out here."

Smith seemed stunned by the action and quickly backed away after turning off his Maglite, but Mack frantically fiddled with his flashlight for several seconds before successfully killing the beam.

Ronan surveyed Mack. He was sinewy and waifish like his nephew Nick.

Nick. Ronan wondered how everything was going back at the house. Ty was right; Ronan did have a lot of explaining to do.

"Who's White?" Daniels asked.

"Lorenzo White. He's the one with the hostage."

Daniels shrugged. "I didn't know. Captain Ashby just told us to come down here, and Bonamico told us to monitor the rear of the warehouse."

Ronan rolled his eyes. Not asking questions or wanting to know the details was Daniels' MO. You could tell him what to do, but you had to be specific because he didn't ask questions, volunteer or do anything other than what he was told. For a cop, the man's instincts were as dull as khaki.

Some time had passed, and there'd been no radio transmission from either team. Ronan tapped his earpiece, trying to engage a transmission. Still nothing. He stepped closer to the door.

Daniels grabbed Ronan from behind. "What are you doing?" he whispered.

Ronan pulled his arm away, slightly annoyed. "I'm just going in to take a look and get familiar with what's inside."

"Sergeant—"

"I know what my orders are, Daniels. I just want to make sure where that doorway leads in case White decides to make a run for it." Not wanting to discuss it further, Ronan grasped his pistol with both hands and approached the doorway, mentally noting the single step at the threshold. That extra step could prove dangerous, especially if someone were in pursuit of an escaping Lorenzo White.

As he entered the darkened room, Ronan smelled something heady and intoxicating; it was the kind of odor that makes someone giddy and nauseous at the same time. Then it clicked. The stench was petrochemicals. Suddenly, ribbons of fire blazed through the darkness directly at him.

CHAPTER 7

Ty ambled into the living room to find Nick admiring the flat-screen TV.

"Like it?"

"Yeah."

Ty smiled. "Thanks. I gave it to Ronan last Christmas. We'd been watching his old box television for a while, and he'd been dropping hints about wanting a new one."

"It's really nice."

Ty rested his hands on his hips, searching for something else to say. He seethed a bit at having to entertain Ronan's nephew—a nephew he only learned existed two hours ago.

The young man stepped away from the television and folded his arms. "This TV will generate a frame of video at 600 times per second, and that leads to smooth images with a high picture quality. Not to mention it has DTS Studio Sound, which means it has speaker correction, immersive sound, plus better bass. And you can have seamless delivery of content across the Internet to web connected devices." He turned to face Ty, and his grey eyes sparkled with interest and envy.

Ty wondered what had happened to the shy kid who had sat on the couch and stared silently at the coffee table earlier while he worked on the fundraising package for the new children's wing at CMH. "That's impressive. You seem to know a lot about electronics."

As fast as the energy of the discussion had invigorated Nick, it went away. He became limp, and the expression in his eyes hollowed. "I do like electronics. Mom and Bruce think I'm wasting my time studying it, because as soon as I learn about something then something new comes out to take its place."

"There's nothing wrong with innovation," Ty replied. "The same is true at the hospital where I work. We nurses are trained to use a piece of equipment, and as soon as we learn about it and get comfortable using it, another device comes along and we have to start all over."

Nick brought his brows together. "And that doesn't make you mad?"

"Not at all," Ty said, sitting down on the loveseat and tucking his legs under him. "If it helps our patients get better then it's worth it."

Nick looked back at the television before returning his attention on Ty. "I guess you and Uncle Ronan both like helping people."

"That's true, although we help people in different ways."

Nick nodded before sitting back down on the couch. He dropped his gaze and locked it again on the coffee table. "The only thing Mom ever said about Uncle Ronan was that he's a police officer."

That comment made Ty sit up a bit straighter. "She never mentioned anything else about him?"

"Well, she did say something else."

"What?"

"Mom said Uncle Ronan was a freak."

Ty curled his lips inward before releasing them. "She called him a *freak*. Why?"

"Because…well…because…" Nick began tapping his foot nervously on the open shelf under the table.

The room seemed to get smaller, and Ty wondered if the kid would rather just shrink away and disappear.

"Because he's a queer."

Ty raised his chin and grimaced, unsure of what to say. He had heard this same declaration before from some of his own family members, classmates, medical-school supervisors, and the like. He was used to prejudice and discrimination, but hearing a woman he'd never met call the man he loved a *freak* made him roil with anger.

When anyone asked Ty about his relationship status, he'd always respond with, *I'm in a committed relationship.* It wasn't because he was ashamed of who he was or of his relationship with Ronan, but because he knew a certain amount of secrecy was prudent and essential. The Charleston law-enforcement community was antediluvian, and not a group that looked favorably upon gay men, especially because of the close-knit nature that cops had with one another. Knowing one of them was gay made that cop an outsider. Eric Bonamico knew about Ronan's sexual preference, but nobody else in the department had any idea. Ty got up from the couch and walked into the kitchen. He rubbed his eyes and sighed deeply.

"I'm sorry if what I said hurt your feelings," Nick said dejectedly as he came up behind Ty.

"It's not your fault, but it's that kind of bigotry and hate that divides people and families."

Realizing what he'd said, Nick began to backpedal, "Please, I don't want you to think that's how I feel. I shouldn't have said anything."

"It's okay," Ty said, speaking softly. "Your mother sounds like a real piece of work. I just want you to know that I love your Uncle Ronan very much, but if that's something that makes you uncomfortable then…"

A cell phone buzzed, interrupting the conversation. Nick looked at Ty and shrugged his shoulders. "That's not mine. I don't have a phone."

Ty ran his hands over his shorts and then followed the buzzing to the living room where he found the phone sitting on the coffee table next to his laptop.

Damn! Ronan left his cell phone. Ty was still vexed at Ronan for working a case despite his vehement disapproval, and now the fact that Ronan had no way to contact him or anyone else had Ty extremely worried.

"Aren't you going to answer it?" Nick asked.

"I'm not sure. This is Ronan's phone, but I don't recognize the number. It's a 305 area code."

Ty sidestepped the loveseat and set the phone on the table.

Nick peered down at the screen and turned as white as a flour sack. "That number belongs to Mom."

CHAPTER 8

The fire's backdraft catapulted Ronan from the door and slammed him into the concrete floor several feet away, knocking him unconscious for a moment. When he opened his eyes, he found himself staring at Daniels' shoes.

"Jesus!" Ronan mumbled, tapping his face to make sure he still had one. "Get that fire out!"

"Huh?" Daniels said, lifting Ronan from the ground.

"Tell Mack and Smith to get fire extinguishers from their cruisers and start putting out those flames."

Both officers were within earshot of Ronan, and all Daniels had to do was make a gesture and they both scurried away. Daniels stepped away and radioed dispatch, asking for the fire department and paramedics. Ronan felt like he was on fire; the feeling of heat still radiated over his body. The leg and back pain that had finally subsided came roaring back with a vengeance.

"Advise the fire department and paramedics to run silent. If White hears the sirens, he might panic and start shooting. We don't want a dead hostage on our hands."

Daniels nodded in the affirmative.

Ronan looked back at the doorway. At first, smoke was

all that filled his view. Then he glimpsed a bright glint of orange and suddenly fire screamed from the narrow opening, and the crackle of burning wood was all he heard.

Mack and Smith returned with two small fire extinguishers and began tackling the flames.

White knew we were coming. He set a trap and used us as bait. FUCK!

"Flash fire," Mack panted. "We got most of it out, but some of it's still smoldering."

Ronan tossed a commanding look at Daniels. "Okay. Watch that door and make sure White doesn't come out."

He retreated to a space near the railroad tracks. The lights on the railroad trestle were a steady red, indicating an oncoming train occupied each track in both directions.

"McCullough calling Unit 1. Unit 1, come in."

Silence.

"McCullough calling Unit 2. Come in, Unit 2."

More silence.

Shit.

Ronan felt his throat tighten. "Come on, Eric. Answer me. O'Neill. Anybody. Somebody answer me!"

After a few seconds, a breathless Eric Bonamico broke the silence. "Unit 1 here. We're safe, but we felt a huge blast of heat. What the hell's going on?"

Ronan felt some relief. "Eric, thank God. Our boy Lorenzo must have poured gas on the first floor and lit it up. He's trying to trap you all."

As Ronan waited for Bonamico's assessment, a groggy and panicked voice interrupted the transmission.

"Unit 1, Sergeant McCullough, this is Unit 2. That blast of fire hit us pretty good. I have two men down, one overcome with smoke and the other with a broken ankle."

Ronan swallowed hard.

"Easy, O'Neill," Bonamico cautioned over the heavy static. "Where are you now?"

"We made it to the second floor on the west stairwell, but when we got to the landing near the first floor, we all got knocked around from the explosion."

"All right. Stay put for now," Bonamico instructed.

For a moment Ronan forgot his location, and his mind raced in several different directions. When Daniels placed a hand on his shoulder, he nearly backhanded him.

"Sorry to startle you. Waddya got?"

Ronan forced out a long breath. "Bonamico's team is fine, but Unit 2 is in bad shape, two men down, one with a broken ankle." Ronan removed the pistol from his shoulder strap.

Daniels' eyes widened as he watched Ronan cock the weapon. "What are you doing?"

"I'm going to end this." Ronan didn't wait for Daniels to respond as he stripped the flashlight from the corporal and began limping toward the door. He clicked the microphone button on the radio earpiece. "Units 1 and 2, this is Sergeant McCullough. I'm proceeding into the west side stairwell entrance. O'Neill, I'll see you in a few. Eric, I'll move up the west stairwell while you guys come up from the east. If White's on the top floor, we'll have him surrounded."

Bonamico immediately objected. "McCullough, you stay put. I've got men down, and I can't afford another one getting hurt."

Ronan tried speaking before Bonamico cut him off.

"Not to mention you're here in a supporting function. Hold the perimeter until we close in."

"We don't have time for procedural shit, Eric. McCullough out!" Ronan removed the earpiece, hearing more forceful objections from his partner as it dangled on the vest.

Approaching the door Ronan held his pistol out with one hand and steadied the flashlight with the other, shining the beam straight ahead. The fire had died, although the heat remained fierce. He could make out the staircase hugging the inside wall and the smoldering, charred hallway that went several feet deep into the structure and then widened at the end. The expanse of space at the end of the hallway was most likely the main room of the first floor, although Ronan couldn't tell how much of it had been damaged.

He craned his neck and swayed the flashlight back and forth across the staircase and then up. The acrid smoke was strong, and Ronan coughed heavily into his arm. No matter what, he didn't want Lorenzo White to know he was coming.

Ronan moved swiftly up the wide stairwell, careful not to drag his boot heels against the metal stairs. The air quality improved the higher he climbed, but the muscles in his leg and back felt like they were tearing away from the bones with each step. Stopping for a moment, he sucked in a quick breath and then continued to the second floor.

As he reached the second-floor landing, an arm reached out and tugged him by the ankle. He jerked the gun and light to the right and found O'Neill shielding his face with one hand.

"It's me, Sergeant. O'Neill."

Ronan crouched on the ground and surveyed the situation. O'Neill and the rest of Unit 2 huddled together in a small space against the brick wall. O'Neill appeared to be the only one in good shape. Two of the men gasped for air as sweat streamed down their faces. A third man sat with his leg propped over the crown of his SWAT helmet, his left anklebone piercing the skin, and his blood-covered foot dangling to the side.

"We're okay, but I'm afraid we aren't much help to you now. I'm sorry, Sergeant," O'Neill said.

Ronan tapped the young man's cheek with a gloved hand. "No need to be sorry. You guys did everything right, and you showed incredible courage," he said as he stood up and turned to leave.

"Where are you going?" O'Neill asked.

"To get this sonofabitch."

"Let me go with you."

Ronan considered the offer for a moment. White would probably not surrender quietly, and the thought of having O'Neill provide some cover during the pursuit intrigued him. He scanned the scene again, surveying the men, and shook his head. "No. You need to stay with your team and take care of the injured."

O'Neill nodded with a slight salute.

"Don't worry. Just sit tight," Ronan directed and then headed for the stairwell.

He ascended the remaining floors without incident. The large entryway to the fourth floor had no doors attached to the hinges, and the panes of glass on the east side of the floor were parallel to the Morris and Smith Street lights. For the first time since leaving the rendezvous point in front of the warehouse, Ronan could see pockets of objects in front of him.

The charred warehouse walls encased him in a suffocating closeness as he tentatively stepped onto the cracked, wooden floor; the distinctive odor of sawdust and wet paint hung cloyingly in the air. Taking small, deliberate steps, Ronan crossed the room, trying his best to avoid tripping over the piles of lumber, slabs of sheet rock, buckets of paint, and paint trays scattered throughout. Nothing unusual. Then suddenly, a chill rocketed from the tip of his feet to the top of his head. He wasn't alone.

To the right of the door, a figure lay slumped against the wall. Ronan cautiously took a long step toward it, steadying his gun as he advanced. Slowly, he scanned the darkened form with his flashlight. In the soft, white light, the Securitas logo and two bullet holes appeared on the left breast of the dead man's shirt. A small stream of blood trickled from the corners of his mouth.

The man appeared to be in his mid-to-late fifties, slightly overweight, with salt-and-pepper hair and large jowls. He stared blankly ahead—eyes empty and unblinking. Ronan scoured the scene around the guard, noting that he didn't have a duty belt, which meant he was most likely unarmed when taken hostage.

Ronan turned off the flashlight, secured it inside the weapons strap, and made the first move. "Lorenzo. Lorenzo White. This is Sergeant McCullough of the Charleston

Police Department. The building is surrounded, and SWAT teams are inside. Your hostage is dead. Surrender yourself now if you don't want to end up the same way."

Looking up, Ronan noticed a series of pulleys dangling down from the exposed ceiling. Some of the pulleys held metal carriages in place. Other pulleys were anchored with large metal widgets and hooks.

Slanted light coming through the windows ricocheted off the construction equipment, splaying jagged shadows onto the ground. Overhead, Ronan saw a pulley quiver and a loud buzzing noise followed. When he lowered his gaze, a steel hook slammed into the side of his face.

The sound of the impact felt like thunder inside Ronan's skull. His head throbbed, and both ears rang almost as loudly as the impact to his face. He fell to the ground, dropping his weapon, and it caromed off a stack of sheetrock and disappeared into the darkness. Ronan tried to pull himself up, but he'd lost all sense of balance, and he couldn't feel his legs under him. He felt detached from the environment, as if suddenly finding himself ten feet under water. With no gun, Ronan swung wildly in front of him with both hands.

A terse, deep voice called out from across the floor. "I thought I killed you in the street! Stupid cop! Sticking your punk ass in something that was none of your business!"

Ronan staggered back and leaned against the wall. "Sorry to ruin your day, but stories of my death have been greatly exaggerated."

"Don't move, or that pulley won't be the last thing in your face."

Ronan thought he heard the safety lock on a gun release. He scanned the shadows, trying to determine the origin of the sound. Pressing himself flat against a wall, he eyed the handle of his pistol illuminated by a patch of light. Automatically, he reached for the weapon but then caught himself and withdrew.

The silence pooled. Ronan could only hear his thumping heartbeat.

White broke the silence. "I know your boys are coming. They think they're going to make it, but they're not."

Sucking in a short breath, Ronan gazed across the expanse of the warehouse floor to see a section of the wall on fire. Flames danced up its side in perfect harmony.

The bastard torched the other stairwell.

Ronan's stomach coiled. Eric and Unit 1 were in that stairwell, and they now faced the same peril as Unit 2—or worse. Anger swirled in his chest. "You crazy sonofabitch! You're going to burn down the whole, goddamn warehouse."

The only noise was the crackling and splintering of wood.

"If I ain't gettin' out alive then nobody will," White finally shouted. "This is just the beginning."

This time White's voice was louder and more direct—and closer.

The temperature on the fourth floor increased with each passing minute. Hot sweat trailed down Ronan's chest and back, soaking his BDUs. He knew he had to evacuate soon. He sized up the distance between himself and the gun. Three long strides, maybe four, would give him the chance to snare his weapon.

As Ronan weighed the risk, he heard a faint clinking noise coming from his right. It sounded like something had brushed against one of the empty paint cans. White was circling, readying to strike. Ronan counted silently then clenched his teeth, pushed off the wall and lunged at the shadow coming toward him.

The leap wasn't quite long enough, but Ronan managed to slap the weapon away. His other hand caught White's arm, and the force pulled them both down.

White responded by driving the heel of his shoe into Ronan's hand. Ronan yelped but scrambled to his knees, reared back and slammed a devastating right cross into his adversary's jaw. White fell back and hit the floor with a heavy thud. As Ronan moved over him, White rebounded and charged, tackling Ronan below the waist. The force of

White's blow slammed Ronan against the floor once more, knocking the air out of him. With a tight, closed fist, White leaned in and punched at Ronan, but Ronan rolled away before the blow made contact.

Trying to gain purchase on the rough floor, Ronan scraped a hand across the worn, wooden planks; splinters and staples sliced open the skin. Finally, he felt the cold steel of his Berretta, and his bloody fingers wrapped around the handle. But White jerked the gun away. A shot rang out, and the bullet tore into the wall. Then another shot exploded, this time humming across the room and ricocheting off something metallic.

With a heavy grunt, Ronan thrust an elbow upward and smacked White squarely in the

nose; blood instantly gushed from both nostrils. As White grasped his face, Ronan seized the pistol.

"You're under arrest!" Ronan shouted as he stumbled to his feet, the pain in his injured leg nearly blinding him.

White let out a maniacal laugh. "It's not over. Getting me doesn't end it. My boys are gonna own this town very soon, and there's nothing your PO-lice can do to stop us."

As Ronan groped for his handcuffs, White caught him off guard and grabbed his ankle, knocking him off balance. Ronan hit the floor. When he rolled back over, he found White standing over him, the gun cocked and pointed directly at his head.

Taking a deep breath, Ronan closed his eyes and prayed. But instead of hearing the voices of angels, a swooshing noise filled his ears. He opened his eyes just in time to see a small sliver of skin explode from White's neck. Another swoosh. This time, a large chunk of the man's face exploded just in front of the ear, and his body jerked violently backward. Finally, three more strikes hit his head and neck. White fell into the wall and then slid limp and lifeless to the floor.

Ronan bolted up and grabbed his weapon. He anxiously surveyed the room, wondering if White had an accomplice. Several shadows descended upon him. The adrenaline pumping through Ronan made the *fight or flight* response an easy one—he'd fight even if he had to shoot his way out.

"Ronan! Are you okay?"

Two members of Unit 1 emerged from the edge of the shadows, flanked by Eric Bonamico.

CHAPTER 9

R onan felt relaxed for the first time in several days. Even the lumpy and stained seat padding in the squad-car seat felt good against his tired and aching muscles.

Officer Mack, impressed with Ronan and the tenacity and vigor he'd shown during the warehouse takedown, offered to take the sergeant home, telling Bonamico it would be an honor. There'd be a debriefing in the morning with Captain Ashby, but right now all Ronan wanted to do was rest.

Mack looked like he had just graduated from the West Virginia State Police Academy. This was due in part to the wide, doleful green eyes that were always permanently fixed in an expression of amazement, giving away his inexperience.

The squad car pulled into the driveway. Ronan leaned forward and scanned the house. Most of the interior lights were off, except for a small light in the upstairs window. As Ronan opened the car door, Officer Mack gave him a long look with those quartz-like green eyes.

"Sergeant Bonamico really thinks you should have gone to the hospital or at least had the paramedics check you out at the scene."

Ronan carefully swung both legs out from the floorboard and onto the driveway, lifting the sore and now swollen right leg up and down with both hands. "I appreciate your concern and Bonamico's too," he said, first speaking into the door and then looking back at Mack. "I'll be fine. I'm just exhausted and sore. That's all."

Mack rubbed his chin and gripped the steering wheel. "All right then. Goodnight, Sergeant. Oh, and great work tonight."

"You too, Mack. If it hadn't been for you and Smith putting out that fire, we could've had a lot of dead cops tonight."

The comment made Mack blush and squirm in the seat. "Thank you. Uh…goodnight then."

Ronan easily navigated the steps leading to the front door of the townhouse despite his right leg having gone numb, most likely from climbing the steps in the warehouse and from the weight he'd placed on it for the last few hours.

A lamp on the small corner table in the dining room provided the light Ronan saw earlier. Upstairs, he heard a low-frequency fluttering. It came in fits, starting and stopping.

Beer. Ronan wanted a beer. The heat and tension inside the warehouse had left him parched. He immediately turned to the right, ignoring anything in the living room. On the island in the kitchen, a note had been left on the granite countertop:

RONAN,

THERE'S SOME LEFT-OVER PIZZA IN THE FRIDGE BUT NOT MUCH. NICK SAID HE REALLY LIKES HUSSON'S PIZZA. HE'S UPSTAIRS ASLEEP. I TOLD HIM HE COULD SLEEP IN OUR ROOM TONIGHT UNTIL I CAN MAKE UP THE GUEST BEDROOM.

I SAW THE STORY ABOUT WHITE'S DEATH ON WSAZ AT 11. I'M GLAD YOU'RE OKAY.

WE'LL TALK WHEN I GET HOME.

I LOVE YOU.

TY

The note made Ronan grin and his heart flutter—mainly because the language was classic Ty: poignant, sweet, and conversational. A pang of guilt soon replaced the contentment. Ronan had bolted from the house, leaving Ty to take care of a teenager. Now Ronan felt awful. Walking over to the sink and turning on the kitchen light, he stared at the words on the paper again. Ty made sure to propose a discussion and include it at the end of the letter. He wanted Ronan to know that they indeed had a lot to talk about: Nick, Melissa, the standoff at the warehouse, and probably more.

As Ronan tossed the note on the counter, his cell phone vibrated. He didn't hesitate to answer it. "I like how you put Officer Mack up to lecturing me about not receiving treatment at the scene tonight."

Bonamico let out a tight laugh. "I've got no clue what you're talking about."

"Save it," Ronan said, opening the stainless-steel refrigerator door and pulling out a cold Budweiser.

"Seriously, though. I didn't get the chance to check on you before you left."

Ronan twisted the bottle cap. The snap and release of sealed pressure from the bottle was accompanied by some droplets of beer that landed on the island. "I'm good. Sore and tired, but good."

Bonamico held the phone away for a moment and then lowered his voice. "I need to whisper. Pat and the kids are asleep."

"As well they should be. Hell! We all should be sleeping." A moment of silence passed between them. "Thanks for saving my ass tonight."

"Don't mention it," Bonamico said. "I'm just returning the favor from when you saved me a few years ago. Remember the house on the East End? I thought for sure I was a goner when that suspect came at me with a knife. If it hadn't been for you, Pat would be receiving a widow's pension now."

Ronan smeared the droplets of beer with a thumb. "I'd almost forgotten about that. Meth is a bad thing."

"Damn right! And that guy was on plenty of it."

Ronan took another generous gulp of beer. "I'll admit I was scared shitless tonight when White set that doorway on fire. I thought your team would be fried for sure."

"Well," Bonamico said thoughtfully, before pausing as if recalling the moment. "We smelled gas when we got to the third floor, and I remember what had happened to you and O'Neill. We waited for a moment just in case he decided to torch it. You must have distracted him because he only managed to light up the doorframe itself and a small part of the landing. We were able to slip through."

Ronan took a long swig of beer and then studied the handwritten note again. He couldn't forget what White had said. *"My boys are gonna own this town very soon, and there's nothing your PO-lice can do to stop us."*

"Oh, yeah," Bonamico added. "Ashby wants my complete report tomorrow morning, but he said you can have the day off to rest."

Ronan pulled the phone back from his ear, mulling over the words. "That's nice of him."

"Well, look," Bonamico said, dropping his voice another octave. "I'm going to check on the kids and head to bed. I'm glad you're okay. Call me if you need anything."

Ronan appreciated the thought. "Thanks, Eric. Oh, one more thing."

"Yeah."

"White said something about him not being the end of things and how *his boys* would soon be taking over Charleston. What do you think he meant by that?"

Bonamico paused again, probably chewing over the words. "Eh, who knows? When a guy's at the end of his rope, he'll say anything to sound important or like he's leaving a legacy. The important thing is he's dead, and we've got the rest of his posse in custody."

Hearing the explanation did make Ronan feel satisfied, at least for the moment.

"Thanks again, Eric."

"You got it, Ronan. Talk to you later."

Ronan closed the phone and walked to the living room, taking two more generous swallows of beer. The frothy liquid tasted better than ever.

A laptop and a large pile of papers sat precariously on the table in front of the loveseat, and next to the computer was *The Charleston Gazette*. Ronan thumbed through the sections until he reached the Sports page.

Sports editor Brian Lipton had a story on the bottom of the page below the fold. Ronan cringed when he read the headline:

CSC'S KICKER WARNER DISMISSED
FROM TEAM FOLLOWING PLEA DEAL

Ronan scanned the first two paragraphs, thankful that the inverted pyramid style of newspaper reporting mirrored those reports required by the Charleston PD, i.e., the most important facts first. He dropped the paper and leaned back into the seat. Locking his hands behind his head, he sighed. He hadn't thought much about Michael Warner since the ordeal with Lorenzo White and the other man began, but Warner had been a part of the situation from the beginning. Normally, Ronan heard details about suspects facing charges, especially from colleagues who served as bailiffs at the courthouse. But with his hospitalization and injuries, he'd missed those discussions.

Upstairs, Nick continued to snore loudly, which made Ronan grin. His cell phone shook again. He opened it and didn't wait for a greeting.

"I guess you couldn't fall asleep."

A woman cleared her throat. "Ronan. This is Melissa."

He grimaced and slapped a hand into the loveseat. *Not now! Not today!*

Ronan used a pause to set the tone of the conversation.

"Melissa. I'm sorry, I don't know a Melissa." He leaned forward. "Oh yes, I think I do know a Melissa." He snapped his fingers. "Ah, that's right, Melissa. Her kid showed up on my doorstep yesterday."

"Aren't you funny," Melissa said, her smoky voice flat and direct. "Where's Nick? How is he?"

"He's fine and upstairs asleep. Don't worry. Ty and I took care of everything. You and Brucie really out did your-selves this time."

"Who's Ty?" Melissa asked.

"Ty's my life partner."

"Don't use that term," she barked. "He's your boyfriend, not that it makes any difference. It's not like you two can get married or have a real life or family."

Ronan crumpled the newspaper slowly, imagining the pages were Melissa's face. "No need to sugarcoat anything. I'm sure you've filled Nick in about me. What was that you called me when I told you I was gay? A freak? Yeah, that's it. *A freak*."

Melissa let out a long sigh. "That was a long time ago, but I still can't believe you're a queer. Growing up, you had every girl in Boston constantly calling you and coming by the house. Ha! You were never interested in those girls. I guess I should've known something was wrong. I just never imagined my brother would be gay."

"Well, thanks for supporting my happiness," Ronan said. He felt the veins in his neck bulging and a headache coming on. "I'm happy, Melissa. Ty's great, and my life's great."

"Really?" Melissa asked, her pitch higher than before. "For God's sake! You're a cop in frigging nowhere West Virginia."

Ronan stood up to alleviate the adrenaline running through him, totally ignoring his sore leg and back. "I like it here. The people are friendly; the life is slower-paced, and I'm just a couple of hours away from the mountains and fresh air."

"Please," Melissa scoffed. "Anytime I've been there, it's reminded me of a Depression-era hellhole!"

"And how many times has that been? How many times have you come to visit me, or called me or checked on me? Hell! I haven't seen Nick in ten years!"

"Don't you put this one on me," Melissa responded defensively. "A telephone works both ways."

"The last time I came to Miami, Bruce got drunk and slugged me in the mouth."

"That's because you brought your boyfriend with you."

"Melissa! Bruce got drunk and called Sean and me every homophobic slur imaginable. So much for Southern hospitality. I don't want to be around someone like that. And you just stood there and said nothing. It's funny how your silence always equates to acceptance." Ronan eyed Ty's note again, feeling blessed to have such a wonderful man in his life, especially in light of what he'd put him through over the last day.

"It doesn't matter—"

Ronan cut her off. "You want to talk about relationships? Let's talk about you getting pregnant by an ex-con during a one-night tryst while he was out on parole." Ronan pressed his lips firmly against the phone, anger coursing through him. "Does Nick even know who his father is?"

Silence.

"Then Mom and Dad basically raised Nick for a few years because you couldn't keep a job. Then you broke up Bruce Copeland's marriage by having an affair with him. You probably targeted him because he was a rich stockbroker. The next thing I know, Mom and Dad are calling me and saying you're moving to Miami with Nick. If I remember correctly, Bruce likes to insult you and throw shit when he's having a bad day. *This* phone call is not about me, Melissa. It's about you and the fact that Nick showing up here in Charleston is just another mess you've created that someone has to clean up!"

Ronan felt droplets of sweat sliding down his nose. He pressed a hand against the cushion and leaned onto it, forgetting completely about the beer. Static infiltrated the line, and he could hear his sister sobbing quietly.

"You can be so cruel sometimes, Ronan."

"Yeah, well, the truth hurts, doesn't it? Now what are we going to do about Nick?"

Melissa sniffed twice, and Ronan could hear her moving the phone around. "I'm not sure staying with two gay men is the right environment for him." Her voice sounded shaky and less confident than earlier.

"Melissa, please. What type of environment does he have in Miami? Watching you and Brucie fight all the time is not what I'd call a good environment. Your son has no confidence. Do you know that? He can barely look at me when he talks."

"Bruce is under a lot of pressure at work trying to recover losses from the real-estate meltdown and—"

"Oh, that breaks my heart," Ronan snapped, mocking the words with a hand resting over his own heart. He felt a presence moving behind him.

"I hope that I can stay."

A startled Ronan spun around to find Nick standing in the living-room entryway.

Melissa heard the comment. A panicked mother emerged. "Is that Nick? Let me talk to him, right now!"

Ronan held the phone in front of Nick. He stared at it like it was an alien object and looked away. "If that's Mom, I don't want to talk to her."

"He said he doesn't want to talk to you."

"That's ridiculous. He has some explaining to do. I'm his mother, and I demand to speak to my son."

Ronan repeated the previous action, and Nick shook his head.

"He still says *no.*"

Before Ronan could say another word, Nick spoke. "I love it here. I like being with you, Uncle Ronan, and Ty. Ty's really nice. He told me about growing up in Hawaii and stories about being a nurse." Nick's voice rose with every word he spoke. "He even told me about the communication and electronics program at the Charleston State College. Ty thinks I could get in. He likes having me here." The expression from his face waned, and Nick looked down. "Did Mom hear that?"

Ronan shrugged. "Did you hear that, Melissa?"

"Every word."

"Well, I guess that takes care of the reason why you called. Anything else?" Ronan could hear Melissa huffing on the other end of the line. "Tell Brucie I said hello, and I hope he drops dead soon."

As Ronan went to close the phone, Melissa barked out, "I'm coming to get my son."

"Goodnight," Ronan said in an impish voice of mockery. He closed the phone and tossed it on the island.

"What did she say?" Nick asked softly.

"She says she loves you."

CHAPTER 10

The sun had been blazing all day, and its unbearable heat had kept Ronan, Ty and Nick locked within the confines of the air-conditioned townhouse for most of the day. Ronan took several afternoon naps while Ty kept a restless Nick company.

When Ronan woke from his nap, Ty suggested they go to a movie. Ronan agreed since it meant he wouldn't have to spend time in the sweltering heat. He then agreed to let Nick pick the movie, which ended up being *Zombies Revenge*.

Nick nearly bounced out of the theater lobby. "That was great! The whole town got eaten by zombies, and then it got wiped out by a bomb!"

Ty reached around and slapped a high-five with Nick. "It was awesome! It reminded me of those *Night of the Living Dead* movies from the 80s."

They both looked at Ronan, who looked pale.

"That movie was awful! I can't believe I let you two talk me into seeing it."

Letting out a short laugh, Ty playfully elbowed Ronan in the side. "Oh, come on. It wasn't that bad."

"Whatever," Ronan scoffed as they stood in the lobby.

The lobby of the Park Place Stadium Cinemas felt suffocating as the hot, humid street air mingled with the stale, recycled air-conditioned air. An overpowering scent of perfumed industrial cleaner further assaulted the senses.

"You know, those are the first real words you've said to me in a while," Ronan added in a whisper, leaning closer to Ty, so Nick wouldn't hear.

"I've been too mad to talk to you."

The intensity in Ty's dark eyes flared.

Nick pushed open the glass doors and exited the lobby.

Ronan slipped close to Ty and held his hand until they both noticed hoards of people streaming into the lobby, murmuring to each other and scrounging around their pockets for money or plastic cards.

"Can we go eat now? I've never been to a real diner before. Mom never takes me out to eat with her and Bruce," Nick stated matter-of-factly.

Ty frowned and looked at Ronan. Ronan shrugged, unsure of what to say.

"I think you'll like the Corner Diner," Ronan said. "It reopened a year ago after being closed for some time."

Nick had gone ahead of Ronan and Ty, but they caught up with him at West Washington Street.

"Man, it's still hot, and it's nearly seven o'clock," Ronan groaned as his nephew ran circles around him, apparently unaffected by the temperature. "Nick, take a left there on Laidley Street."

The young man stopped at the corner and pressed the walk button as Ronan and Ty stepped under the glass bus-stop canopy and waited for the light to change.

Looking around and seeing little foot or vehicle traffic, Ronan pulled Ty close. "The weather's not the only thing that's hot."

Ty squirmed playfully as Ronan pulled him close and nuzzled the soft space below his ear. Ty smelled heavenly: clean and fresh with a faint smell of sweet cologne. Softly, Ronan licked the spot with the tip of his tongue before applying a wet kiss.

The kiss made Ty pant slightly, and it made Ronan's crotch swell. A ringing bell followed by a repetitive clicking noise chimed from the walk signal, interrupting Ronan's romantic gesture.

Nick stayed ahead of them, craning his neck back and forth, drinking in downtown Charleston. Despite the oppressive heat and time of evening, smartly dressed men and women hurried down the sidewalks on both sides of the street, heading to the movie theater or to the Town Center Mall.

Too seasoned to trust the traffic lights, Ronan grabbed Nick by the shirt once the crosswalk light signaled for pedestrian traffic. The cars coming down Quarrier Street screeched to a halt behind the white lines, except for one that made a dash into the intersection despite the lights having already changed back to red. Some pedestrians shook their fists, but no one was hit.

When they reached the Corner Diner, Ronan placed his hand against the cool glass door and smiled appreciatively. *Thank God for air-conditioning!* As he opened the door, the wonderful aroma of onion, garlic, meat, pepper and spices greeted him, and his stomach growled in anticipation.

"Wow!" Nick exclaimed. "This place looks just like the diners on those old black-and-white TV shows."

The diner had undergone a remarkable transformation. For years it had been a frequent haven of the homeless. Broken windows and graffiti routinely plagued the old landmark, and Ronan and his colleagues had responded to more than one vandalism call there. After many years of abuse and finally abandonment, the Pollitt family purchased the property and began extensive renovations, restoring the building to its original 1946 status.

Waitresses scurried around the diner, taking orders and bringing customers trays of piping-hot food and cold drinks. Ronan looked around, admiring the newly restored interior with its red tabletops, decorative lamps, shiny black and white tile floor, and cushy leather booths accented with polished decorative wood paneling.

A plump waitress with fuchsia-colored hair and too much makeup seated them in a booth near the door.

Ronan sat on the outside of the booth seat next to Ty while Nick eased himself into the opposite seat. The same woman dropped menus on the table and mumbled that a waitress would be with them shortly.

Nick opened the menu and studied the entrees.

Ty smiled and nudged Ronan, who returned a faint smile.

"Get whatever you want, Nick. It's our treat," Ronan directed.

"Really?"

"Of course," Ty replied. "You're our guest."

Nick's eyes widened. "They have everything—macaroni and cheese, mashed potatoes, fried apples, and ten different kinds of burgers! I always have enough to eat at home, but Mom never makes mac and cheese. She said it would make me fat like Grandpa McCullough."

Ronan grimaced at the remark. The dark blue veins running through the young man's thin arms and small hands, coupled with his frail physique, made Ronan think the kid needed all the carbs he could get.

The same woman who had seated them reappeared at their booth. She looked at Nick for a moment and then turned to Ronan and Ty. "Anyone been here yet?"

Ty shook his head, and the woman grumbled. "What can I get you?"

"I want the double bacon cheeseburger with a side of mac and cheese, mashed potatoes, applesauce, and a piece of banana cream pie for dessert. Oh! And I want a chocolate milkshake too."

Nick looked up to see Ronan and Ty staring at him. He slouched in the seat and blushed. "Sorry. That's too much food, isn't it?"

"Nothing to worry about. We'll have the same," Ronan said with a wink.

The woman pulled out a small notepad, scribbled down the order and then disappeared without saying a word.

"There's always room for cheeseburgers and milkshakes," Ty said.

Nick grinned.

"By the way," Ronan added, "your Grandpa McCullough wasn't fat. He was short and stout and incredibly strong. He was a longshoreman at Boston Harbor."

"Mom never really had too many nice things to say about grandpa, just that he was fat."

Like Ronan, William McCullough was mortified that Melissa had had a baby out of wedlock. For a while, William shunned her and didn't acknowledge the baby, but he eventually took them both in for a time. When Melissa decided to move to Miami with Bruce, all contact between them ceased. She didn't even attend her father's funeral, which devastated their mother and the rest of the McCullough clan.

Ronan swallowed hard and decided not to share the family history with his nephew at this point in time. He looked out the diner's glass door to see three people loitering nearby. Two of them were smoking, and Ronan recognized the outline of the third person.

Ty and Nick were laughing about something when Ronan interrupted. "I'll be right back."

Ty cupped his hand on Ronan's arm. "Where are you going?"

Ronan didn't look back but instead focused on the figure closest to the door. "I think I see someone I know."

He pushed open the diner doors and was hit again by a wall of humid air. The two smokers froze and stopped speaking as Ronan appeared. The third figure turned slowly around when he noticed the reaction of the others.

The kid sucked in a breath. Ronan studied him, recognizing the sandy blond hair with caramel-colored streaks and the ice-blue eyes.

"Michael Warner."

Michael stiffened.

Ronan sensed panic. "It's okay. I just wanted to talk for a second."

"Who's this?" the young man standing next to Michael asked.

A young woman stood to the left of Michael, and leveled an incredulous look at Ronan. Ronan looked at the three of them for second. The male friend was tall like Michael but dressed in all black clothes, and his face was coated with white powder and dark lipstick. The girl looked exactly the same.

Ronan reached into his pocket and pulled out his shield. "Sergeant Ronan McCullough, Charleston Police."

"It's okay, Justin," Michael added, his voice quivering slightly as he spoke.

Justin held his breath and nudged the girl next to him. They both put out their cigarettes on the sidewalk and then deposited the butts in a nearby trashcan. "Later, man."

As they walked away, Justin looked back at Ronan and Michael and then shook his head.

"I don't want any more trouble," Michael said, watching Ronan slowly clip the shield onto his belt.

"And I'm not here to start any," Ronan replied.

Michael appeared agitated. He shifted his weight from one foot to another and clenched his jaw. Unlike his two departed friends, Michael wore gray sweatpants and a maroon tee shirt that hung loosely over his waist and was splotched with sweat stains.

"Are you here to arrest me?"

"No."

"Good."

Michael lowered a shoulder and pushed his way past Ronan, but Ronan grabbed him by the arm.

"Let go of me!" he shouted, drawing the attention of some people passing by.

A plump woman with a cherubic face winced at them and shook her head as she walked past and into the diner.

"I don't know you."

"I know," Ronan said. "I just wanted to ask you a couple of questions. That's all." He looked through the diner's glass door to see the waitress lowering a tray of food onto the table. "Do you know those men who attacked us outside of The Two Minute Warning?"

Michael stopped wiggling and pressed his lips tight against his face. "Look, man, I meant to find you and say thank you for helping me. So, thank you. But I don't want to talk about what happened."

Ronan stepped closer, looking deeply into Michael's eyes. "You'd better, son. You seem like a good kid, so I can't figure out why you'd be protecting thugs like that."

Michael was silent.

"Was it drugs? I read that you lost your spot on the CSC football team because you got busted for weed."

"So what? I like to smoke a little from time to time."

"That's not the point," Ronan said. "Did you owe those men drug money?"

Michael ran a hand through his hair. The pale blue rings around his dark pupils contracted. Ronan's interview training and experiences told him the kid was trying to formulate a credible response.

"The man who attacked us was named Lorenzo White. He's dead now, and that other prick's in jail. White said trouble was coming to town. Do you know anything about that?"

Michael shook his head repeatedly. "I can't say anything. The others will know if I squeal."

"What others?"

"You know…others…like the guys who came after me. I was in some trouble. I was warned…"

"Are you a drug runner for them?"

"No. I just needed some money for school."

"You deal for them? Sell drugs at CSC?"

The faded pools of sweat staining Michael's shirt grew dark again.

"Look, I just want to forget all this happened."

Ronan stomped on the sidewalk and turned away. Inside the diner, he saw Ty and Nick eating and slapping high-fives with each other.

"Michael," Ronan said, turning back to look at the young man, "if you know what's going down, you need to tell me. If you don't then you're an accessory to anything that happens. Do you understand what that means?"

"Yep."

"And if you decide to do whatever you've been doing again then you're right back in the middle of it all."

Before Ronan could continue, an old pewter-colored Honda Accord pulled up into the middle of Quarrier Street. The exhaust coming from the vibrating tail pipe spewed a white plume of smoke into the air. The car heaved and rattled as the girl who had been with Michael earlier leaned out of the passenger-side window.

"Michael, come on. Let's go," she called out over the noise coming from the old car.

He looked at her, then at Ronan, and then back at her. "Just a second, Raina." Michael's facial expression remained flat, but his eyes relaxed. "Again, thanks for helping me that night."

Before Ronan could say another word, Michael was in the car. Ronan reached into his pocket and pulled out his phone, noting the license plate as the car chugged away.

CHAPTER 11

After saving the car's license plate info in his phone, Ronan walked back to the diner. But instead of going in, he stopped out front and called the precinct.

Ty tapped Ronan on the shoulder. "We're finished with dinner."

Ronan spun around and brusquely waved Ty away. "This is Sergeant McCullough, shield number 1178. I need you to run a license plate for me."

Perturbed, Ty moved in front of Ronan and searched his face for an explanation.

"Ready? West Virginia license number AWS 166. Who's the registered owner? Any priors? Has the vehicle been reported stolen?" Ronan looked down and dappled the corners of his mouth with the tip of his tongue. "Okay. Great. Let me know when you find out something. By the way, I'm off-duty right now, and this isn't an emergency." He paused. "Okay, thanks."

Ronan ended the call and finally made eye contact with Ty who rocked back and forth on both heels waiting for an explanation.

"In case you're wondering, I had your dinner boxed to go."

Ronan clicked the power button on his cell and noticed over twenty minutes had passed since he'd stepped outside. "I'm sorry. I didn't mean to be gone for so long, but I saw Michael Warner and wanted to talk with him. Is Nick okay?"

"He's fine. He's eating his banana cream pie."

Ronan studied Ty, waiting for an expression of aggravation or disappointment to cross his handsome face.

Ty's dark brown eyes twinkled with delight. "Thanks for dinner," he said, holding up Ronan's wallet with the tips of his fingers and swaying it back and forth. "You left it on the table, so I used your Visa to pay for dinner…and dessert."

Ronan grabbed his wallet.

"Did you see the newspaper article on that Warner kid I left for you in the living room?" Ty asked.

"Yeah, I did. He seems like a good kid. I can't for the life of me understand why he'd get mixed up with a guy like Lorenzo White."

Ty bobbed his head, contemplating the statement. "The article said Michael was from San Jose. He's a long way from home. CSC's a private school and tuition's expensive."

"No, there's more to it than that." A hard edge formed around those words. "He was probably recruited to play football. Why would he risk that?"

Ty held up his hands. "Just a thought. That's all."

Ronan wiped the sweat from his brow and leaned closer to Ty. "Sorry. I didn't mean to be rude."

"I know," Ty responded softly. "I just wish you could move on from this. I've never seen you get so consumed over a case before. What is it you always tell me when I get worked up over patients at the hospital? *Ty, you have to learn to compartmentalize everything.* I think you need to heed your own advice."

"I know. You're right."

"Like always," Ty said with a tight laugh, thumping Ronan on the chest with a loosely clenched fist.

Nick opened the diner door and broke into the conversation. "Are you guys coming back in? Dessert was great! Can I order another one?"

Both Ronan and Ty turned around and simultaneously said, "No!"

———

Ty jammed the Jaguar's gas pedal, and Ronan stared silently ahead as the elegant sports sedan glided up Lee Street and onto Interstate 64.

Looking out the window onto the Kanawha River, Ronan watched the orange haze of the setting sun dance over the moving water, reflecting off every ripple. August had been hot and miserable, but he enjoyed the late summer sunset, its tranquil beauty hovering above the damp, sticky air that cloaked everything at the surface.

The Jaguar effortlessly merged onto Route 119 and headed for Autumn Road. Ronan liked the fast motion of a darkening landscape. By the time they'd pulled into the driveway, Nick had awakened from his nap in the backseat. "I'm going to watch some TV and then go to bed," he mumbled as he stretched out of the car.

Ty followed and unlocked the townhouse door while Ronan remained inside the car. The interior was still cool from the air-conditioner, so he'd be comfortable enough as he waited the obligatory ten minutes. Ronan and Ty agreed to this arrangement early on. If they'd been out together, Ty would enter the house first, and Ronan would go into the garage or get back into the car and wait ten minutes. Ronan assumed that anyone in the neighborhood who saw he and Ty constantly together would know they were a couple. A gay couple in Los Angeles was one thing, but a gay couple in Charleston was not as readily accepted, especially when one half of that couple was a cop. It was best to lay low and keep the neighborhood gossip to a minimum.

Ronan checked the clock on his cell phone. An illumi-nated green light under the time display blinked. Perhaps by now someone on the dispatch desk had run the license-plate numbers for him. He clicked on the *V* character at the bottom of the screen, unlocking the voicemail inbox. Melissa's number was the first in queue. Ronan didn't want to argue with her over Nick or anything else. "Not tonight, sis. Nick is my nephew too, and I like having him here. If you and Brucie boy don't want to take care of him, Ty and I will," he almost shouted into the phone.

Ronan half expected Melissa's voice to rise from the microcomputer inside the phone and scold him. When only silence ensued, he scrolled through the recent calls, but there was nothing from work. He turned off the phone and walked quickly inside.

Entering the living room, Ronan could hear the Science Channel blaring on the television. Nick lay on the sofa, an arm covering both eyes, snoring softly. Ronan lowered the TV's volume and slipped quietly out of the room.

As he climbed the steps, Ronan could hear Ty shuffling in between the bedroom and bathroom. When he reached the top of the stairs, the phone rang again. "Ronan McCullough."

The bathroom door clicked shut when he reached the bed and sat down.

"Sergeant, this is Todd Epperly at dispatch."

Ronan didn't recognize the voice or the name. Hunter McDowell normally manned the dispatch desk, but it was Friday—McDowell's day off.

"Go ahead, Epperly," Ronan instructed.

"I ran the license plate you requested. The car is registered to a Justin Collier who lives on Noyes Avenue in Kanawha City. Nothing came up. He's clean."

"Nothing?"

"Nothing at all, Sergeant. No priors, no arrests, no warrants, not even a speeding ticket, and there haven't been any reports of stolen vehicles within the last seventy-two hours."

"Okay. I appreciate it, Epperly. Everything quiet tonight?"

"So far, other than the usual traffic jams and accidents.

It's the last Friday in August which means it's the first weekend for high-school football, so that always keeps us on our toes."

Ronan remembered working security for those high-school games when he first joined the CPD. Every high-school game venue was different. Some nights were calm and incident free, while other nights he felt like a high-paid babysitter trying to control a mob of unruly teenagers.

Epperly spoke again. "Everything okay, Sergeant?"

"Yeah, I think so. Thanks again."

"Sure. Have a good evening."

As Ronan hung up the phone, his thoughts once again turned to Lorenzo White. *Maybe Eric was right. White knew the end was coming, and he wanted me to think something bigger was going to happen.*

Two warm hands slipped around Ronan's chest, interrupting his solitary reflection. He absent-mindedly stroked the smooth, delicate hands, relishing their power and tenderness. When he turned around, he saw Ty standing before him, dressed only in a pair of low-hanging plaid boxers, the material hugging his square, narrow hips.

"You look disappointed. Bad news from dispatch?"

Ronan watched Ty hold his breath. "Not really. Those kids who picked up Michael Warner checked out. The car wasn't stolen."

"See, you were worried about nothing," Ty said as he rested his head on Ronan's chest. Ty could feel Ronan's strong, steady heartbeat and even breathing, and he was content. Ronan was safe in his arms.

Ronan delighted in Ty, finding his quiet strength and manly beauty always surprising and constantly exciting. Playfully, Ty unbuttoned Ronan's shirt and removed it, exposing the hard chest and flat abs that sent a shattering wave of desire through him. Ronan kissed Ty's neck and shoulders, and Ty trembled slightly as Ronan's lips trailed tiny kisses across the soft hollow of his throat and down across his chest. Willingly, Ty mirrored the action, and Ronan moaned, trying desperately to contain his passion.

Gently, Ronan slipped his fingers beneath the waistband of Ty's shorts and seductively pulled them down his long, lean legs. He gazed with awful reverence at Ty's perfect form, and then dropped to his knees and teased Ty's anxious flesh with his tongue, giving him pleasure beyond imagining.

"Take me now," Ty whispered.

Ronan obeyed Ty's command. Scooping him into his arms, he carried him to their bed where together they explored one another's body with hands and lips and tongues. When Ronan could contain himself no longer, he rolled on his back and pulled Ty forcefully to him. With one swift and deliberate stroke, he entered Ty. Ty gasped and tensed in response then yielded completely to Ronan, entreating him beyond his finite threshold as Ronan ran his hands down the length of his back and pulled him deeper with each shattering thrust. As Ty was brought to his pleasure, Ronan acknowledged his climax and spent himself deep within him. Their bodies jerked helplessly together with spasms of passionate satisfaction, and Ronan never wanted this moment to end.

When their pas de deux was complete, Ty rolled onto the bed to catch his breath. Ronan gathered him into the warm circle of his strong arms and kissed his sweet-smelling hair.

"I love you so much, Ty Andino," Ronan said, the words getting garbled in between kisses.

"I love you too, Ronan McCullough."

Suddenly, a noise from outside the bedroom startled them both. Ty rose up first, and his chin clipped Ronan on the nose. Ronan yelped.

"Be quiet," Ty hissed as he looked at the bedroom door that had been unintentionally left ajar.

"Okay!" Ronan replied as he rubbed his nose and then followed Ty's gaze out to the hallway.

A large, square shadow tightened and shrank as it slowly moved across the open expanse.

CHAPTER 12

R onan didn't remember falling asleep, nor did he remember Ty waking up. As he stared at the ceiling, the passionate sex from last night still raced through his mind. He felt like a teenager in love. Although he wasn't a teenager, Ronan was in love. There was nobody more important to him than Ty. No matter what happened, Ronan knew Ty loved him and wanted the best for him. The best for *them*.

Ronan had to admit Ty was normally right about everything when it came to him and their relationship, and he was especially cognizant of Ronan's fixations. Ty knew Ronan could get so obsessed with something that he didn't know when to let it go. A prime example of that was the White-Warner case. White was dead, and Michael Warner had suffered the consequences of his involvement, which included losing his football scholarship.

Ronan closed his eyes for a moment. *Case closed. Move on, Ronan*, he thought. His focus shifted to Nick. Now that Nick was living with them, Ronan would have to make room in his life for his nephew. His mind snapped back to last night. *Nick*. Nick was the one in the hallway. "Shit!" Ronan said aloud. He wondered how much the kid had seen, and if he had already packed his bag and was headed back for Miami, scarred forever.

Leaning up, Ronan felt a warming ray of sunlight angling through the gap in the window curtains. The ray splayed on the bed, accentuating the squared-pattern comforter. Ty believed in making their bedroom as comfortable as possible, and even though the bedroom with its corner exposures, en-suite bathroom cum stall shower and high-end finishes, coupled with a surround system, seemed too much for Ronan, he did appreciate a comfortable room.

Ronan put on a light-blue tee shirt and cotton shorts and then headed downstairs to the kitchen. Nick was nowhere in sight, but Ty was standing at the stove watching something sizzle and pop in the pan. Ronan slipped up from behind and pressed himself against his lover, suddenly finding himself hard and erect again.

Ty playfully shook him off. "Hey, you. Didn't you get enough last night?"

"I can never get enough of you," Ronan replied, kissing the soft, delicate skin beneath Ty's ear. "Where's Nick?"

Ty reached into a drawer beside the stove and removed a skillet. "Nick's going with us to the Charleston State game today. He said he wanted to get a team shirt, so I sent him to the Town Center. Can you get me a cup of water?"

"Yep," Ronan replied before stopping and turning back to face Ty. "Wait. He doesn't know his way around. How's he getting to the mall and back?"

Ty laughed as he placed the skillet on the stovetop. "I gave him my phone and plugged in the directions using the GPS tracker. He'll be fine. And before you say anything else, he took my car instead of your big ole' truck."

Ronan fetched the cup of water as Ty stood tending breakfast, all shoulders, two-day scruff and intense dark eyes focused on the task at hand. Carefully, he dabbed coconut butter into the little skillet, toasted two pieces of bread and simmered one egg at a time over low heat, dusting the surface with garlic salt and checking it frequently so it wouldn't burn.

Two pieces of bread sprang from the toaster, and Ronan pulled out another piece before the timer-bell dinged. Stuffing the toast into his mouth, he reached into the refrigerator and pulled out a Diet Pepsi.

"You nervous about today?" Ronan asked as he opened the can.

The snap and hiss from the punctured can pulsed in the air between the crackling of cooking eggs.

"A little," Ty replied as he absent-mindedly turned over the egg. "This new children's wing is important to the hospital, and I support it. But…"

"But what?"

"I had no idea I'd be put in charge of the fundraising team and asked to hit up sponsors for money."

Ronan swallowed the piece of toast mixed with a large swig of diet soda. "Well, you picked a big fish to ask first. Charleston State has plenty of money. I'm sure they were happy to be asked.

Ty rolled his shoulders. He lifted the skillet from the stove, rocked the hot pan back and forth and then let the egg slip onto a plate. "Well, they're getting the ICU named after them."

Ronan nodded and slipped through the side door into the dining room. "Keep my eggs warm. I'm going to get dressed."

"Wait, I thought you weren't going."

"I changed my mind," Ronan called back. "You know I couldn't care less about the football game, but I want to see how much cash CSC is going to pony up."

———

The Charleston State College stadium had been home to numerous high-school football games, band competitions, and state high-school track meets throughout its long and illustrious history. Over the years, the 18,500-seat stadium—located near the state Capitol Complex on Elizabeth Street—had fallen into disrepair. Its owner, the Kanawha

County Schools, had lacked the funds to maintain the stadium, so the school system entered into a joint venture with the Charleston State College. The university had invested over $1.5 million in repairs and improvements in exchange for access and naming rights, and the stadium eventually became home to the Charleston State College Falcons football program.

"Over one million dollars. That's a boatload of money," Nick remarked as he pushed a wave of hair behind an ear. "I can see why Ty picked the school to be a donor for his hospital."

"That's what I told him," Ronan added. "CSC has plenty of cash, and schools love being in the media and having buildings named after them. I'm curious how much money they put up."

Ronan led Nick down behind the east stands. The concrete pad, which served as a walkway for guests, was chipped and faded and bordered tightly by a barbed-wire fence and railroad tracks. Catching a glimpse of the tracks made Ronan shiver. The last time he'd been this close to railroad tracks was the night of the hostage situation on Smith Street.

"There's really not much to this place," Ronan said as he and Nick passed by the Falcons' locker room where the team was preparing for its opening game against Southern Virginia. "I imagine Ty's on the field by now or in one of the luxury boxes doing a lot of talking and shaking hands," he added.

They emerged from the concourse and walked up a narrow ramp to the stands. Ronan saw two Charleston Police Department officers' slipping through a small gate away from the concourse and recalled when he'd worked the Capital-Riverside football game back in 2004. Over 20,000 people attended. It had been a great matchup.

The day was calm and clear, but oppressively humid. Nevertheless, the Falcons football fans packed the stands, many of them clad in bright yellow and maroon-colored jerseys.

"Let's sit at the 50-yard line," Nick suggested.

As Ronan and Nick took their seats, a no nonsense voice came over the P.A. system and announced that the stadium had a no-smoking policy. The voice then proceeded to list the food items available at the concession stand.

Nick leaned forward, creating a shield from the sun with his hands, and watched a group of well-dressed men and two police officers amble onto the field. Ronan glanced at his nephew and then leaned back, listening to the stillness the fell over the field.

College president Gerald Iddings and the Charleston Mercy Hospital CEO John Morris were introduced to the CSC fans. After the announcer read a lengthy list of accomplishments and credentials for each man, Ty's name was finally broadcast. Afterward, all three men made their way to midfield.

"There he is! There's Ty!" Nick exclaimed like a child who had just seen a famous cartoon character in person.

Each of the men on the field raised a hand and waved at the crowd. The crowd responded with a smattering of polite applause.

"Look, Uncle Ronan, the football team is out on the field too."

Turning away from the scene at midfield, Ronan watched as the Charleston State football team began doing several rudimentary exercises, including stretching, running in place and jumping jacks in the end zone. Coaches with whistles and headsets weaved in between the men, mouthing words and slapping players on the helmets and shoulder pads.

Ronan looked at Ty, who stood politely off to the side of the group. The announcer finally said what he'd been waiting to hear. "Dr. Iddings is proud to present Mr. John Morris of the Charleston Area Medical Center, and the hospital's lead fundraiser Mr. Ty Andino with a check for 1.1 million dollars…" The announcer held onto the last syllable of the word *dollars* for an extra second, causing the entire statement to reverberate around the stadium.

"For this generous donation, the new ICU in the children's wing will henceforth be known as the Charleston State College Intensive Care Unit."

The applause grew louder, and Dr. Iddings shook hands with John Morris and Ty once more. The two cops, who had escorted them to the field, inched closer. One of them leaned in and whispered something to John Morris. Morris nodded and motioned for Ty to walk back to the sidelines.

Ty led the men to the end zone and then down the white-painted goal line. The college president and the hospital CEO followed slowly behind, engaged in conversation.

"I'm so glad he did it," Ronan said, nudging Nick. "Ty's been worried for weeks about today, but now that he has a substantial donor others will follow." Ronan crossed both arms and smiled, proud of his boyfriend.

Southern Virginia emerged from the locker room on the east side of the stands and took to the field. The Falcons team sprinted to their sideline where Nick began reading the names and numbers on the back of their jerseys.

Southern Virginia didn't engage in the same pregame warm-up ritual as the Charleston State College did. Instead, half of the team headed to the far sidelines while the captains headed to midfield and talked with the referees.

Nick tapped Ronan on the arm. "I'm going to get something to drink, Uncle Ronan. Do you want anything?"

"No thanks. You need money?"

"Nope," Nick said, reaching into his pocket. "Ty gave me some this morning."

Spoiled rotten already.

The university drum corps began slapping their drums, producing a razor-sharp sound that carved into every groove of the stadium. The fans clapped along as the drums' pace quickened with each beat.

Ronan hated football and wondered how long it would be before they could leave. Ty said he'd text Ronan when he was ready to go.

Visiting Southern Virginia was ready to kick off the

game, but as both teams braced for battle, a man dressed in a maroon shirt and matching shorts bolted past the Falcons' sideline. He tugged on the official's shirtsleeve, and the official immediately blew his whistle in response to the unexpected intrusion. Meanwhile, another man dressed in the same maroon attire emerged from the walkway under the concourse and began sprinting up the stadium steps, followed by one of the police officers who'd been on the field earlier.

A lump formed in Ronan's throat. Something was wrong. In an instant, his tactical training took over, and he began surveying the scene in quick bursts.

The referees motioned both teams to the sidelines as their respective coaches flailed their arms and shouted, demanding an explanation. The fans booed and whistled, annoyed at the game's delay.

"Ladies and gentlemen," came the voice over the P.A. system. "We have a game delay. Please be patient. The game will begin shortly."

Ronan stood up. He knew better than to heed the words from the press box. He'd worked enough games to know teams were not brought onto the field and then sent back to the sidelines unless something was wrong. Seriously wrong.

Nick emerged from the concourse ramp, sweating profusely, accompanied by the other cop. "Uncle Ronan," he blurted breathlessly. "You need to come quick. There's been an accident. A really bad accident."

CHAPTER 13

Adam opened up the cabin door, seeking some fresh air.

The stale, hot wind wailed between the distorted tree trunks. The light was fading, creating new shadows and dark patches around the cabin. The cracks of light that did break through the trees came down in a golden stream. Adam lifted his face, letting the light and shadow dance across his skin. He inhaled the minty smell; the thick, green pillars of the conifers created a dense curtain, forbidding an easy path to anyone who ventured through the woods.

The stillness filled Adam with confidence. He stepped back into the cabin and closed the door, pushing the deadbolt across the handle, locking everything into place.

Miles, Adam's friend and partner, stood at one of the rustic pinewood tables, stacking unmarked, cardboard boxes into groups of six. Adam grabbed his knife and with a fast, broad swipe slit open one of the boxes. He grinned as he greedily gazed at its contents. Then he locked his beady eyes on Miles and nodded. Miles acknowledged the silent command, stepped forward and tore the box apart.

"What's this stuff called again?" Miles asked, his thin,

nasally Michigan accent heavily accenting the vowels in his words

"The pharma companies named it desomorphine. On the streets it's called krokodil."

Miles broke the jar's seal, and the pungent aroma of the clear fluid inside made him step back with a jerk. "Fuck! This damn stuff stinks. What the hell's in it?"

Adam released a deep, throaty laugh. "Who cares? But this shit's in everything; codeine, lighter fluid, gasoline, and industrial cleaners."

Miles set the jar down on the table and stepped away, fearing contamination. Adam grinned again and carefully reattached the lid.

"And people drink this shit?"

"Not really," Adam replied, lifting another box from the stack and cutting it open. "They inject it. You can drink it or smoke it, but it tastes awful. If you want a fast high, you stick yourself with it like this." Adam pulled up the pants leg of the faded green slacks he'd been wearing since yesterday.

The stench of the drug mixed with rotting flesh assaulted Miles as he stared down at his friend's leg. "Shit! Your damn leg's all green and scaly and covered in bloody, open sores. And it smells like a swamp too."

"That's krokodil. It's ten times more powerful than morphine, and the high is fucking fantastic!"

Miles shivered, turned and then coughed into his shirt-sleeve as he desperately tried to expel the caustic odor from his lungs.

"Never you mind about my leg. You're just here to help distribute the product."

"Like Lorenzo and Troy."

"No, not like Lorenzo and Troy," Adam replied, waving the knife as he spoke. "Lorenzo and Troy were sloppy. They went after Michael and then stabbed that damn cop. Got too many other people involved."

"And Troy's been arrested and Lorenzo's dead," Miles said, barely above a whisper.

"Lorenzo's dead because he panicked. He wanted to be

the big man and run the Charleston territory. But he panicked and got sloppy, and that's when he made mistakes. I didn't tell Lorenzo to break into that warehouse and kill that damn security guard. I didn't tell him to lean on Michael Warner, and I sure as hell didn't tell him to stab a cop! The only task I gave that fucking loser was to find us a warehouse where we could store the krokodil — and look what happened. Both of those damn fools got exactly what they deserved."

"It doesn't matter now. That cop is still sniffing around, and the entire police department is going to be waiting for us."

"Even if they are, it'll be too late," Adam sneered, removing more jars from the box and checking their lids. "We've already infiltrated Charleston. Soon every college kid and redneck lowlife who does nothing but sit on his ass all day and collect a government paycheck will be on this shit. And it ain't cheap. Once they get hooked, they'll do anything to get more. You know those West Virginia rednecks are addicted to everything: food, cigarettes and prescription meds. Hell! Most of them bastards are looking for one kind of fix or another."

Miles nodded his head in agreement.

Adam felt the excitement burgeoning inside him as he caught himself speaking louder and louder. He swallowed hard and collected himself. "The point is, my friend, the Charleston cops will be so busy trying to get this shit off the streets that we'll be able to take it statewide. Once we do, we'll have markets north and south.

"Is that why you chose Charleston? For access?"

Adam pointed his finger at Miles. "Damn straight. Three interstates run right through that town, the 64, the 77 and the 79. We'll be able to ship krokodil from Detroit, down Route 23 and onto I-64. From there we can go north to Pittsburgh and South into Virginia and the Carolinas. After that, who knows?"

Miles chewed on his lower lip for a moment. "That's a lot of money."

"It's a shitload of money. We're talking hundreds of thousands of dollars."

"So, what are we doing out here in the sticks?"

"Getting ready for the second part of the plan. But first, we have to tie up some loose ends."

"Like what?"

"Don't you bother yourself with the trivial details of the operation. I've got everything in motion."

"Usually, when you say, 'Everything's in motion,' bad things happen to people who get in our way."

Adam felt a new swell of confidence wash over him. "By now, the bad things have already happened."

CHAPTER 14

Ronan dashed down the ramp and stairway, taking two steps at a time. Nick fell behind while a uniformed officer radioed ahead, stating they were on their way.

When they reached the concourse underneath the stands, the cop stopped and pointed to the left. "The locker room's this way."

The blurred faces of fans, clutching their snacks and drinks, whisked by Ronan like ribbons of color that darkened and then faded. With each step, he could feel the bile rising in his throat and wondered if this situation had something to do with Ty.

A shaft of sunlight at the edge of the stadium momentarily blinded Ronan. He winced and shaded his eyes with his hand. As he moved out of the sun, his eyes adjusted and he could see a stout man with a carefully trimmed brown beard and wire-rimmed glasses standing by the locker-room door. The man was trembling, and his lips quivered.

As Nick rested both hands on his hips and collected his breath, the sturdy young cop with a wide-open face spoke to his superior. "Sergeant McCullough, this is Frank Ater, the team trainer for the Falcons."

Before pleasantries could be exchanged, Frank began

talking, spilling out words in clips and fragments. "I, I can't believe it. He's…he's a good kid and far from home."

"It's okay, Frank, just tell me what happened," Ronan calmly said as he planted his large hands firmly on the shoulders of the anxious man standing before him.

"I was gone…gone for just a few minutes…to get ice for the Gatorade. When…when…I came back…I found him."

Ronan felt the muscles in his stomach coil. "Who, Frank? Who did you find?"

Frank began trembling again, and the shaking forced Ronan to loosen his grip.

"I think you'd better come with me, Sergeant," the young police officer said. His anguished face and tightly pursed lips told Ronan something bad had happened.

Before he took a step, Ronan looked back at Nick. "I want you to stay here with Officer…"

"Keenan."

"Right. Keenan. I've seen you around the station before, but I'm bad with names. You stay with Keenan, Nick."

"But Uncle Ronan, I want to—"

"Nick! Do what I tell you."

The color and emotion drained from Nick's face.

Keenan swallowed hard and spoke again. "We've got backup coming and paramedics are on their way."

As Ronan walked through the locker room filled with blue metal lockers and worn wooden benches, he noticed a faded yellow vest lying on the floor. Taking a step closer, he gazed at the large black letters embroidered on the back of the vest. The word *security* stood out.

"There's some evidence over here. We need someone to bag and tag it," Ronan hollered to Keenan who was still standing at the locker-room door.

"On it!" he hollered back.

Ronan found Ty kneeling next to a wooden bench, his gray sports jacket tossed carelessly across it. Ty glanced over his shoulder, regarding Ronan for a moment before returning his attention to the young man who lay on the floor beside him. Ty's white shirt and red tie were rumpled and loose, and his black dress pants were covered in blood. Remnants from an overturned first-aid kit littered the floor.

"He's alive. Barely. So much damn blood. How did this happen?" Ty rasped as he tried to staunch the flow of blood that gushed from the kid's throat like water from a ruptured pipe.

Ronan pulled his gaze from Ty and focused on the victim, immediately recognizing the tousled blond hair and slender figure of Michael Warner. Between Ty's latex-gloved fingers, Ronan could see the ugly gash transecting the young man's throat.

"Michael," Ronan gasped as he instinctively reached out to touch him.

"Ronan, don't," Ty barked. "Please."

Frank Ater appeared with an armful of clean gym towels. Ty grabbed one and immediately pressed it to Warner's throat. Within seconds, the white terry cloth was stained crimson with the thick, red fluid.

"Will he live?" Ronan asked softly.

"His carotid artery has sustained damage. We need to get him to the hospital."

The locker room felt like it was growing smaller by the second.

"Who did this? Someone wore that security vest and got in here. Michael wouldn't have noticed anyone trespassing," Ronan said to no one in particular. "He didn't deserve this."

Paramedics interrupted Ronan from his desperate reverie as they arrived on the scene, pushing him and Ty aside.

Nick stumbled in behind them, searching for his uncle.

"Get out of here!" Ronan snapped.

Nick screamed and staggered back, tripping and landing hard on the floor. "Ah, ah, ah!" he moaned, covering his mouth.

"Get out of here, Nick! Where's Keenan? Keenan, get him out of here!"

The young officer grabbed the kid's arm. "It's okay. Come on."

"We need to get you cleaned up and find something for you to wear," Frank Ater stated as he walked up to where Ty stood.

Ty stepped back and looked down at himself, unaware he was covered in Michael Warner's blood. "Don't bother. It doesn't matter. I need to go with the paramedics."

Warner was loaded into the ambulance while Ronan and Frank stood helplessly by and watched. Ty joined the paramedics, giving Ronan a slight wave before the doors slammed shut. Lights flashed and a piercing siren hushed the rowdy voices as the van eased through the crowd and headed for Charleston Mercy.

After the paramedics were safely out of sight, Ronan looked around for Nick. He found him sitting against the concrete ramp with both knees drawn to the chest, his head bowed. When Ronan approached, Nick didn't look up.

"You okay?"

Silence.

Searching for something to say, Ronan looked to his right and watched as the passing CSX train whirled by the stadium. "I'm sorry you had to see that," he finally whispered.

Nick dug both heels into the concrete and pulled his legs tighter.

"Come on. Talk to me."

"Seeing something like that on TV isn't the same as seeing it in real life," Nick said as his chin rubbed against both knees, muffling the words. He looked up at Ronan, tears trickling down his cheeks. "What happened to him?"

Ronan ran a hand over his mouth, tugging at the corners of his lips. "I don't know, but that's exactly what I'm going to find out."

Nick reached out a gangly, trembling arm. Ronan pulled him up, and Nick sniffed deeply, wiping away the granules of dirt and gravel from his shorts.

The crowd continued to swell at the entrance of the locker room, but more Charleston police arrived, and soon the inquisitive spectators began to disperse. Ronan assumed the game would be cancelled any minute, and the disappointed fans would obediently, if reluctantly, depart the stadium.

Scanning the scene, Ronan contemplated his next move. He knew Keenan and his partner needed to return to the station and file a report as soon as possible. He also needed to file his own report, but he wanted to be with Ty.

Ronan turned to his nephew and gently said, "I'm going to ask one of these officers to take you home, and then I want you to stay there until you hear something from me or Ty. Okay?"

Nick didn't refuse. "I…I'd like to go home."

Ronan patted his cheek. "Good. Let's find someone to take you."

As Ronan and Nick sidestepped the rushing movements of fans and first responders, Ronan caught a glimpse of the college's president. The man paled as several other university officials delivered the news of what had happened in the locker room.

Ronan felt the phone in his pocket vibrate. Amidst the chaos and confusion, he'd forgotten about it being there, much less using it. He glanced at the screen: five missed calls. Perhaps Ty had called with an update on Michael Warner. As he searched through the missed calls, only one name flashed across the screen: Captain Ashby.

CHAPTER 15

Ty leaned against the ambulance door while paramedics circled Michael Warner, monitoring his vital signs. Although the bleeding was under control, it was still a life-or-death situation.

By the time they'd reached the ER, Warner's blood pressure had fallen dangerously low. The paramedics shouted numbers and phrases to each other as they unloaded their patient, but Ty could make out only certain words amid the traffic noise and other approaching sirens.

Passing by one of the exam rooms, Ty noticed two sweating and shivering men, one leaning forward and filling the space with harsh, hacking coughs and the other sitting with his head in his hands. Warner was taken into the last exam room where Sarah Gilmore was waiting to triage his injuries.

Sarah worked with Ty in the ER. Ty liked Sarah. She had a soft, kind face and a razor-sharp sense of humor. Despite her happy-go-lucky nature, Sarah was a consummate professional with extremely high standards, and she expected nothing but excellence.

When she saw Ty covered in blood, her large, brown eyes widened even more. "Ty, what's going on? Do you know this man?"

"Sort of...his name's Michael Warner. Who's the doc on call today?"

"Stevens. Why?"

Ty felt relieved. Dr. Joe Stevens was one of the best ER doctors Charleston Mercy had. Strong, smart, principled, and compassionate, Stevens was the doctor every nurse wanted with them in the emergency room.

"Warner was found in the locker room at CSC Stadium. He'd been viciously attacked. Luckily, I was attending the endowment ceremony for the new children's wing and was there to help."

Joe Stephens pushed back the curtain and entered the exam room. His portly frame filled the small, cramped space, and his forehead, which was already sprinkled, began to sweat in earnest. As he pulled on his latex gloves, he walked swiftly toward his patient, silently commanding the nurses and techs with a nod of his head.

"We've got it under control. I'll come out when we know something," Sarah said to Ty as she prepped the I.V. bag.

Ty headed to the nurses' station where he grabbed a hazardous-materials bag from the supply cabinet behind the horseshoe-shaped desk. Inside the employee dressing room, Ty removed his blood-soaked clothes and deposited them into the red, plastic bag. He knew the clothes might have evidence from Warner's attacker, so he'd make sure Ronan took possession of the clothing as soon as possible. After the evidence had been secured, Ty gratefully headed for the showers.

When he returned to the nurses' station after changing into a fresh pair of scrubs, Sarah was there waiting for him. "Warner's still critical, but he's in surgery now."

"It's amazing he got that far. I think the plan was to put him in the morgue," Ty replied, immediately thinking how much he sounded like Ronan.

Sarah raised an eyebrow at the remark.

"Thanks, Sarah."

She touched him lightly on the hand and then headed back down the hallway to the waiting room.

Ty picked up the desk phone and called Ronan. After several rings, the voicemail system activated. Ronan sounded stern and official on the recorded message; nevertheless, the husky, no-nonsense voice was reassuring.

Somewhat dejected, Ty hung up the phone and walked back to the ER, unsure of what to do next. At the end of the hall, the doors swung open. Ty clenched his fists and felt his stomach muscles tighten, expecting paramedics to push through another critically ill or injured patient. Instead, a lean, wiry man entered the ER and stopped. Thin, wispy strands of sandy-colored hair hung down over his face, and his pale gray eyes were vacant and unblinking. Slowly, he scanned the area side-to-side and then searched through each room, grabbing the curtains and peering in before stepping back and moving down the hallway to look into another room.

A male nurse approached the man, but the intruder grabbed the nurse and pushed him into the wall.

"Hey!" Ty shouted. "Get your hands off him!"

The man parted his greasy hair and glared at Ty, sending a chill down the entire length of Ty's body. One lip curled back, revealing a sharp, dark-stained canine. As Ty looked down, he saw the open, oozing sores and dried, yellowing scales covering the stranger's hands and fingers. The natural nursing instinct in Ty kicked in, and he stepped forward, preparing to offer his help.

Sarah emerged from the waiting room, startling Ty for a moment.

"Sarah, call security. Now!"

She stopped abruptly, but Ty frantically motioned her to get away all the while holding his gaze on the man. As Ty stepped forward again, the man pushed him aside and bolted out the door. Ty's heart thudded hard and fast against his chest as he followed down the narrow hallway, dashing and weaving between paramedics, patients and techs.

"Stop that man!" Ty called out to a paramedic pushing a gurney.

As the paramedic reached out to grab the fleeing man,

he swung around and grabbed the gurney and tossed it onto its side. Ty stopped, moved left, and then pivoted right and around the overturned gurney, but he was still unable to catch up. The man was incredibly fast and soon disappeared through the sliding glass doors and onto Morris Street. Once outside, Ty bent over and tried to catch his breath before continuing his pursuit. When he looked up again, the man was nowhere to be seen.

CHAPTER 16

R onan swerved around the corner of Hansford Street. His truck groaned and heaved like some alien being as he continued to thrust the gas pedal home. Appalachian Power Park and Highland Pharmacy were nothing more than mere blurs, and the warehouse, where Lorenzo White and the security guard had been killed, disappeared from his view just as quickly.

Ronan's stomach churned the more he thought about that night—and everything that had transpired since. His thoughts were blessedly interrupted when he spied a parking space in front of police headquarters. He angled his vehicle into the spot with barely an inch to spare and then ran up the front steps of the sand-colored brick building, nearly knocking over a descending civilian and two uniformed officers.

Inside, the waiting area was peppered with a handful of people lounging on faded green chairs and well-worn couches. Karen Paxton, the front-desk guard, mindlessly scribbled on a notepad. She looked up and winked at Ronan as he walked by.

Hurriedly, he passed the cubicles, desks and offices of various departments, including Metro Drug Enforcement, Street Crimes, the Bicycle Unit, Professional Standards,

Training, Informational Standards, Vice, SVU, Criminal Investigations, and Internal Affairs.

One hundred and sixty-one sworn officers were responsible for enforcing an area of Charleston that extended approximately thirty-three square miles. That was 0.245 officers per square mile, a burden all members of the department felt.

The evening briefing of the patrol division was just getting underway as Ronan passed by the command room. He smiled, remembering that shift well; it was his first assignment as a rookie.

He stopped in front of the assignment board and carefully scanned the night's schedule. Captain Ashby was the Captain of the Day; Eric Bonamico was listed as one of the three sergeants assigned to this shift and to the next.

Bonamico emerged from Captain Ashby's office at the back end of the building. His face was flushed, and his movements were anxious. He wore a dark-blue dress shirt and a red tie that appeared to have been loosened before his shift had even begun. A case file clutched tightly against his chest hid the folds and wrinkles in the unkempt neckwear.

"Where in the hell have you been? Ashby's been trying to call you."

Ronan wanted to explain, but he didn't know where to start. "I just came from Laidley Field, or Charleston State College Stadium, or whatever it's called…"

"I know all that," Bonamico said, cutting Ronan off. "One of the patrolmen heard the call go out on the scanner. Keenan radioed in and said you were on the scene aiding the victim."

"More like trying to save his life," Ronan grumbled. "I was with Ty for the endowment ceremony. He found Michael Warner in the locker room."

"Did you see what happened?"

Ronan felt a pang of guilt and nodded in the affirmative.

"Well, you'd better get in there and see Ashby. He's hot and wants to know what in the hell's going on."

"Where are you going?"

Bonamico tossed the case file onto a desk and turned back to face Ronan, coiling two fingers under his shirt collar as he spoke. "We've had four drug busts this weekend all over town, and I've worked three of them. I'm heading to Mercy now. Ashby wants me and a couple of patrolmen to go with Criminal Investigations to see if we can question Michael Warner."

"Question him? His throat was slashed. He may not even be alive when you get there, much less be able to talk to you."

The heaviness and sadness that tinged Ronan's words caught Bonamico by surprise. Ronan swallowed hard and looked down at the floor for a moment. Then he stared back at the door leading to Ashby's office. "Who's the detective handling the case?"

"Sean Carter, I think, but check with Ashby," Bonamico replied as he patted Ronan on the shoulder. He scooped up his sports coat from a neighboring chair and left.

Ronan let out the deep breath he'd been holding and entered Ashby's office without knocking.

A mountain of papers and case files covered Ashby's desk. When he saw Ronan, he tossed aside the report he'd been reading, pulled off his glasses, flung them across the desk, and stood up. "There you are. What's going on?" he demanded.

Ronan started the story from the beginning and left out none of the details. Ashby had a sense for detecting omitted information, and he tended to be more rational in difficult circumstances if he knew all of the information.

"That's all of it?"

"Yep."

The captain walked around his desk and sat down on the corner, casually crossing his arms. "Bonamico tells me you think something big is going down, and this Warner kid is up to his armpits in it."

"I do, Cap," Ronan replied, his mouth suddenly feeling parched. "It's something White said to me in the warehouse. He said we wouldn't be able to stop *them*. When I saw

Warner outside the Corner Diner, I asked him what he thought that meant, but he wouldn't answer me. His two Goth friends didn't want to talk to me either."

"Trust your instincts, but don't question anyone who has ties to Warner if they're out on the street. Warner was let off easy on that possession charge, and some bleeding-heart attorney could construe your interview of his associates as police harassment. But if you think something's up, you're probably right. I'll have Bonamico and my lieutenants be on the lookout for suspicious activity. I'll also increase patrols in some of the trouble spots in town, especially on the West Side and East End."

Ronan watched the captain search him with those piercing, focused eyes. A moment passed between them. "And I thought you were going to give me a tongue-lashing for inserting myself in what happened at the stadium today."

Ashby thought for a moment and set his jaw. "I think you should have let Keenan and Mathers handle it," he said. "After all, they're not paid to watch the game, but you did the right thing. I just can't figure out why you can't seem to stay out of this thing, whatever it is."

Ronan shrugged. "I wish I knew."

The phone on Ashby's desk rang. He raised his eyebrows at Ronan and reached around to answer it. "Captain Ashby."

Ronan leaned back in the chair. Ribbons of sun streaked through the window, making the room feel warm and stuffy and even more uncomfortable than usual.

"All right. Thanks."

Captain Ashby dropped the receiver back on the handset. His face was grim as he rolled both shoulders, sighed, and gazed out the window. "That was Bonamico. Warner didn't make it out of surgery."

CHAPTER 17

A symphony of coughing, hacking and wheezing greeted Ronan in the ER waiting room. He found the closest antibacterial hand dispenser and feverishly started working the lever. Wringing both hands together, he moved back through the sliding glass doors. He could never remember where the second entrance for emergency personnel was located. Consequently, he wandered through the patient waiting room, past the check-in desk and then out the side door to the restrooms.

In the narrow hallway, a brace of security guards clad in charcoal-gray uniforms stood against the wall, casting suspicious glances at everyone. When two paramedics ambled by pulling an empty gurney, Ronan pressed his back flat against the wall and nodded at them. He leaned forward on his bad leg and then bent his neck to the right, but he couldn't see past the guards. One guard became skeptical of his movements and approached. Ronan removed his shield from his wallet, holding it still as the thin-faced, beady-eyed guard scanned it. The guard's face softened, and he stepped back.

"I'm here on official business," Ronan stated.

The guard simply shrugged.

"The exam area is down that hallway, right?"

The guard nodded, and Ronan moved past him, flashing

his shield to the other security officer as he passed. When he pushed through the swinging doors to the emergency room, a broad-shouldered, stocky male nurse met him almost instantly.

"I'm sorry, sir. Only authorized personnel—"

Ronan displayed his shield again.

"How can I help you, Sergeant?" he said, relaxing his stance.

"I need to speak to Ty Andino and Eric Bonamico."

"I haven't seen Ty, Sergeant, but two cops did come through here earlier. They went upstairs to the surgical floor. I imagine those are the men you're looking for."

"Where can I wait for Mr. Andino?"

"Wait in the lounge by the nurses' station. I can page Ty if you'd like."

"Thank you."

The nurses' station buzzed like a swarming bee hive, and hospital personnel scurried from room to room, their conversations with patients and family members dissolving into a loud cacophony.

Ronan remembered when he'd been brought to the ER after responding to a hostage standoff on Charleston's west side. A slovenly, overweight man had held his wife hostage after she'd served him with divorce papers. As Ronan and several other officers surrounded the house, the man started shooting, shattering most of the windows on the first floor of the house.

Several shards of glass lodged in Ronan's forearm, and Captain Ashby demanded that every injured officer be treated at Charleston Mercy. The paramedics rolled Ronan into the ER and parked him against the wall to await treatment.

As he waited to be examined, Ronan couldn't help but overhear Ty arguing on the phone. Ronan was immediately struck by the young man's beautiful face and attractive physique. For the next few months, he found any excuse he could to go by the ER. When Ronan learned Ty's relationship with his boyfriend Chris had ended, he got up the courage to ask Ty out on a date. That was the beginning of their love affair.

Ty maneuvered past the chaos in the exam area and locked eyes on Ronan. Ronan wasn't sure how much time had passed since he'd entered the ER, but it seemed like an eternity. Ty looked disheveled and tired, and his hair, which was normally perfect, looked matted and unkempt. He grinned when he saw Ronan.

"Hey, you," Ronan cheerfully said, trying to buoy Ty's heavy spirits.

Ty looked around and motioned for them to go down another small hallway to the nurses' locker room. Once inside Ronan wrapped both arms around Ty, pulling him close, never wanting to let go. He kissed Ty on the top of the head.

"I'm sorry I didn't call sooner, and I'm so sorry you're mixed up in this mess."

"It's okay," Ty replied through muffled breaths. "I needed you, and now you're here."

"Always," Ronan said, before Ty loosened his embrace.

"Have you seen Eric?"

Ty smoothed his uniform and hair with both hands. "He and a detective from your department are upstairs talking with Dr. Mason. I'm sorry Warner didn't make it. The blood loss was just too great. He's in the morgue until his family can be notified."

Ronan thought for a moment about the shock and pain Michael's family would face. "I know. I was at the station talking to the captain when Eric called. How long was he in surgery?"

Ty looked up at the digital clock in the corner of the room. "Only about an hour. The massive blood loss coupled with the trauma led to cardiac arrest."

"I need to get up there. Sean Carter is the detective on this case, and he's tenacious about protocol."

As Ronan turned to leave, Ty stopped him. "Wait! You'll have to be escorted by security."

"What? Why?"

"We had an incident earlier."

"What kind of incident?"

Ty told Ronan about the disheveled man who'd barged into the exam area right after Warner had been taken to surgery.

"Shit! Are you all right?"

"I'm fine."

Ronan touched Ty's check. "I'm serious. Don't go all nursey on me. Are you okay?"

"I'm fine. I promise."

"Good. Well, that explains why the security guards out front made me show my ID."

"We all have to show I.D. now. Direct orders from the hospital Chief of Staff."

"Have you reported this to anybody?" Ronan asked.

"No. I should've called the police, but I didn't get a real close look at the guy. When I approached him, he took off. I couldn't prove what he was doing there, or if he was looking for Warner. But he sure looked disappointed when he didn't find who or what he was looking for in those exam rooms."

Ronan bit down on his lip. "That's too much of a coincidence."

"There's something else. Can you go to the morgue with me? I don't really have authorization to take you down there, but I want you to see something," he said as they headed for the elevator.

The elevator opened into a small hallway. Ty swiped his ID card on the keypad that was located on the wall directly outside a double, stainless-steel door, and the blinking red light immediately changed to solid green. When the soft click sounded a second later, Ty pushed open the door.

The morgue smelled of chemicals, and the cool air emanating from the vents overhead sent chills over Ronan's warm skin. The bright white walls, stainless-steel tables and instruments shimmered under the light. Faded, white-painted metal arms with round lights attached at each end bent downward from the ceiling at odd angles. The lights were all turned to one side, and to Ronan they looked like large alien eyes, scrutinizing everyone who entered the room.

"This place is even worse than upstairs," Ronan whispered. He drew his hands to his side, making sure not to touch anything.

"Jack. It's Ty Andino. I've got Sergeant McCullough here from the Charleston Police Department."

Jack emerged from a back room, dressed in a teal-blue apron, latex gloves, a surgical mask, and hairnet. "What can I do for you?" he asked politely. "If you're here to see Dr. McAndrew, he'll be back in a minute."

"We just need to see Michael Warner," Ty stated with authority.

"Be my guest," Jack replied and returned to his work.

Ty led Ronan to a table where a thin, narrow object lay covered with a sheet. "When Warner was in surgery, Dr. Mason discovered this."

Ty pulled back the sheet. Warner's eyes, once so full of life, were now closed, and the smooth, young face was cold and ashen. The bright, jagged red line running under his chin had dulled to a dark maroon, but the cruel curves in the skin served as evidence of the brutality he had suffered.

Ronan felt the muscles in his throat tighten, and he desperately wanted to lift the young man up and take him home to wherever that might be. "I don't see anything here other than a dead body," he said, shaking off the incredible waves of sadness washing over him.

"Look down here," Ty said, removing the temporary shroud.

"My God! What's that?" Ronan gasped, taking a step backwards.

"You tell me."

The shins on both of Michael Warner's legs were splotched with rough, greenish-yellow patches. Swollen, red lesions filled with puss erupted from the ugly scale-like formations, leaving streaks of trailing, dried blood around each sore. The smell of rotten flesh nearly made Ronan gag, and Ty wiped his watering eyes with the top of his forearm.

Michael Warner may be dead, but the lesions seemed very much alive.

"What a stench!" Ronan hissed.

"Shh! Keep it down. I don't want Jack or anyone else getting suspicious."

"Cover him back up, and let's get out of here," Ronan demanded, bolting for the door.

Once outside even the hospital air smelled better than what he'd just inhaled. As Ronan coughed and collected himself, he remembered the last time he saw Michael Warner upright and alive and what he was wearing: sweatpants in the middle of a sultry August afternoon.

"What you saw in there was one of the reasons why we have security upstairs."

"I'm listening."

"I didn't get many details on the man in the ER, but I did get a good look at his hands, and they were identical to Warner's legs."

CHAPTER 18

Ty followed Ronan to the truck where he grabbed his pen and notepad that he always carried for moments just like this.

"When Eric and Carter find you, you need to tell them the same thing you told me," Ronan said as he took several deep breaths of the humid summer air. Compared to the ripe, putrid smell of the morgue, it was surprisingly invigorating. He scribbled notes onto the paper. "What time do you say that man showed up?"

"Around 15:20," Ty replied. "He didn't stay long. Maybe ten minutes."

The patter of feet disrupted the conversation. Eric Bonamico and Sean Carter surrounded them. "Thank you, Sergeant, for your assistance, but Criminal Investigations can take it from here."

Ronan took a step back.

"Are you Ty Andino?"

"I am."

"I'm Detective Sean Carter. I'd like to ask you a few questions about what happened today."

Ty folded his arms tightly across his chest, glancing defiantly at Ronan.

"It will only take a few minutes of your time, Mr. Andino."

"Okay."

"Why don't we go back inside where it's cooler?" Sean suggested, leading Ty away. The detective looked back at Ronan, eyed him from top to bottom, and then shook his head disapprovingly.

When enough space had passed, Bonamico grabbed Ronan by the shirtsleeve. "What are you doing, McCullough?"

Ronan jerked his arm forward, dislodging the hold. "I'm trying to piece together a mess. That's what I'm doing."

Bonamico pursed his lips and scratched his dimpled chin. "Investigations has the case now. All Carter's got to do is tell Ashby or Chief Toler that you're meddling and—"

"Cut the crap, Eric," Ronan said, the edge in his voice sharp. "Aren't you doing the same thing?" Ronan studied Bonamico's face for a moment and then wagged a finger at him. "I know that you marched into Ashby's office and put your name in to come over here and *assist* Carter. You want to know what's going on as much as I do."

"That may be true, but—"

"You know it's true."

"Ashby will have me step back as soon as today is over, and if he finds out you're trying to run your own inquiry into what's going on here, he's going to tear you a new one."

"I don't give a damn about that. Don't forget I was the one White was shooting at on the top floor of that warehouse. And that's after he damn near set fire to the entire SWAT team."

"I told you to forget about White and what he said."

"Well, I can't!" Ronan yelled back. Inquisitive bystanders stared at the two men, so he leaned closer to Bonamico before speaking again. Ronan could feel his colleague's breath against his face. "Michael Warner was the only consistent link I had to everything that's happened recently, and now he's dead. Someone killed him and made it a public spectacle. If someone was trying to silence him and wanted us to know he'd been silenced, I think the message was received loud and clear."

"Carter and the crime-scene response unit went over the stadium for any and all probative evidence. No fingerprints and no DNA were found other than the victim's. It's possible we'll get more evidence after the autopsy, but as of right now we've got nothing," Bonamico replied as the descending scream of an ambulance siren drowned out the force of his words.

"Maybe not," Ronan said. Looking at his notepad, Ronan licked a finger with the tip of his tongue and flicked back a page. "Ty told me a man came into the ER while Warner was in surgery. Seemed like he was looking for someone. Maybe it was Warner. When Ty confronted him, the man took off."

The statement piqued Bonamico's interest. "Did he get a good look at the guy?"

Ronan shook his head. "Not really, but he said the man had mangled hands and was wearing a long-sleeved sweat-shirt with a hood, trying to disguise himself. And Michael Warner had some messed up skin on his shins. The last time I saw him conscious, he was wearing long sweatpants on a fucking hot, miserable day. So, we do have something."

Bonamico stepped back and thought for a moment. "Wait a minute, you've seen Warner's body?

Ronan ignored the question and turned another page on the notepad.

"I won't tell Carter or Ashby about that."

Ronan flashed a toothy smile. "I'm hoping you won't."

"But what you're saying means that whoever was supposed to kill Warner wanted to make sure the job had been finished."

Ronan held the tip of the pen in the air. "Right. And that also means the killer is obviously sloppy because you don't brutally attack someone like that and then leave them barely alive in a public place."

Bonamico finished the sentence. "You'd want to make sure that it was done right the first time."

"Exactly. But right now, we need to wait on the autopsy and the tox-screen reports. Something caused that rash or whatever it is on Warner's skin, and it may be tied to our visitor in the ER."

Bonamico checked his watch. "I'd better get in there."

"If you find out anything—"

"I'll let you know. Even though sharing this information could get us in big shit."

CHAPTER 19

Jason held up the syringe and flicked the plastic barrel twice with his long, bony middle finger. He anxiously watched on as the opaque, green liquid reacted, forming tiny bubbles. When the solution had settled, he depressed the plunger ever so slightly until a thin stream of liquid shot out of the needle. Hastily, he snatched the syringe and jammed it into the one patch of skin on his forearm that wasn't covered in oozing, red lesions or blackened with gangrene. An instant cool sensation coursed through his body, making him shiver like a cold winter's day in deepest January.

Taking the scissors from the chipped and faded gray Formica countertop, Jason gripped them tightly. As he waited for the body tremors to wane and his hands to quit shaking, his thoughts drifted to Michael Warner. *There was no way in hell Michael has survived the attack*, he thought with satisfaction.

When the rush had evened into a calm, steady sensation, Jason began attacking his hair. With each snip of the scissors, the greasy tendrils fell like dirty-blond snakes into the sink and coiled around the rusted-out drain. Cutting, looking in the mirror, and cutting some more, Jason was finally content. As he regarded his new hairstyle, he realized that the blunt cut only accentuated his angular cheekbones and pitted skin. His anger flared white-hot. "I can't fucking believe I still have zits," he hissed, slamming a hand into the mirror.

With his high now gone, Jason wrapped his bleeding hand in a dirty bathroom towel and shuffled into the bedroom. Flopping onto the bed, he looked around the room and sneered. The ambiance of the Ivy Terrace Motel certainly fit his bad mood. The faded brown carpet and bedspread were burned in spots, likely from cigarette butts, and the room smelled like a mixture of musty old men, whores and stale tobacco smoke. A loser of a motel room fit for a loser like him.

Jason didn't know how to tell Adam that although Michael was most likely dead, he could still be alive. Following him to the stadium hadn't been Jason's original idea. He'd planned to take Michael somewhere secluded and then sedate him with chloroform before killing him. But when Michael left the CSC campus earlier than expected, Jason panicked and followed him to the football stadium.

Michael had been startled to see Jason, but his surprise quickly turned to terror as Jason overpowered him. Before one syllable could escape Michael's lips, Jason slit his throat, silencing him—hopefully forever.

Jason picked up his cheap burner phone and punched in Adam's number. After several rings, he hung up. *Where the hell is he?* Jason dialed Adam again. Still no answer. When he'd finally given up, the phone buzzed. "Hello."

"How's Michael doing? Has rigor set in yet?"

Jason twitched nervously, watching the small droplets of blood leak from the needle puncture on his forearm.

"Did you hear what I asked?"

"Michael's been taken care of," Jason finally replied. "So, when do I get my money and my krok?"

"Soon, my friend. I'm sending Miles down next week. He'll be in a moving van filled to the gills with krok. I want you and Aaron to meet him at the 69-mile marker rest stop. He should be there by three a.m."

"Let me write that down," Jason said as he grabbed the pen and notepad that sat next to the old-fashioned, rotary dial phone on the nightstand. "Yeah, mile marker 69, West Virginia Turnpike Rest Area."

"Right," Adam said. "By the way, there'll be two more moving trucks identical to the one that Miles is driving. Help him unload the shipment and then divide the rest of the product equally between the other two. Miles will have your money and krok. We're sending a shipment down to the coalfields, and another's being sent north on I-79."

"You want me to keep spreading it in Charleston?"

"Damn straight! Since Michael's Catholic-school conscious got the better of him, it's your turn now. Start with the college frat houses. Then hit the downtown party scene and the strip clubs. Start in Jefferson. Work both ends of the city. And make damn sure you don't give away any freebies or discount the merchandise. Full price for the shit. Got it?"

"Okay, boss. Got it. I'll wait for your call next week."

As Jason started to hang up, Adam hollered, "Oh, one more thing."

"Yeah."

"Did anyone see you at the hospital or at the stadium? Tell me you didn't screw everything up like those stupid assholes, Troy and Lorenzo, Purcell sent down from Detroit."

"Well," Jason hedged. "There was this Asian guy. I think he was a doctor or maybe a nurse. I don't know. He saw me looking for Michael in the ER."

"And?"

"He caught a glimpse of me. Not up close or anything. I hightailed it out of there as fast as I could."

Adam growled. "Would you remember this guy if you saw him again?"

"Yeah. I think so."

"Good. Then find him before he finds you and get rid of him. Now!"

CHAPTER 20

Ronan ambled through PD headquarters; his slate-blue eyes searching for Sean Carter amidst a sea of uniforms and suits. As he passed two officers busily working on case files, he thought they resembled the officers who were with Carter at the hospital when Ty and the doctors were questioned. *I wonder how they made it back so fast?* Ronan also noticed Officer Keenan sitting at a desk piled with paperwork, trying his best to look important.

A flurry of activity greeted Ronan as he pushed open the door to the Criminal Investigations Division. The workspace in CID mimicked the main department area with desks pushed together and tables and chairs circling the outer edge of the perfectly perpendicular space. Dry erase boards covered with pictures of anonymous people were situated along the walls with red arrows pointing to names, descriptions and details of the indiscriminate faces. Several detectives looked over the information contained on the boards, comparing it with the info in their case files.

Ronan found Sean Carter sitting at his desk, talking on the phone. As he approached, Carter held up a hand.

"Right. Okay. Good. Thank you," he said as he hung up and pushed himself away from his desk; the wheels of the chair squeaked as they wobbled across the well-worn linoleum. "That was the medical examiner's office. The autopsy is scheduled for Tuesday."

Ronan rested both hands on his hips and studied the detective for a moment. Carter had loosened his blue tie, but his white shirt and dark trousers remained perfectly crisp.

"What can I do for you, Sergeant? If you're looking for details on the case, I don't have anything more than what you already know, or should I say, *witnessed*."

"That's what I came to talk with you about," Ronan said. He hated verbally jousting with detectives; they were so damn cocky, feeling superior to everyone on the thin blue line. "I want to be on this case. I know it isn't my division, but for better or worse, I've been a part of this thing since the beginning, and now my nephew Nick and Ty…I mean, the nurse at the hospital are involved. I want to make sure this stays a police matter."

Carter rested the sole of his black dress shoe against the desk and peered at Ronan. "Did Ashby send you over here?"

"No. I came on my own."

The detective settled his gaze onto the notes and files scattered across his desk. "The way I see it, drugs had to be the motive for Warner's death. I know you saw that crap on his legs when you were down in autopsy."

"Carter—"

Carter raised a hand to stop Ronan. "Warner had already been kicked off the football team for drug posses- sion. Both his legs were riddled with needle marks. Jesus! They looked like fucking pincushions. It's likely he owed the wrong people money. When he couldn't pay with cash, he paid with his life."

The callous way in which Carter described his theory caught Ronan by surprise. "But that doesn't explain why Warner's body would be dumped in the locker room prior to the Charleston State game."

"I have a theory about that too," he replied, dislodging the arched leg and pulling the chair closer to the desk. "I think Warner was using and dealing. His teammates should know what he was selling. Now if Warner was giving out freebies or skimming money from the collections then that would have really pissed off his supplier."

"Then where does White fit into this scenario?"

Carter rested his chin in his hands. "White was probably the supplier. Remember, it was him and his posse who attacked Warner."

"How could I forget?"

"Since White didn't finish the job, maybe one of his associates did."

"But what doesn't make any sense is why White would take the warehouse guard hostage and kill him and then attack the SWAT team. If Warner were the target, White would have killed him and not some poor schmuck rent-a-cop."

"Thanks to you and Bonamico, we won't know why White did what he did because the son-of-a-bitch is dead," Carter replied with more than a hint of aggravation in his voice.

Ronan thought back to the incident at the warehouse; the pain flared in his leg as if it too could remember that terrible night.

"As you can see, Sergeant, we're back to square one—drugs."

Ronan rapped his knuckles against the desk before pulling up a metal chair and plopping into it. "White told me that—"

"I know what he told you. So does Bonamico and so does the captain."

"I'm telling you, Carter, there's more to this case than some random drug deal gone bad. I've never seen abscesses like the ones I saw on Warner's legs. There must be a new drug on the street; crack or heroin, not even meth, does that to the skin."

Carter settled back into his chair. "As I said, we'll know more after the autopsy. But I can tell you what I do know now and that's the drug statistics for this miserable, Godforsaken state. Last year West Virginia had 28.9 drug deaths per 100,000 people. That's an increase of over 600 percent since 1999. CID spends more time on drug cases than on anything else, so I can't see how Warner's death is any different from any other drug-related death other than the drug de jour."

Ronan's jaw tensed.

"And I also know how you operate, McCullough. You like butting your Irish nose into cases that aren't yours. We do all the work, but you take all the credit for saving the day. Isn't that how you made sergeant?"

Ronan had heard enough. "I'm not going to sit here and be insulted. The only reason you got that federal circuit judge corruption case last year was because your daddy was the sitting mayor of Charleston. He put the screws to the Chief of Ds to let you in on the action. But I was the one who did the legwork and solved the case. If you want to come after me, you'd better look at yourself first. You're one of the most opportunistic, self-serving bastards on the force. So, don't get all fucking sanctimonious with me. I was just doing my job. And one more thing. Get ready. This case is going to take everything you've got. And you know what? Your pompous ass just might need *me* to solve it!"

With that, Ronan kicked over the seat and stormed off.

CHAPTER 21

Feeling disrespected and angry after his meeting with Carter, Ronan was in no mood to talk with anyone else. He exited headquarters through the rear of the building and headed home. The pain in his leg had returned and so had the throbbing headache he'd had earlier in the evening. *What a way to end an already miserable day*, he thought.

Ronan intensely disliked Sean Carter. He was a good detective though. For a moment, Ronan felt embarrassed for accusing the man's father, the former mayor, of calling in a favor to help his son get assigned to a high-profile case. Ronan had no proof to corroborate his theory, but a junior detective didn't normally get the chance to investigate a case that questioned the integrity of anyone in the judicial system, let alone a well-respected, federal circuit court judge. But Sean Carter had clearly taken charge of the investigation and made it clear that his theories would be actively pursued. Perhaps Bonamico had been right: Captain Ashby had passed the case off to the Criminal Investigations Unit, and it was CID's responsibility to solve Michael Warner's murder and any connections it might have to other crimes.

The townhouse was dark when Ronan pulled into the driveway. Cautiously, he got out of the car and removed his duty belt from the passenger seat and secured it around his waist. Then he quietly climbed the steps to the front door and jiggled the doorknob: the door was unlocked.

Ronan checked the perimeter of the end-unit town-house, his hand resting on his Glock as he maneuvered across the front lawn, down the side of the building and behind it, and then back across the lawn. When he didn't see anyone, Ronan returned to the porch and pushed the door slightly open with one hand.

The door swung back, revealing a dark, empty foyer. Ronan eased through the door with his weapon drawn. As he turned on the light, he felt movement to his right. Before his heart could beat again, Ronan tackled the figure to the ground. Gripping his weapon with both hands, he aimed at the intruder's head.

"God! Don't shoot, Uncle Ronan. It's me!" Nick shouted, palms extended, his face whiter than the boxer shorts he wore.

Ronan stood up and re-holstered his pistol. "Damn it, Nick! I thought you were a burglar," he said through gritted teeth as he bent toward his nephew.

Nick hesitantly reached out and accepted Ronan's strong hand.

"I'm sorry. I'm just a bit wound up. I see Officer Keenan got you home okay."

"Yeah, he's really nice," the young man replied, more than a little bent out by his uncle's 'shoot first, ask questions later' mentality. "I'm tired. I'm going to bed."

Dull sunlight spilled into the room from the opened front door. "It's not even dark yet."

Nick closed the door and swung the lock into place. "I'm tired. Ty is too. He's already asleep."

"I think we need to talk about what happened today."

"I don't want to talk about it. I wish I'd never gone to that stupid game."

"Look. I'm sorry. You shouldn't have seen such a thing, but everything's okay now."

Ronan cupped a hand over Nick's shoulder.

Nick lowered his head and softly asked, "Did he die?"

Ronan pressed harder into the shoulder. "I'm afraid so."

"Then everything is *not* okay."

Nick broke away from Ronan's grasp and marched down the hallway and into the bedroom, slamming the door.

The house fell silent. All Ronan could hear was his own breathing.

———

Ronan wrapped his arms around Ty and kissed him lightly on the nape of the neck. Ty cuddled closer; Ronan smelled like evergreen soap, and the clean, fresh scent sent shock-waves of desire through him. Ty didn't remember Ronan coming to bed or how long they'd both been asleep, but it didn't matter. He was here now in his arms, and Ty could feel every movement Ronan made, including the small breaths that entered and escaped him and how both their bodies rose and fell in unison.

A loud banging on the front door jarred Ty from his bliss. He slipped from Ronan's embrace and grabbed a pair of pants from the dresser.

"What's going on?" Ronan mumbled, groggy and disoriented.

"Someone's knocking on the door. I'll be right back."

As Ty descended the stairs, the pounding grew louder and louder with each knock, and he could hear the door-knob being jiggled. He opened the door to be greeted by a full-figured woman wearing white sneakers, dark pants, and a gaudy flowered shirt.

"It's about time someone answered the door," the woman said, huffing. "I've been standing here knocking for ten minutes!"

Ty shielded the sun rising from his eyes with a hand and tried to make eye contact with the woman. Behind her, a small, square black suitcase sat on the porch along with a small canvas beach purse.

"I'm sorry to bother you. Wait a minute! No, I'm not.

It's eight in the morning. People shouldn't be asleep at this time of the day."

"Well," Ty replied, his tongue filling up the inside of a dry mouth. "The occupants in this house are exhausted."

The woman stepped back and regarded the handsome young man standing before her. "You're Japanese."

"Actually, I'm Polynesian, but thanks for noticing. What can I help you with? If you're selling something, we're not interested," Ty said as politely as he could, considering the rude interruption by this strange woman—the emphasis on the word strange.

"I'm looking for my son. Is this Ronan McCullough's house?"

Ty leaned against the doorframe. He could almost feel the synapses firing as his brain made the terrible connection. "Are you Melissa?"

The woman stepped back and furrowed her brow. "How do you know who I am?"

"I think you'd better come inside. Bring your suitcase too."

Melissa kept her eyes locked on Ty as she stepped down and retrieved the suitcase and purse. She slowly slipped into the foyer before dropping the suitcase to the floor.

"This is ridiculous," she said, before stepping back onto the porch step. "I'm not going into a stranger's house. This is how women end up missing or being kidnapped."

"I assure you, madam, I have no intention of kidnapping you," Ty said as he politely extended his hand. "I'm Ty Andino."

"I, I think you need to put some clothes on," Melissa replied, looking at Ty's uncovered chest.

"What did you expect? You woke me up."

"Is this Ronan McCullough's house or not? Is my son here?" Melissa demanded as she removed a picture of Nick from her pocket and held it in front of Ty's face.

"Nick's sleeping. First room on the left," he replied, pointing down the hallway.

Melissa stepped back inside the foyer, her face ashen.

"Oh, my God, Melissa!" Ronan hissed as he came down the stairs. "What the hell are you doing here?"

"I've come to get Nick. Where is he?"

"I'm right here, Mom," Nick mumbled.

Melissa rushed to her son and hugged him tightly. "It's all right. Mama's here."

Ty stood still as Ronan circled them. "And I trust *you'll* be leaving just as fast as you got here."

Melissa let go of Nick and asked, "Are you okay? I'm so sorry about the trauma you've experienced."

"Trauma?" Ronan asked.

"That's right. Nick called me last night and told me what happened yesterday at the football game. My goodness! Nobody should have to experience anything like that, let alone a boy."

Ronan locked both hands behind his neck. "Nick, you called your mother?"

Oh, no! Ty said to himself.

Ronan stepped in between Nick and Melissa and then pushed Melissa out of the way. "Answer me, Nick. Did you call your mother?"

Nick dropped his head, looked away and nodded in the affirmative.

"What for?"

"What for? He went to a football game and wound up seeing a murder! Jesus, Ronan! Are you that dense?"

"Yes, that was unfortunate. I never intended to expose Nick to such a thing, but it happened, and I can't undo it. Nick's a strong kid, and he'll get over it and life will return to normal."

Ty cleared his throat. "With all due respect, Nick showed up here unannounced, sort of like you just did. It's not Ronan's fault what happened."

Ronan shot Ty a grateful look.

"Despite what's happened, we're both glad Nick's here," Ty added.

Fury roiled in Melissa's eyes; she marched across the room, reared back, and slapped Ty hard across the face.

"What the fuck do you think you're doing?" Ronan demanded.

"Mom!" Nick called out.

"You aren't part of this family, so butt out, you queer!"

Ty touched his cheek, still hot from Melissa's wrath.

Ronan went to comfort Ty.

"No. Don't bother. It's okay."

"I suppose everyone here thinks this is just fine. Do you actually think I'm going to allow my son to stay here and be exposed to this violence while everyone plays house and acts like nothing happened? I won't have my son living with two men, much less two men who—"

"Love each other," Ty said.

"Please," Melissa replied, shaking her head. "My brother's been confused for a long time now. He doesn't know what love is, so he thinks this is love. This isn't love. It's something sick and un-natural. I thought you were going through a phase when you brought that man to Miami, but now you're acting like a married couple with this, this... Are you the man or the woman, Ronan?"

Ty and Ronan glared at Melissa, unable to comprehend the hatred that enveloped this woman's heart and soul.

"You're disgusting!" Melissa added as she walked up to Ronan and slapped him across the face as she had Ty.

Ty could feel the hot tears welling up in his warm brown eyes both for himself and for the man he loved.

Melissa grabbed Nick by the wrist. "Get your things. I booked us on the evening flight to Miami."

As she opened the door, Ronan pressed a flat hand against it and slammed it shut. Melissa turned around. A perplexed look crossed her face.

"I don't know why the fuck you're here, but if you ever come back, you'll be sorry that you did."

"Oh, big Mr. Policeman. Please, don't arrest me," Melissa said, rolling her eyes.

Ronan pulled his hand from the door, balled it into a fist

and then slammed it into the frame. The smack ricocheted throughout the house.

Before Ty could do or say anything, Ronan cut him a look that could have severed steel. "Stay out of it, Ty."

Ty backed away. Ronan leaned in near to Melissa, but she turned away and inched closer to the door.

"Please, do something," Melissa begged, looking at Ty for help.

"This is family business," Ty replied, trying to suppress a frown.

"On a good day, Melissa McCullough Copeland, you're a sanctimonious ass, and the rest of the time you're nothing but a wretched, nasty bitch. I didn't ask Nick to come here, but he's here with me and with Ty. And I love Ty. He's the love of my life, and we're going to spend the rest of our lives together. I don't give a flying crap whether you accept us or not. I don't need your blessing. I never have, and I never will."

Melissa began sobbing. "Stop it, Ronan! You're scaring me."

"Bullshit!" Ronan shouted, slamming his fist into the door once again.

Melissa's sobs grew louder and louder with each breath she sucked in.

"I haven't even begun to show you what scary looks like. You wanted a fight and damn it, you've got one. Except this time I'm having the last word."

Ty approached them. "Come on, Ronan. Back off."

Ronan jerked away. From the corner of his eye, he saw Nick and turned to face him. "Son, I don't care if you stay or go. But your mother has to leave now, or I'll have her ass thrown in jail for trespassing."

Nick stood staring at Ronan, his mouth agape, hardly able to believe what he was hearing.

Ronan stood back and huffed, took a deep breath and composed himself. He licked his lips and took another slow breath. "I'm sorry, Ty. This is your home, and my family has disgraced it."

"No, Ronan. This is *our* home. You could never disgrace it or me."

Ty went to embrace Ronan, but Ronan backed away and retreated up the stairs, slamming the bedroom door in his wake.

CHAPTER 22

Ronan didn't remember falling back to sleep, but he awoke to the sun streaming through the covered bedroom window. He rubbed his eyes and rose up, finding Ty's side of the bed still undisturbed.

Thick with sleep, Ronan ambled into the bathroom. He splashed some cold water on his face, swiped a toothbrush across his teeth and then slipped on a black shirt and a pair of jeans and went downstairs.

Ty was coiled on the couch, watching television. He didn't respond when Ronan entered the room. It took Ronan a moment to remember what had transpired earlier. Although he couldn't remember every word that burst from his mouth during his altercation with his sister, he knew the words had been cruel…and true. Melissa knew just how to push Ronan's buttons, and her greatest calamity was not knowing when to stop pushing.

"Where are Nick and Melissa?"

"They took your advice and left, but they missed the last flight from Charleston to Charlotte."

"Where are they now?"

"Melissa rented a car at the airport; they're going to drive to Charlotte and take a flight to Miami from there."

Ronan waited for Ty to say more, but instead Ty picked up the remote and began scrolling through the channels.

"Ty, look I'm—"

"Save it, Ronan," Ty snapped back as he turned off the TV and flung the remote into the easy chair near the opposite wall. He got up and circled the couch. When Ronan reached out to touch him, he shrugged it off and headed for the kitchen.

"Why are you mad at me?"

Ty stopped in midstride. "Don't take your anger at Melissa out on me."

"I'm sorry about that. There's just a lot of history between Melissa and me, and it's personal and complicated and—"

"And you never told me a thing about it until Nick showed up here." Ty moved deeper into the kitchen as Ronan followed.

"I need to speak with Nick and Melissa," Ronan said.

"Maybe you can catch them at the airport."

"Ty—"

"My evening shift starts in an hour. I'll call you later on break," Ty replied and left.

Ronan stood staring at his reflection in the shiny marble countertop, wondering how he could make amends with Ty. When nothing came to mind, he went to the closet and found his service weapon and duty belt. He clipped on his shield, grabbed his Glock, and slid the handgun into the holster until it was wedged tightly into the leather. Then he grabbed the truck keys and headed out the door.

———

Jason surveyed the room. What a dump! He couldn't wait to get out of the Ivy Terrace Motel. As he glanced around one last time, he was careful to make sure everything, especially the bathroom, had been thoroughly cleaned. He'd meticulously wiped up any droplets of krok or spots of hair color, and any loose hairs had been flushed down the toilet.

Once Jason locked the flimsy motel room door behind him, he'd vanish like a ghost. If truth be told, Jason knew he couldn't vanish completely, but at least with shorter hair and a new color, he'd be unrecognizable to the cops and to many folks who knew him.

With his duffel bag slung over his shoulder, Jason shuffled along the motel hallway and down the outside stairs. He tossed the room key into the deposit box by the office and then checked his watch. It was 8:10 p.m. The truck would meet him in the parking lot in front of the DMV at 8:15.

With purposeful strides Jason walked toward the rendezvous spot at the Kanawha Mall. By the time he reached the shopping center, a seventeen-foot moving van sat waiting in front of the DMV entrance. Not wanting to attract attention or suspicion, he walked around the truck, flung open the door and pulled himself into the cab.

Inside, he found Miles leaning forward with his arms wrapped around the steering wheel. Miles was dressed in the same all-black ensemble as himself: black sweatshirt, jeans, boots, and bandana. Another man, wraithlike and younger with an arched nose and wide eyes dressed in similar attire, sat quietly in the back of the cab.

Jason shoved his duffel bag into the narrow space behind the seats, only to hear a loud groan as he tried stuffing the bag closer to the floor.

"Stop it! Shit!" the female voice commanded.

Jason shot Miles and the other man a puzzled look.

"We picked up some extra help," Miles said matter-of-factly as the other man licked his lips and chuckled.

"What type of extra help?"

"Me."

Jason turned to face the sound. A round, white-powdered face with glossy black lips and dark eyes trimmed in jet-black eyeliner squinted back at him.

"Her name's Raina," the younger man offered. "Adam's decided to give us something nice to look at during our trip."

Jason folded his arms and looked out the window as

Miles revved the engine and slammed the moving van into drive.

As the truck lunged forward, Jason looked at Miles. "Who is she, and why is she here?"

"Raina's one of our distributors. She took over that Warner kid's territory."

Raina leaned back and pressed herself against the cool metal of the truck wall. "I told Adam a cop had been sniffing around Michael. Michael got scared and wouldn't deal anymore. I got his job."

"So you're more than just a pretty face."

"Shut up, Jensen," Raina said.

"All of you, shut the fuck up!" Jason barked. "Lorenzo and Michael both screwed Adam over, and they paid the price for it."

The cab grew quiet. Miles gripped the steering wheel tighter as the truck bobbed up the onramp and onto the turnpike.

"We're going to pull off at the rest area just past Mahan. It's closed for renovations, but repairs haven't started yet. One of you will guard the entrance. If you see a cop coming our way, click the radio button twice, and we'll stop loading and unloading and pull the hatch down to cover the goods. We need to work fast. Understood?"

Everyone nodded. "How many trucks are meeting us?" Jason asked.

"Two more," Jensen replied, a twinge of excitement in his voice.

"Yep," Raina said. "We'll divide the merchandise evenly between the two trucks."

"And then we drive home with the money," Jason said, finishing off the thought. "An easy payday for us all." He closed his eyes to savor the idea of being rich, but his thoughts soon turned from his good fortune to Adam and what he had said: *Find the nurse and get rid of him.* Suddenly, Jason didn't feel so lucky.

Passing the Chelyan and Cedar Grove exit, Miles made a sharp right turn and stopped at the first tollbooth on the

West Virginia Turnpike. Hurriedly, he dug into his pocket for the $18.00 toll, and moments later he and his crew were back on their way. When they arrived at the rest area, only a single wooden barricade blocked the entrance. Miles parked and turned on the hazard lights. "Thank you West Virginia Parkways Authority for making this easy," he muttered through a raspy laugh.

"Jensen, help me move the barrier," Jason ordered. Then he looked at Raina and said, "Sweetheart, you sit here and check the mirrors. If you see any traffic pulling up behind us, I want you and Miles to get the truck into the parking lot as fast as you can. Got it?"

Raina nodded as she pulled her black hair into a ponytail and tied it with a rubber band.

"Two minutes and we're in," Jason said as he stuffed the gun Raina had given him into the waistband of his jeans.

Raina watched on as Jason and Jensen quickly removed the barrier. When it was safely out of the way, Jensen banged on the rear of the truck, giving them the go ahead to move in.

Miles dropped the lever, and the truck heaved and groaned as it bypassed the narrow entrance into the rest area and then pulled up alongside two other white, unmarked moving vans. He shut off the engine and motioned for Raina to get out.

Jason and Jensen made their way to the cab as several other men, also clad entirely in black, carefully began transferring the merchandise. Nearby, two men clutching tactical short shotguns and flashlights stood guard.

"Let's get it done," Jason commanded. "We move out in ten minutes."

CHAPTER 23

"My name is Sergeant Ronan McCullough of the Charleston Police Department. I need to know if you rented a car to a woman named Melissa Copeland."

The ginger-haired young man standing behind the Hertz rental car counter at Yeager Airport cautiously eyed Ronan's shield, unsure if he should or could answer the question.

"Did you rent—?"

"Don't you need a warrant?"

"No. I don't need a warrant," Ronan answered in a deep, authoritative voice, his cool blue eyes scanning the employee's nametag.

"Kevin," the young man said as he felt his knees starting to buckle.

"I need information, Kevin, and I'd appreciate you giving it to me now."

"Yes, sir, yes," Kevin stammered as his fingers flew across the keyboard. "Mrs. Copeland rented a 2014 Toyota Corolla."

"License-plate number?"

"I'll give you a printout."

"That would be excellent. Thank you."

Within seconds the rental agreement was printed, and Ronan was on the road and headed down the hill to Greenbrier Street and the Turnpike.

Traffic was normally light on Sunday evenings, but, of course, tonight the traffic was as thick as the summer air. "Where the hell did all these cars from?" Ronan hissed as he weaved in and out of the left passing lanes, trying to make up lost time. Relentlessly, he pushed the gas pedal closer to the floorboard and prayed no Smokeys were within radar range.

He reached for his cell phone in the cup holder and viewed the *received calls* menu. For once, Ronan wished he had stored Melissa's number, or at least had memorized it, so he wouldn't have to scroll through the entire call list.

Several cars pulled in front of him, and one blared its horn. Ronan looked out the passenger-side window to see an elderly man mouthing the words *slow down* as he extended his middle finger. For a moment Ronan dutifully returned his attention back to the road but then soon found himself scrolling through the *received calls* menu once more. Finally, Melissa's number appeared, and he punched the *dial* button.

The phone rang several times before going into voicemail. Ronan cancelled the call and re-dialed. Again, it went to voicemail.

"Damn it, Melissa! Answer the phone!" Ronan shouted, slamming the phone into the empty seat cushion. He crossed over the Chuck Yeager Bridge on I-64 and merged onto the West Virginia Turnpike. "5EU 364, 5EU 364," Ronan chanted as he scanned both lanes, looking for the dark-maroon rental car. He dialed Melissa's phone number again, and this time she answered.

"I have nothing to say to you, Ronan," Melissa said, a hard edge cutting her words into sharp slivers. "I think you said enough this afternoon for everyone."

The comment made Ronan clench his teeth. "If you think I've called to apologize, think again. What I said needed to be said. Besides, I didn't call to talk with you. I want to talk with Nick."

"Nick doesn't have anything to say to you."

Ronan rapped a clenched fist into the steering wheel. He didn't want to get into it with her again. "Where are you now?"

"We're on our way to Charlotte. Our flight in Charleston was cancelled, so I'm hoping we can catch the 12:30 a.m. flight from Charlotte to Miami."

"I don't want Nick to leave."

Silence fell over the line. Ronan could hear Nick asking Melissa something, but the words were garbled through the static in the connection.

"It's too late now. Nick needs to be home with his family. With me and Bruce."

"Jesus, Melissa! I'm his family too, and so is Ty. And you know how unhappy Nick is living with Bruce. Give the kid a chance."

"And what do you suggest I do?"

"Let Nick come live with me. I'll get him enrolled in classes at CSC, and he can start making something of himself."

"What's Uncle Ronan saying?" Nick asked as he grabbed at the phone.

Melissa swatted at the hands tugging at her cell.

"Did you hear what I said?"

"Yes," Melissa huffed.

Again Ronan heard muffled words coming from Nick.

"Your Uncle Ronan wants you to live with him and Ty."

"That's awesome sauce! Let me talk to him!"

Melissa knew when she'd been beaten and handed Nick the phone.

Nick and Ronan spoke briefly and then Nick handed the phone back to his mother.

"Tell me where you are, Nick?"

"We just passed a place called Sharon...I mean, Standard or something." Melissa snatched the phone back from Nick.

Ronan processed the location. "I have a good idea where

you are. In a couple of miles, there should be a Morton Travel Plaza on the left, I think."

"Okay," Melissa replied as the little rental car effortlessly cruised down the turnpike.

"Over there," Nick said, pointing to the exit.

"Oh, no! We missed the turnoff, Ronan," Melissa wailed into the phone.

Ronan cleared his mind, trying to remember the next exit off the turnpike, a place where they could turn around safely and head back to Charleston.

"Look, Mom!"

"Ronan, there's a rest area up ahead just before a place called Mahan. We'll stop there and wait for you."

"Great! See you in a few," Ronan replied as he looked at the passing road signs, figuring he was about eleven miles behind them.

"Okay. We'll wait."

The cell phone chirped and then silence. Ronan held the phone away and looked at the lighted panel. *No signal.* A sudden chill crept up his back and over his shoulders, but he shook it off and continued driving, although he slowed to the speed limit just in case one of those State Smokeys were lurking behind a billboard or parked on the side of a turnpike entrance ramp.

As Ronan approached the Morton Travel Plaza, he saw several orange signs announcing the rest area closure at exit 69. The next available rest area was at exit 44 near Tamarack and North Beckley. He grabbed his cell to see if he could get a signal. He was in luck and immediately called Melissa to tell her to meet him at the rest area off exit 44. The call went straight into voicemail.

"Damn!"

———

Jason stood behind the trucks, his pistol facing the ground but still tightly resting against his thigh. He checked his watch: five minutes had passed. Turnpike traffic continued to whoosh by, and so far nobody had noticed them or what they'd been doing.

Miles came around the side of the truck. "Two more minutes, and we'll be done."

Jason nodded. "Where's the money? We ain't doing this for free."

Miles peered behind the edge of the truck as one of the guards with the shotgun and flashlight stepped aside. "The money's under the driver's seat of the truck we're taking."

Jason felt his face burn and his brow furrow.

"It's fine. The money's there. I checked it myself," Miles said reassuringly.

Jason reluctantly nodded again and then walked to the other truck where boxes of liquid krok sat neatly pressed into stacks of eight, secured by leather straps and tied to joists. As he counted the boxes, he caught a flicker of light from the corner of his eye. When he turned to look where it was coming from, he found a panting Jensen standing before him.

"Someone...someone's coming," Jensen said in between swallowing gulps of air.

"Cops?"

"No. Just a normal-looking car. Two people in it."

"How the hell did they get through the barricade?"

"I guess we didn't get it put back exactly the same way we found it," Jensen offered with a timid smile.

Jason growled.

The smile fell way from Jensen's face. "There was a little bit of space on the left side of the barricade. It's a small car. It must have slipped through."

Raina climbed down the ramp from the deck of the middle truck and joined in. "What's going on?"

Jason reached down and cocked his pistol. "We've got company. Finish getting the trucks ready. I'll check it." With long, angry strides, he headed toward the entrance of the rest area but stopped abruptly when he heard footsteps.

"What do you mean you're going to check it?" Raina said as she caught up with him.

"Stay out of it, sweetheart. Do as I told you. I'll take care of it."

"And what does that mean? You're going to shoot up that car and kill whoever's inside?"

"Maybe."

"I don't think so."

Raina reached out and placed her hands on the gun barrel. Jason tried dislodging the gun from her grip, but she wouldn't let go.

"Take your hands off the gun," Jason snarled.

"No way. Our orders were to switch the cargo, move the krok, and get paid. Nothing was said about shooting anyone."

"That happens sometimes. It's called collateral damage."

"So, Michael was nothing more to you than collateral damage?"

Jason started walking toward the barricade. "What do you think? I'm the one who took him out."

Raina tried another tactic. "If you shoot up that damn car, we're going to have cops all over this fucking place, and we'll be the collateral damage this time!"

"I'm touched by your concern," Jason replied as he grabbed the pistol from Raina's hand and slapped her hard across the face, knocking her to the ground.

Melissa's rental car pulled closer into view. Jason squinted. Flecks of color momentarily dotted his vision as his eyes adjusted to the light. Looking through the windshield, he could make out the two figures: a driver and a passenger. Jason smiled a mean smile and aimed the gun.

CHAPTER 24

Ronan pulled slowly into the rest area but stopped abruptly when he came to the wooden barrier impeding vehicle access to the parking lot. He heard two loud pops. Cautiously, he surveyed the area ahead and the parking lanes to the right. A solitary car sat just beyond the barricade, its taillights gleaming like two red eyes in the darkness.

He grabbed his Glock and stepped down onto the still-warm blacktop. Ronan's heart thumped hard against his chest as he noted the car's license-plate number: 5EU 364. Just past the faint glow of the car's parking lights, a jagged shadow milled about. Ronan listened for sounds of life or movement to come from the car, but there was nothing. Holding his breath and his weapon tightly, he crouched down and made his way along the side of Melissa's rental.

Suddenly, his bad leg gave way. The pain shot through his knee and up into his thigh, and he tried desperately to muffle the groan that escaped his pursed lips. The shadow stilled and then ran, disappearing into the blackness beyond.

Ronan sat down heavily on the blacktop and sucked in a couple of shallow breaths, hoping to quell the pain and regain his momentum. As he tapped the driver's-side window, a pitiful cry pierced the silence. He counted to ten and then stood up and peered into the car.

Nick sat in the passenger's seat, leaning forward with his face in his lap. His mother's arm lay across his back, her hand gently cradling her son's head. Melissa's free hand still clutched the steering wheel in a deathlike grip.

"Roll down the window," Ronan mouthed with a circular motion of his finger, fearing the shadow still might be within earshot.

"Is the shooter still here?" she mouthed back.

Ronan shook his head negatively.

"Are you both all right?"

"Oh, God, Ronan, I'm so scared—"

"Shh," he whispered. "I know you're scared, but are you both all right?"

Melissa bit the inside of her lip and nodded her head quickly.

"Good. Now be quiet and listen to me." Ronan looked past Melissa to his nephew. "Nick. It's Uncle Ronan. Can you hear me?"

Nick slowly raised his head and sat back into the car seat, a faint grimace creasing his lips.

"Melissa, put the car in reverse and back up slowly. Nick, I want you to move my truck and that barrier out of the way for your mom. Then drive until you get cell service and dial *star SP* on the phone. That'll connect you to the state police. Tell them where you were, what happened, and to send help. And do it fast." Ronan wiped at the sweat dripping down his face and then added, "I'm going to stay here and try to find out what's going on—"

"Uncle Ronan!" Nick interrupted. "Someone shot at us!"

Ronan glanced at the bullet hole in the middle of the windshield. It was a miracle neither of them had been injured.

"Come on! Get out of here. And remember, *star SP* as soon as you get a signal."

"Got it, Uncle Ronan."

Melissa heaved, and her entire body began shaking from head to toe.

"It's going to be fine. Nick's strong, and he can do this," Ronan said as he patted his sister's hand. Ronan locked eyes with Nick, who nodded, silently acknowledging the compliment. "Now go!"

Melissa backed up the car, leaving Ronan alone and exposed. Seeing a large, steel trashcan a few yards ahead, he crouched down again, ignoring the pain, and scurried toward the squat, cylindrical sanctuary. Another trashcan sat several yards ahead and a dumpster beyond it. In the distance, he heard what sounded like commands being given, and the sound of heavy doors opening and closing. Ronan waited for a moment and then crawled to the second trashcan. When his movements went unnoticed, he continued.

Hesitantly, Ronan stood up and surveyed the area. To his right the automated spotlight on the restroom building flickered on, giving off enough light for him to make out several individuals unloading and loading boxes. He narrowed his focus on one person standing near the first truck. As Ronan crawled around the side of the dumpster for a closer look, he caught sight of the long, narrow barrel of a shotgun gleaming in the phosphorescent light.

Ronan clutched his Glock tighter and quickly assessed the situation. One person armed, perhaps more. Three trucks with possible contraband. One shot fired. Did they notice the Corolla had vacated the rest area? Would these men be on the lookout for other interlopers? Had he been seen by anyone? If so, were these men waiting for him to show himself? If they were, did they have orders to shoot?

The questions pinged through Ronan's brain like a pinball bouncing off bumpers. Despite having no idea what the trucks contained or who the people were, it was clear to Ronan they had trespassed into an area that was closed to the public. For that matter, so had he.

Ronan stepped closer to the scene. The pain in his leg was excruciating, and he became lightheaded, losing his balance for a moment. He took a deep breath and tried to shake the feeling and center himself, but it was too late. He careened forward and toppled hard onto the ground.

As he lay twisting in pain, Ronan heard the unmistakable click of a shotgun being cocked somewhere quite near. He turned and stared into the sky, but the stars were blocked from his view. The only thing he could see was a man dressed entirely in black.

"Someone's here!" the man called out to his cohorts. A mean smile curled his lips as he pointed the shotgun directly at Ronan's head.

The adrenaline coursed through Ronan's veins, and without another thought he pulled himself up, knocked the man to the ground and scrambled away just before two shots rang out. The deadly pellets ricocheted off the steel trashcan. More shots followed.

Ronan raced to the dumpster, yanked open the lid and heaved his battered body into the black expanse below. The heavy plastic lid slammed behind him as a pungent mixture of paint, rotten food, beer, and sawdust assaulted his nostrils. He gagged and prayed that he couldn't be heard above the din outside. When the shouting and shooting finally waned, Ronan could hear someone breathing heavily, all the while circling the metal container with stilted, uneven paces.

"You've been on the krok too long," Jason spat.

"I swear I saw someone!" Miles angrily shouted back.

"You're seeing ghosts, asshole… "Come on. Let's get out of here. We're already ten minutes behind schedule."

The words *krok* and *schedule* immediately piqued Ronan's attention. As the men retreated, Ronan groped for his Glock. He'd dropped it into the dumpster as he sought refuge from the hail of buckshot. Wincing, he reached into the refuse. Something soft and slimy slid through his fingers. Eventually, he came across the roughened finish of the Glock's grip but not before raking his fingertips across a chunk of two by four. Splinters bit mercilessly into his flesh. He found the weapon, climbed out of the dumpster, sighed, and proceeded to remove the splinters with his teeth.

In the distance Ronan could hear the rumbling of engines warming, and despite the pain in his leg, he charged toward the trucks. The trucks sat next to each other in the middle of the parking area surrounded by swaths of empty parking spaces on either side. The churning noise of the idling truck engines allowed Ronan to approach undetected. One of the men, who was securing a truck latch, was caught unawares by Ronan's presence. Grabbing the man by the arm, Ronan spun him around, and struck him forcefully in the face with the Glock. The man stumbled back and let out a wheezing laugh.

"So! You ain't no ghost after all," Miles said as he reached for the pistol in his belt.

But Ronan grabbed the weapon first and slung it several feet away from where they stood.

"No ghost! Just a cop."

Miles lunged forward and grabbed Ronan by the ankle. Ronan swiftly countered, reached down and gripped Miles by the throat with one strong hand to keep from being pulled to the ground. Then Ronan slammed Miles as hard as he could against the truck.

"What's in the trucks?" Ronan demanded in a voice that left no room for deceit.

"Fuck off, pig!" Miles hissed, revealing a mouth full of stained, yellow teeth. He yanked Ronan by the belt and jammed a knee into his groin.

Ronan doubled over in pain as the handgun flew from his grasp. Both men dove for it,

but somehow Ronan managed to retrieve the Glock a moment before Miles's dirty hand clasped the black, polymer-covered weapon. A sharp pop sounded, and a 9mm bullet nailed Miles squarely in the shoulder.

The truck's backup lights flashed, and the vehicle started to lurch toward them. Ronan jumped out of the way, landing on the blacktop, clearing the truck's path with only inches to spare. The other truck then throttled quickly back, forcing him to escape once more.

Ronan scrambled to his feet as three bullets hit the side

of the stationary truck, piercing the steel frame and shattering the side mirror. Two more shots were fired as the trucks sped away. Ronan watched the trucks disappear from view while Miles lay writhing on the ground, blood gushing from the gaping wound.

"Damn cop! You shot me!" Miles wailed.

"And now this damn cop's arresting you," Ronan said as he clamped the handcuffs down hard on Miles's wrists.

CHAPTER 25

Ronan chose to violate his initial instinct to wait for the state police and instead went in pursuit of the men who'd shot at him. He left Miles handcuffed to one of the outside drinking fountains and could still hear the man cursing his name as the truck's tires sputtered for a moment, tossing rocks and dirt everywhere, before reconnecting with the concrete and gaining traction. Throwing the truck into drive, Ronan pulled out onto the turnpike without even checking oncoming traffic.

A passing car flashed its lights, and the flat sound of a horn blared as Ronan's pickup swerved too closely to the left lane. For a moment he lost sight of the truck amidst the endless stream of taillights. But it didn't matter. Ronan knew even at the rate of speed the truck was moving, it wouldn't get too far ahead of him in this traffic. Luckily too, this flat stretch of turnpike went on for several miles, allowing him the chance to make up lost time.

The adrenaline and anxiety made Ronan's head throb. As he approached the next exit, he caught up with the truck and pulled alongside it. Wide, deranged eyes stared back at him from the driver's side. Jensen grinned, baring his ugly krok-rotted teeth before slamming his truck into the side of Ronan's pickup. The smaller truck swerved and rattled in response. Jensen pulled deeper into the right lane and cut another sharp, fast turn, slamming into the pickup once more. This time the angle of the impact was sharper, and the front bumper collided with the pickup's front tire so powerfully that Ronan was nearly thrown over the steering wheel and into the dashboard. The truck violently shook and tilted, but he corrected for the movement and regained control before the vehicle could flip and then careen down the embankment to his right.

Jensen exited the turnpike at the next exit, and Ronan followed down into the darkness and onto a frontage road where both vehicles stopped. Jensen jumped from the cabin, taking flight toward the heavily forested mountains. Glock in hand, Ronan pursued his adversary on foot, stopping every few moments to catch his breath and assess the location.

The sound of heavy breathing and equally heavy footsteps, accompanied by the sharp snapping of dried, fallen branches and crunching leaves, led Ronan to the edge of the mountain slope. He jammed his gun into the waistband of his jeans, took another deep breath and tackled the slope.

The angle of the hillside made Ronan's calf muscles burn and ache while the sting of evergreen branches slapped and bit at his face. But he kept climbing, willing himself on. With one hand extended forward, he felt the branches bend and crack as he pushed through the sylvan shadows. Further on he could see where the branches thinned out, and just beyond that point a small clearing stood beneath the warm, yellow moon. The celestial light shone through the surrounding canopy of the trees but not enough to fully illuminate anything or anyone in the glade ahead.

Ronan briefly ceased his trek and tried to ascertain the distance between himself and Jensen. Jensen was near. Very near. Suddenly, the muddy ground below Ronan's feet gave way, and he tumbled head over hind down the mountain slope. Dead branches, twigs and small rocks grazed his exposed face, arms and hands as he crashed through the unforgiving underbrush.

Ronan collided with Jensen, momentarily halting his

descent and knocking the wind out of them both. With a grunt, Ronan rose up and punched Jensen twice in the face. The sound of cracking cartilage in Jensen's nose was like a branch snapping in half, and the warm, red castoff instantly spattered Ronan's sweat-drenched face.

Jensen flailed about, desperately trying to protect himself from another one of Ronan's devastating punches. When his fists failed to make contact, he leaned back and drove his forehead squarely into Ronan's face. Ronan's vision blurred, but he instinctively reacted and delivered a swift punch into Jensen's gut. Without a word, Jensen fell heavily to the ground.

"Get up, you piece of shit!" Ronan shouted, grabbing his adversary by the collar. As Ronan lifted Jensen up from the mountain floor, his back heel slipped again and both men hurtled down the mountainside.

The stink of rotted wood and pungent earth filled their nostrils as they slid faster and faster, branches catching at shirts and jeans and skin. A boulder at the base of the slope finally halted their tumultuous descent. Bruised and battered, Ronan closed his eyes for a moment and inhaled the minty smell of the leaves and twigs stuck to his face and clothing. When he opened his eyes again, two state troopers stood silently over him, their guns held inches from his head.

"Don't move!" one young trooper yelled.

"I'm a cop!" Ronan shouted, raising his hands high into the air.

"I said, don't move!" the trooper repeated.

Jensen groaned and stirred, coming out of his brief, unconscious respite.

"That's your man," Ronan said, pointing as he struggled to his feet.

The other state trooper lowered his weapon and ran over to Jensen.

"I'm Sergeant Ronan McCullough of the Charleston Police Department."

"A little bit out of your jurisdiction, aren't you?"

Ronan nodded. "It's a long story."

"I can't wait to hear about it," the trooper said, lowering his Sig Sauer. "We got the call about the incident at the rest area. It's blocked off and secure, and the wounded man was taken away by the EMTs."

"Good." Ronan felt some relief for the first time in several hours.

A single shot rang out, and Ronan instinctively dropped to the ground. He looked to his right and then to his left where the young trooper lay. Ahead, he saw Jensen scrambling back up the mountain slope. Ronan checked the fallen trooper's pulse; the pulse registered faintly but steady. Then he ran to the other trooper who slowly collected himself and stood up.

"Your partner's been shot. Call paramedics. Now!"

Two gunshots punctuated the sentence.

Within seconds Jensen's body careened from the darkness of the mountain, coming to rest a few feet from where Ronan and the trooper stood.

CHAPTER 26

Ty examined the size and depth of the various wounds covering Ronan's arms and legs. Dabbing a gauze square into a clear, opaque ointment, he hesitated for a moment before inserting it into the bloody mess on Ronan's knee.

Ronan grimaced, and the sound of sucking air hissed through his teeth. "Damn! That burns like a son-of-a-bitch!"

"It will for a while," Ty replied, sliding a gentle hand under Ronan's calf to steady his leg while increasing the pressure on the wound.

The white gauze quickly turned crimson, the trailing tentacles of blood flowing down Ronan's leg until they'd pooled at the edge of the material.

"Murpirocin will kill any bacteria and stop the spread of infection. It's hard to say what got stuck in these wounds."

Ronan gave Ty a blank look, wondering if he'd begin speaking in medical-techno babble, something Ronan didn't like or understand. He clearly understood the succinct tenants of sick and healthy, life and death, criminal and victim. Everything else was incoherent nonsense.

"Don't give me that look," Ty ordered sweetly, while applying the antibiotic cream to another gauze square. "I know things like infection and bacteria don't mean anything to you, but if you want these wounds to heal, you'll trust me."

"I do," Ronan said softly.

He grazed Ty's smooth, small hands with his large, rough fingertips. For a moment the gesture made Ty smile like a lover, but then the smile faded and was replaced with the stern, serious look of a medical professional.

Ronan looked down at the raw, reddened cuts and scrapes, which curled and twisted down both arms and legs.

"Thanks for being there for Nick and Melissa during this ordeal."

Ty gave Ronan a furtive look. "You're welcome, but trying to keep them calm while I was going crazy wasn't a walk in the park."

"I know," Ronan said, dropping his head. He winced again as Ty pressed another piece of gauze onto a bleeding section of skin, this time on Ronan's right forearm.

"I hadn't expected to be crawling around in a dumpster and dodging bullets. I'm just glad they left the rest area before things got ugly."

"Do Nick and Melissa know what happened after they left?"

Ronan shook his head. "They don't need to know the details. It's bad enough they're involved in this mess as it is."

Ty wrapped a strip of clear surgical tape around the gauze patch, holding it in place. "Like it or not, Ronan, I think we're all involved in whatever is going on."

Ty reached down and helped Ronan up. Looking in the mirror, Ronan thought his face resembled a battered chunk of roadkill, all bruised, swollen, and lumpy. His normally square jaw and tight muscles seemed cobbled and doughy, splotched with red and purple bruises and cuts.

"Use this until your leg and back stop hurting completely," Ty said matter-of-factly as he handed Ronan his cane.

Ronan looked down at the cane with utter disgust.

"I don't want any argument," Ty commanded. "We'll let the Murpirocin settle into the wounds and change the bandages again later."

Ronan gripped the cane tightly with one hand and pulled Ty close with his other. Softly, his lips brushed across his boyfriend's mouth. The kiss was soft and flirtatious at first. Then Ronan opened his mouth and let his tongue explore the warm wetness of Ty's lips and tongue. Ty returned the kiss in kind.

"Thank you for coming home," Ronan said as he begrudgingly tore his lips from Ty's.

Ty's face brightened. "There's nowhere else I'd rather be. Besides, things were a bit slow tonight." He turned off the lights in the bathroom, and as they moved through the bedroom into the hallway, Ronan watched Ty's face tighten with worry.

"Ty, what is it?"

"The last few days in the ER have been absolute hell. We've had more drug overdoses and gunshot victims than normal. Tonight, someone came in with the same scaly, abscess-covered skin as Michael Warner. The people are young, not the type to have been heavy, long-term drug users or gangbangers."

Ronan processed the information.

"The more I think about it, the more I think there's a connection to everything that's happened...just like you feared."

Ronan put an arm out to stop Ty from going down the stairs. "Have you called Eric and told him?"

"I did."

"What did he say?"

"He said he'd look into it. By the way, a cop from CID came and took my statement, but I'm walking a fine line here. The Chief of Staff is very serious about any HIPPA violations by CMH employees."

Ty let out a long breath and crossed his arms. Ronan slid next to him and wrapped an arm around his shoulder. "Call me from now on. I'll handle it or make sure someone else does. That way it will look like a CPD-driven inquiry and not information being leaked by hospital staff."

Ronan watched the strain melt away from Ty's expression. "Thanks. I hate to whine about it, especially with everything going on—"

"It's okay," Ronan soothed. He kissed the top of Ty's head, delighting in the fresh, clean hair that smelled of jasmine and ginger.

Voices from downstairs drifted up to the bedroom, breaking Ronan's enchanted spell. Melissa was talking to someone. Ronan hadn't heard the doorbell ring, and a bolt of anxiety shot through him.

Ty sensed Ronan's nervousness and placed a hand on his chest. "It's okay, my love. My car is in the garage. It will look like you're the only one home. I'll stay up here for a bit. It's fine. Go find out who she's talking to."

As Ronan hobbled to the top of the stairs, the abraded and bruised skin on his arms and legs burned like fire. It almost made him forget about the pain radiating down his leg and across his back, pain that had been reignited thanks to the tumble down the mountainside.

When he reached the bottom of the staircase, Ronan found Sean Carter and Eric Bonamico standing at the opened front door, their features highlighted by the porch light.

"...I'm actually Melissa Copeland," Melissa said to the men as Ronan came closer.

"That's right. She renounced her affiliation with the McCullough clan a long time ago."

Melissa turned sharply, the hurt flickering in her eyes.

Ronan held up an open palm and pushed it in her direction but then thought better of his comment and his action. He withdrew his hand, realizing what Melissa had been through, and silently chided himself for not giving her credit for following his orders.

"I'm sorry. It's a brother-sister thing."

Melissa clipped a tight breath, putting her hands over her mouth as she looked at Ronan. "My God, Ronan!"

"I'm getting too old for this," he sighed. "I see you've met Detective Carter and Sergeant Bonamico."

"Don't try to change the subject," Melissa said. "You really are hurt. I'm glad to see that Ty—"

"Melissa," Ronan said sharper than he'd intended. "Why don't you go into the living room for awhile and relax. Let me have a word with my colleagues in private."

Melissa cut a quick look at Carter who didn't object.

"M'am, it was nice meeting you. Don't forget we'll need you and your son to come down to the station and make a formal statement."

Melissa bobbed her head and then gave Ronan another wide-eyed look. He touched her arm lightly, saying, "It's all right. I'll just be a minute."

As Melissa retreated to the living room, Ronan lifted up and then planted the rubber-knobbed cane firmly onto the hardwood floor. The noise made Bonamico blink, snapping him out of whatever mental fog he'd been in.

Carter stiffened. Bonamico looked uncomfortable standing next to the detective as he kept clutching and releasing his grip on a leather-padded notebook.

Sharply outfitted in brown khakis and a seersucker dress shirt, Carter smiled. "How are you?"

"I've been better."

"The department is grateful for your actions."

Ronan detected the insincerity in the words spoken. "But I take it that *you* view my actions as meddling in *your* ongoing investigation."

"Captain Ashby sent us here to speak to you and your sister," Bonamico said, sounding deflated.

"And now you have," Ronan replied, flashing an irreverent grin at them both.

Carter continued. "Troopers searched the area, but they didn't find anything other than a few small footprints leading into the woods. Forensic techs made some plaster footwear impressions of the tracks."

A moment passed before Bonamico spoke again. "Thankfully, the kid you shot in the arm is going to make it. We were able to ID the civilian who was shot. His name's Jensen Williams from Detroit. He's got a pretty active criminal record, including arrests for drugs, robbery, forgery, assault, and battery."

"What a guy," Ronan replied.

Carter spoke again. "There's more. While checking Williams' rap sheet, we discovered that he and Lorenzo White were cellmates at Alger Maximum Security Correctional Facility in Munising, Michigan. He's also done time with Miles Thompson."

"For what?"

"Drug possession, drug distribution and assault," Bonamico said.

"Where's he now?"

"Jensen's at Mercy in critical condition. Doctors don't know if he'll pull through, but right now he's stable. The captain assigned a 24-hour guard outside his room."

"Hopefully, you'll get some credible information out of the scumbag, and after you do, pull the plug on him on the way out."

A nervous moment passed between the men. Ronan absorbed the words and began piecing together the information. Some of the threads of the last several weeks were beginning to make sense. Michael Warner had been kicked off the CSC football team for drug possession. Jensen had been involved with Lorenzo White. White had drug connections. The ER had recently admitted more patients than normal for drug-related problems. The letters D-R-U-G-S kept bouncing around in Ronan's mind. But the fact that Sean Carter had made it more than clear to stay away from the investigation made Ronan reticent to share the information Ty had provided, or the connections he was making as he pieced the details together.

Carter stopped speaking, and even though Ronan hadn't been paying attention to the last bit of what Carter had said, he waited for a response.

"What did the troopers find in that truck?"

"Nada. Not a damn thing."

"Shit!" Ronan hissed.

"McCullough, I know what you're thinking," Bonamico said.

"So, I come off looking like the overzealous cop. Here I am operating out of my jurisdiction, going into a rest area the Parkways Authority closed, initiating a confrontation that leads to a shootout, and then I pursue one of the trucks in a high-speed chase on the turnpike, endangering myself and other passing motorists—"

"McCullough, come on, man, it's not like that."

Ronan talked right over Carter. "Then the state police show up and eventually one of them gets shot; the driver of the truck gets shot, and for what? An empty truck? I imagine that's how the report was written and presented to the captain."

"Ronan," Bonamico said, trying to diffuse his partner's temper. "That's not true. Those men assaulted you and from what we've learned from Melissa's call to the state police, they shot at her too. You're on to something; there's no doubt about that."

Ronan regarded Bonamico for a moment before looking back at Carter. "But as Detective Carter no doubt will add, there's not enough evidence at the scene to justify a Charleston Police officer operating unilaterally, leading to actions that could have gotten himself and others killed. Isn't that right, Carter? Isn't that why you're really here? You never miss an opportunity to throw your weight around, do you?"

"Some of what you just said is true and is the real reason for my visit."

"Ah, ha! I was right! You guys in CID are so damn busy investigating idiot criminals that you think everyone on the force except you has the same mental capacity. If you two came here to lecture me, you could've saved your time and effort."

Carter gazed at the bloody bandages covering Ronan's arms and raised an eyebrow. "Make no mistake, McCullough. I want you to stay away from this case. By the way, I think Captain Ashby might temporarily transfer you to Narcotics. That is, when you're healed."

Ronan stared at Bonamico. He looked exhausted. The dark circles rounding his bloodshot eyes made him look like death warmed over. His normally glowing olive skin seemed sallow and pale.

"Rumor has it everyone in the department is buried in drug cases," Ronan said, not taking his eyes off Bonamico. "As I've told you both before, there's something going on here, and I think it's all connected somehow."

Carter leaned closer to Ronan, his eyes softer and tone more mellow. "And we're going to find out why and how, and then we're coming down on everyone responsible for it. The captain and the chief have made it the department's top priority."

Even though Ronan still didn't completely trust or believe Carter, he didn't respond with a sharp retort. Instead, he waited to see if he or Bonamico had anything more to say.

"Please remind Melissa that we need her and Nick to come down to the station tomorrow morning and give us a statement," Carter reiterated.

"I'll bring her down myself."

"Rest up," Bonamico said.

Carter's face knotted into something between a grimace and a smile as both men stepped off the porch and headed down the walkway to their cruiser.

After Carter had reached the car, Bonamico returned to the porch.

"What the hell was that? What's with you being Carter's lackey?"

"Shh," Bonamico hissed. "We'll talk later. Find me tomorrow when you bring by Melissa into headquarters. I've got Warner's autopsy report."

"Yeah?"

"Yeah, and you're going to be interested in what it says."

CHAPTER 27

"Let me go, Jason!" Raina demanded.

He clutched the black duffel bag in one hand, and squeezed her arm with the other. The moonlight angled through the treetops, casting odd shadows on the pair as Jason dragged Raina through the woods and behind the farm, with her kicking and squirming.

"Adam's going to be pissed," he said through gritted teeth.

"Why's he going to be mad? We did what he told us to do!"

"Shut up! I'll talk to Adam. All you need to do is be quiet."

Jason pounded on the cabin door, first with a quick thump, then several small thuds, followed by a door-jarring slam with a tight, clenched fist. A radio, which had been blaring beyond the door, was switched off.

A bald, medium-sized man in his mid-fifties opened the door. He looked haggard as he nodded at them and smiled. As he stepped aside, his sloped shoulders and shapeless arms resembled those of a once strong, brutish man who had lost his strength and physique at some point in midlife.

"Adam, this is Raina. Raina, Adam."

Raina seemed to shrink into the wall after the introduction. Adam looked at her, his eyes filled with lust. "Yes, the girl who shot Jensen."

Raina panicked. "I...didn't—"

"Here's the money," Jason said curtly, tossing the bag onto the wooden table. "The rest of the desomorphine should be on its way to Charlotte as we speak."

Adam tore into the pouch, greedily pulling out handfuls of cash.

"I didn't count the money," Jason said.

"Don't need to," Adam answered authoritatively, his eyes growing wider and wider as he stacked the money on the table. "The buyers in Charlotte want this stuff, and I told them no bullshit, or I'd cut them off and kill 'em."

Jason moved aside as Adam ambled over to Raina and pressed himself against her. Mortified, she collapsed into the wall. "She's a pretty one," he hissed, stroking her cheek with a dirty finger, smearing a swath of white makeup.

Raina squealed under a frightened breath.

A mean grin crossed Adam's full lips as his knee spread her legs apart.

Her body quivered and her voice shook in terror, as Raina mumbled "No," repeatedly between the brutal, grinding thrusts of Adam's hard, angry body against her own.

"Maybe I ought to give it to you right here, huh?"

"No! Please! I'm sorry. No!" she screamed.

Adam froze for a moment and then stepped back, gazing at Raina with complete disdain. Who was she to rebuff him? His hand came down hard and loud against her cheek, knocking her to the floor. Raina clutched her cheek and cried, the sobbing becoming louder with each labored breath.

"Stupid bitch nearly ruined the operation," Adam huffed.

Jason shrugged.

Raina's eyes quickly set upon Jason, but he turned away and shrugged again.

"She's good with a gun. I'll give her that. I told her to

follow that jerkwad and get rid of him if the cops got too close. She did what she was told," Jason said, sounding almost proud.

"Is that so?" Adam crouched down in front of Raina again. She tucked her legs in and lowered her head in response, afraid of another vicious hit. "The bitch has spunk. I like that."

"What's next?"

"Things are going better in Charleston than expected," Adam replied, returning to counting the money. "The police are overwhelmed. The krok is being used and distributed by every low-life junkie in the city, and the money is flowing in like milk and honey. We're getting ready to double our next batch. I'm going to send a truck to Parkersburg and Wheeling next week, and then we'll move to Huntington and Morgantown and deal to the college kids at Marshall and West Virginia University."

Jason walked over to the file cabinet and removed a syringe filled with a rust-colored liquid. He rolled up his shirtsleeve and jammed the needle into the crease of skin above the elbow.

"No! Not yet!" Adam shouted.

Jason tossed back his head as he pushed the plunger of the syringe with all of his might. "Consider it a down payment for future work," he replied, his words instantly sounding calm and relaxed.

Raina had pulled herself up from the floor and now stood at the corner of the table, hands gripping the corners.

"You want some too, sweetheart? Here." Jason tossed a syringe at her, which landed on the table and rolled around before coming to rest in front of her right hand.

"No, I'm fine," Raina mumbled.

Jason reached out and grabbed the empty syringe, tossed it back into the file cabinet, and kicked the door shut. Then suddenly, he charged the money-filled table and began wildly grabbing the cash and stuffing it into the duffel bag.

Adam struck Jason on the side of the face with his pistol, and Jason dropped to one knee as Raina yelped.

"Greedy prick," Adam growled. "I wasn't finished counting the money yet."

Jason massaged the side of his head, staring incredulously at his fingers, looking for blood.

"Get up!" Adam said. The words sounded more like a challenge than a command.

Jason did as instructed, and when he reached an upright stance, Adam pressed the

cold barrel of the pistol against the younger man's temple.

"Don't you ever forget who's in charge here. You work for me, and if at any time I get tired of fooling with you, your life is over. What happened to Lorenzo and Jensen will pale in comparison to what I'll do to you."

Raina stood shaking and sweating, still clutching the table, trying to find a way to escape the madness.

"That goes for you too, honey," Adam shouted. "And don't think this idiot boyfriend of yours can protect you. You, Justin, Jensen, and Miles…you all work for me!"

Jason curled back one side of his lip, revealing a sharp, stained white canine. His breathing was heavy and deliberate, but he showed no weakness. He didn't want Adam to sense his fear.

It seemed like an eternity before Adam slowly lowered the gun, and Jason cautiously backed away. The anger gradually subsided from the older man's face, and he resumed his business-as-usual attitude.

"Now you can take your money."

This time Jason slowly approached the cash and quietly shoved eight stacks into the duffel bag. He reached back into the pile of money and tossed six neatly wrapped stacks in Raina's direction. "That's $10,000 there. Count it, if you want."

Raina quickly grabbed the money.

"Who's the cop that got Jensen shot?" Adam asked as he walked up to the table.

Jason stopped stuffing the bag. "Some Charleston cop.

Raina saw him talking to Michael after he'd been busted for pot and kicked off the football team."

Adam sighed. "Are you certain it's the same cop?"

Jason deferred to Raina.

"It was dark in the woods, but I recognized the voice when he was talking to those two state troopers. His name is Ronan something," Raina said in a soft, childlike voice as she clutched the money to her chest.

"What about the two in the parked car at the rest stop?"

"They didn't see anything," Jason said. "Honest."

"But they got shot at," Raina blurted out. "I mean, we shot at them before they took off."

Adam slammed his fist on the table. "Fuck! That means there'll be slugs lodged in their car. That's just fucking great! I knew that I should've led this transfer myself."

"Adam, I—"

"Shut up and let me think. Okay. So, we have a cop who's in the way. What about that nurse at the hospital?"

"I haven't had a chance to get back in yet. Security has been tightened on every floor of the hospital. You've basically got to be an employee or lying on a gurney before they'll let you in."

Adam set the gun down on the table and pressed both palms against the edge. His eyes blazed, and he looked as if he could send the table crashing into the wall at any moment.

Jason and Raina exchanged anxious glances.

"Raina, I want you and Justin to hit the college parties at West Virginia State and CSC. Start passing the krok around at frat parties and off-campus parties too. With Warner gone, it's up to you two now to keep the product moving. Now get the hell out of here and take a couple stacks of cash and drop it into the farmer's mailbox on the way out."

Jason nodded, careful not to make eye contact again with Adam.

"One more thing," Adam said as Raina and Jason headed toward the door. "See to it that the cop and nurse are taken care of, and do it sooner than later."

CHAPTER 28

Ronan, Nick, and Melissa sat in the Charleston Police Department reception area, patiently waiting for Detective Carter. Melissa looked nervous and guilty, like she had swallowed a secret she didn't want the police to know. Nick stared absentmindedly at the floor with both hands folded.

"I'm so sorry about the car," Melissa said, her voice creaky and uncertain.

"Don't worry about the car. Eric's taken care of everything with the rental company. The car was insured, and besides, it's evidence in a criminal investigation. Hertz isn't holding you liable for anything."

Melissa looked up at Ronan, her eyes misty and forlorn. "I'm nervous, Ronan. I've never been in a police station before, much less been questioned by police."

Ronan dismissed the concern. "Remember what I told you. Neither you nor Nick is under investigation. Detective Carter just needs to know what you saw. Tell him what you saw. No more. No less."

Nick looked away for a moment before Ronan slapped him on the arm, regaining his attention. "This is important too. Don't speak for each other. Answer your own set of questions, and don't say anything else unless Detective

Carter directs a question specifically at you. Otherwise, he's going to think you're omitting information, or that your stories have been rehearsed."

Melissa squirmed in her seat, appearing annoyed with her brother's instructions. "Are you our lawyer now too?"

"I think Uncle Ronan would make a good lawyer," Nick said, momentarily animated before his face became expressionless again, and he looked back down at the floor.

"No way," Ronan said. "The last thing our society needs is more trial lawyers. Besides, I've done enough of these interviews to know how things work."

Ronan knew if Nick and Melissa were actually suspects in the case, Sean Carter would have charged into the interview room, blue eyes blazing, and begun using deductive reasoning to interrogate them, i.e. asking questions based on questions they'd previously answered. If they had no probative information, he would summarily dismiss them. However, if Carter thought they were part of the incident and would be privy to future information, he would definitely keep them under surveillance and interview them periodically. But he had already come to the house and spoken with Melissa, so Ronan surmised that Carter didn't think Nick or Melissa would be of any use to him in his investigation.

Carter materialized through the door near the receptionist cubicle. Dressed in brown pants and a light-blue shirt and blue tie, he immediately extended a hand to his visitors, which they both unenthusiastically shook. At first Carter ignored Ronan and then casually glanced at him when he asked Nick and Melissa into his office.

"This shouldn't take too long," Carter said as he opened the door.

Melissa gave a long look back at Ronan and then without a word followed the detective.

Carter liked to use the interview room in the Criminal Investigations Division of the building, so that everyone would know the investigation was *his* and was taking place under *his* careful supervision.

Ronan checked his watch. It was 9:15. He knew Captain Ashby would soon finish briefing the dayshift cops on what had transpired the night before and with any special directives for the day. Ronan pulled himself up from the chair and instantly felt something warm trickling down his leg. He bit his lip, realizing one of the bandages had come lose.

Walking the best he could, he headed to the main squad room where he found Captain Ashby finishing up morning muster. Bonamico stood in the back of the squad formation, reading a case file, his eyes burning with intensity. Dressed in the standard dark navy-blue CPD uniform, he looked more like a beat cop than he did a detective.

Ronan knocked on the desk next to where his partner was standing. "I'd like to speak to Sergeant Bonamico. I need to log a complaint."

Bonamico welcomed Ronan with a wry smile. "Let's find an empty interview room," he suggested. "I know this report will interest you."

They found a vacant interview room in the back of the building. The room was sparsely furnished, just a table, two chairs and a large two-way mirror. The harsh fluorescent lights overhead gave a slight bluish-green tint to everything in the room.

Bonamico pulled an aluminum chair from beneath the worn wooden table and sat down with a heavy sigh.

"What's in the medical examiner's report?" Ronan asked, cutting to the chase.

"You certainly don't waste any time getting to the point. But first let me say, you're looking a helluva a lot better than the last time I laid eyes on your ugly mug. Getting good care and some rest, no doubt."

"It pays to know a nurse."

Bonamico gave a little harrumph.

"It looks like you got some rest last night too."

The sergeant inhaled a deep breath and then spoke. "Yeah, I went home after Carter and I left your house. It's the first night in about ten days where I've gotten more than four hours of sleep and been home before midnight. My kids were starting to forget what I looked like."

"I think Ty feels the same way."

"Anyway, back to the business at hand. The autopsy report has the typical findings you'd expect," Bonamico began. "Warner died from exsanguination caused by severe sharp force trauma. He had several fractured ribs and a punctured lung as well."

"Ouch."

"Exactly. Someone wanted this kid to really suffer."

"What else?"

"Warner had small patches of genital warts around his dick, no doubt a result of getting plenty of action from all those college coeds who wanted to sleep with a football player."

"He was a good-looking kid."

Bonamico peered at Ronan and then shook away the remark. "The rest is basically physical notations, but here's where it gets interesting."

Ronan leaned back into the aluminum chair and crossed his arms. "I'm all ears."

"There were traces of a drug in Warner's system."

"Pot, right?"

"Nope, not even close." The sergeant paused and then walked to the room next door on the other side of the two-way mirror. "Sorry, I just wanted to be sure no one was listening in on our conversation," Bonamico said when he returned.

Ronan nodded.

"The M.E. found traces of a synthetic form of desomorphine in Warner's bloodstream."

Ronan stared incredulously back at Bonamico.

"When running a mass spec on the blood, he found codeine, formaldehyde and gasoline compounds."

"Gasoline?"

"Yep." Bonamico turned the folder around and pushed it at Ronan. "The M.E. notated the compounds with a special entry regarding desomorphine."

Ronan scrutinized the file. *Desomorphine: 10x more addictive than morphine or heroin.* Staring at the plain plaster walls of the interview room, Ronan counted the cracks and pitted flakes of paint as he tried to process the implications of the M.E.'s findings. "Warner started out using pot, and it progressed into harder drugs. That's nothing new; we see it all the time," he finally said.

Bonamico waved a finger. "Not like this. Desomorphine leaves users with gangrenous limbs, scaly, rough skin, and abscesses, and the addiction threshold is extremely low."

Bile formed in Ronan's throat as he remembered the smell of Warner's rotten flesh and the puss-filled sores covering his leg.

"The M.E. said Warner's lower leg would have been amputated in a few weeks due to the severity of the infection. It was literally eating away his damn bones."

Ronan swallowed the bile and grimaced. "If you want to kill yourself one piece at a time, it looks like desomorphine is the way to do it. How's the drug administered?"

"With a needle, which explains the small puncture marks on Warner's leg. The M.E. noted over seventeen puncture marks in several places. I don't think the kid was a seasoned user."

"No, probably not. Got any leads on the guy Ty chased from the emergency room?"

"Nothing yet, but we're working on it. Seems like the guy just disappeared as fast as he appeared."

Ronan stood up and stretched. The time on the clock in the interview room read 10:02. "Thanks for sharing the report with me."

The sergeant nodded. "I don't need to mention that you never saw this report."

Ronan held up both palms in a submissive gesture. "I saw nothing and heard nothing. I need to go check on Nick and Melissa. I can't imagine what kind of shape they're in after being grilled by Carter for the last forty-five minutes."

"Be nice," Bonamico said, extending the vowels for extra emphasis.

By the time Ronan and Bonamico entered the squad room, Carter had emerged from the CID's wing of the building and had seen Nick and Melissa to the front door.

Ronan moved quickly across the room to intercept them.

"Everything went fine," Melissa said.

Carter provided a convincing charm-offensive, prattling on about the high level of cooperation and how Nick had been great at providing specific details about the sequence of events.

"Nick gets that from his uncle," the detective said, flashing a toothy smile that made Ronan want to vomit.

"So long, Carter." Ronan pushed open the door for his sister and nephew. As they went through, he turned around and locked eyes with Carter. "Good luck on *your* case. The McCullough's will stay out of your way from now on."

"That's where you're wrong," Captain Ashby said as he came up from behind. "I want you on the case, McCullough, until we get it solved."

CHAPTER 29

Indignation swept over Sean Carter's face as he waited for some kind of an explanation from his captain.

Captain Ashby stuffed his hands in his pockets and set his jaw. "As I'm sure you know, Carter, ninety percent of the police work is normally handled by ten percent of the force, and McCullough has been a large part of that ten percent in this case."

"With all due respect, Captain, Sergeant McCullough embarrassed our department by instructing his sister and nephew to access a closed rest area on the turnpike. That led to an unauthorized investigation out of our jurisdiction. And the result? One state trooper wounded and a suspect in the hospital on life support."

"What happened to all of the cooperation Nick and Melissa provided in the investigation?" Ronan asked.

"I don't want to hear any of that procedural crap, Carter. Miles Thompson and Jensen Williams are career criminals, and I'm damn sure they were doing something illegal at that rest area. McCullough showed true courage investigating, and I can assure you that society isn't going to miss Thompson as he rots in prison or Williams when he dies."

"Captain—"

"Carter, you'll still be the lead detective on the case, but I want you and McCullough to work together. No withholding information from one another. Got that? Bonamico will assist you both with anything you need. We're only going to find out how to stop these drugs infiltrating Charleston if we work together, not against each other. I want formal reports on my desk at the end of each week, so I can keep Chief Toler apprised of your progress. Have a good day, gentlemen."

Ronan watched Carter glare at the captain as he walked off. He cleared his throat, folded his arms and asked, "Does this make us partners?"

"Shut the fuck up," Carter said before stalking off and back through the door to CID.

When Ronan returned to the front reception area, Nick and Melissa were gone. He managed to catch up to them as they headed out of the building. "Sorry about that. I needed to talk to the captain. It looks like the interview made quite an impression. Detective Carter and I are going to be working together on the case thanks to all of the cooperation from the McCullough clan."

Melissa bit her lip and lowered her gaze. Nick brightened. "That's great, Uncle Ronan. It sounds like a promotion."

The thought of spending significant time with Carter made Ronan think twice about the comment. "Yeah, something like that."

"Nick says Ty is taking him for a tour of the CSC campus."

"Uncle Ty and I have been discussing it. He wants to take me over there today."

"Don't call him *uncle*," Melissa said tersely, shaking her head.

"Ignore your mother; call him whatever you'd like."

"I can't believe Nick wants to stay here after being shot at by thugs at a deserted highway rest stop." Melissa shivered after finishing the thought.

"They don't call it *Wild and Wonderful West Virginia* for

nothing," Ronan said, chuckling. "Nick, can you get home from here?"

Nick nodded and shot a devastating grin at his uncle.

"Well, I can see I'm outnumbered," Melissa said with a huff.

"Go home and meet up with Ty. I've got something I need to do. If I can, I'll see you later on campus."

———

The man had been to the farm at night but never during the day. At the edge of the property under an old oak tree, there was a small metal box covered with a blanket. Adam described it as the offering plate, and each time someone passed through the property on his or her way to the woods, they were expected to drop a donation in it as they passed. The money bought the farmer's silence while giving Adam a safe base for operations.

He drove the Ford Focus down the worn path as the trees, set wide and deep against the road, blocked out most of the sunlight, except for a few bands that provided just enough light to see ahead.

Slowing down, he nearly passed the cabin. Slamming on the brakes in a fit of disgust, the man threw the car into reverse, and then rolled backwards until the front door was in sight.

He walked up the path and pounded on the door. Normally, Adam expected a series of knocks, something agreed upon by himself and his employees. The pounding continued for several seconds until the door suddenly flung open, and Adam emerged, a Smith and Wesson 500 Magnum separating the space between them.

Adam instantly paled, and his hands began trembling violently as he stared at the man with the horribly burned face.

"I wasn't expecting to see you again after what happened," Adam said, gulping.

With eyes full of malice, the man took one long look at

Adam and then spat in his face. As Adam wiped away the spit, the man shoved him back into the cabin and slammed the door behind them.

The pistol dropped to the floor, and the man nonchalantly kicked it aside. Squinting from one eye, Adam tried to regain control of the situation.

"I didn't stop looking for you. I hadn't forgotten about you or our arrangement. But killing Michael wasn't part of the deal. I had to spend a lot of time convincing my associates that your actions were part of the bigger plan."

"Shut up," the man said coolly, the steely resolve in his voice silencing Adam's frantic breathing. "I wanted that sloppy, stupid, snot-nosed brat dead to send a message. I'm in charge, and as of right now I'm changing the rules and the players in this game."

The man took a meaty hand and pressed it over Adam's nose and mouth and then slammed him hard against the wall. Adam's eyes went cold and black, and he squirmed and flailed until his fingers found purchase in the scorched skin on the man's face. The man instantly recoiled in excruciating pain, letting go his of grip.

As Adam leaned back against the wall gasping for breath, the man took advantage of the lull and grabbed the hunting knife on his belt. With one quick thrust, he buried the knife deep into Adam's ample gut.

Adam screamed and clawed at the disfigured face, peeling back partially healed layers of flesh. The man growled in agony and thrust the blade deeper in response. The anger in Adam's eyes slowly faded, and his fingers fell away as his lifeless body slumped heavily onto the floor.

Bright red castoff streaked the cabin floor as the man circled his late associate—the knife still held firmly in is meaty hand. Momentarily captivated by the strange patterns, the man stopped and gazed with satisfaction. He wiped the blood that trailed down his face with the back of his hand, grinned and then slammed his steel-toed boot into the uncaring corpse.

CHAPTER 30

onan stood in the parking lot of old Charleston High School and gazed across Morris Street to the Emergency Room entrance of Charleston Area Medical Center: "Mercy." Since his arrival in Charleston, Ronan had heard endless stories about Charleston High, which had stood on the corner of Quarrier and Morris until 1989 when the high school was demolished, and the students were relocated to Capital High School. Ronan hated high school in Boston and remembered very little about the experience. He never understood the personal attachment so many of his colleagues at the CPD had to a school and to a building that no longer existed.

As he surveyed the scene, Ronan watched several people enter a small door near the ER's covered walkway. He rushed across the street and followed the group in. Once inside, he glanced up at the electronic marquee on the west wall. It couldn't be, but he checked his cell phone just to make sure. Eight days had passed since Michael Warner's murder, and Ronan hoped today would be the day he discovered the name of the person responsible for it.

He located the directory and found the ICU listed under the heading "2 East" and grabbed the first elevator available. Stepping off onto the second floor, Ronan followed the smooth curved walls and sparkling tile floors that eventually led him to his destination. When he arrived at the nurses' station, a plump, round-faced, young woman paused from filling out paperwork and smiled pleasantly at him. Ronan displayed his shield and asked where he could find Jensen Williams. She responded Room 214, and Ronan politely thanked her. As he walked down the hallway, the nurse gazed at Ronan's backside until he disappeared from her appreciative view.

The eerie silence of 2 East made him shiver. It was more like the morgue here than a hospital unit. The only sounds he heard were the hushed whispers of family members talking to and comforting mostly comatose loved ones.

At the end of the hall, Ronan recognized the tall, handsome, boyish officer standing near the open door.

"Officer Keenan. Nice to see you again."

It took a moment for Keenan to recognize Ronan, but once he did, a sense of relief washed over the young cop.

"Sergeant McCullough, good to see you."

They exchanged handshakes. "Please, call me Ronan."

"Oh, okay then. Ronan. What are you doing here?"

The question locked Ronan's thoughts. "Uh, I'm helping Sergeant Bonamico," he stammered. "We're investigating the recent disturbance in the ER by a suspect in the Michael Warner case."

"Yeah, some guys at the station were talking about that the other day."

"We're reviewing security tapes to see if we can positively ID the unsub." Ronan glanced back up the hallway, detecting no movements. "How are things here?"

"Great! Captain Ashby assigned me as day guard and Gavin at night until something happens to Williams one way or the other. By the way, I heard what happened on the turnpike. That was awesome…what you did, I mean."

Ronan smiled at the candor and politeness that most young cops displayed. "That's good," he said as he slipped his hand around Keenan's neck and pulled him close. "I never did thank you for watching out for my nephew at the football stadium last week. I really appreciate you stepping up in the middle of a chaotic situation."

Keenan blushed. "It's was nothing, Sergeant, uh... Ronan. Just doing my job."

Ronan patted the kid on the cheek and stepped back. "How's our patient?"

"He's stable, but serious. The doctor came in this morning and mentioned that Williams had regained consciousness and was talking. I think they're going to question him later."

"Who are they?"

"Detective Carter and maybe some other officers. He's been calling every hour wanting to know if Williams is awake yet."

Ronan could hear the hissing inhale and exhale of a ventilator in the background.

"How long have you been standing here?"

Keenan checked his watch. "About three hours now."

"Since I'm here, why don't you take a break and go sit down and have a cup of coffee?"

"Sir, I've got orders not to leave this prisoner unguarded."

"He won't be," Ronan insisted. "I'll stay here until you get back. I've already checked in at the nurses' desk; they know I'm here."

Keenan leaned against the wall and whistled, the air rushing between his teeth. "I don't know. I've never been put on this type of duty before, and if it gets back to the captain that I abandoned my post—"

"It'll be fine, Keenan. I promise. If anyone says anything, I can vouch for you."

"Okay. I could really use some coffee."

"Atta boy," Ronan said, slapping him on the back. "Don't be in a rush."

"Thanks." Keenan seemed relieved and strode confidently down the hall, stopping at the nurses' station before disappearing around the corner.

Ronan let a few beats pass and then walked into the

room. Pushing the door partially closed, he looked at Jensen lying in the bed. A trach tube had been inserted into his windpipe through a hole in the front of his neck, and the ventilator pushed air into his lungs as the machine wheezed and beeped with each blast of pressure. The rhythmic tempo was almost annoying.

"Wake up you sonofabitch. Wake up!" Ronan said as he pulled up a stool and sat down at the side of the bed.

Jensen moved slightly at the command, and Ronan reached out and touched his hands. They barely moved. But they were warm, and he knew this despicable man still had life within him.

Ronan leaned forward, forcing himself into Jensen's field of vision. "Wake up! Come on! You've had enough beauty sleep."

Jensen's eyes fluttered open, and Ronan stared into the watery depths.

"Are you here to arrest me?" His hoarsened voice and garbled words made him sound like he was speaking with a mouth full of rocks.

"Later," Ronan replied. "I'm here now to ask some questions. After that, I don't care if you live or die."

Jensen tried to chuckle, but he coughed out a dry, wracking hack. He closed his eyes and smacked both lips, drifting back to sleep.

"Stay with me, Jensen, or believe me, I'll make sure this is your last day on earth."

"I guess I'd better play along since I've nowhere else to go."

"I've got nowhere else to be either, Jensen, and I'd be more than happy to stop your air flow if you don't tell me what I need to know."

The machines around Ronan hummed, making faint noises that filled the room with an ambient rhythm.

"Who killed Michael Warner and why?"

Another pulse of air puffed from the machine.

"I don't know."

"Really?" Ronan stood up and walked over to the ventilator. A clear, corrugated tube ran from the port in Jensen's throat to the machine. Ronan watched intently as the plastic tubing expanded and then retracted with each pump of air. He lifted the tubing and held it in front of Jensen. "Tell me who killed Michael Warner."

"I…I told you, I don't know. He wasn't my responsibility."

"That's too bad," Ronan said, pinching the tube.

The machine beeped frantically, and Jensen hacked and gagged as his body lurched violently upward from the bed. Not wanting to alarm the nurses, Ronan reluctantly let go of the tube. The frenzied beeping of the ventilator slowed and finally returned to normal. Jensen settled back into the bed, his breathing calm.

"I…I…"

"Ready to talk again and give me the information I want?"

Jensen rolled his head completely to the right, locking eyes with Ronan. "We were instructed to leave the kid alone. I don't know how he died. Nobody in the group was allowed to touch him."

"Why? What was so special about a college kid who smoked a little weed and got kicked off the football team?"

"Warner gave us access."

"Access to whom?"

"To college students, football players at parties and games…people who would want…"

Jensen grimaced.

"Come on. Keep talking. What would the players want? Who are you working for? I know you and Lorenzo White did time together. Who's calling the shots?"

"We push a drug…" Jensen let out a long breath, his voice barely above a whisper.

"Desomorphine. I know all about it. The M.E. found traces of it in Warner's blood during the autopsy."

"We made a fuck load of money on that shit," Jensen replied.

"We who? How many of *you* are there?"

"A few. We work for Adam."

"Not good enough. That's probably an alias anyway. What's his real name?"

"I don't know. We only know him as Adam."

"Still not good enough."

This time Ronan reached over and turned off the ventilator. The frenetic beeping resumed, matching the rhythm of Ronan's own rapidly beating heart.

Jensen began trembling violently. His mouth popped opened, and he gagged and hacked as he started swallowing his tongue. Ronan grinned and flipped the switch back on. "Isn't this fun? I could do it all day. I wonder what would happen if I turned off this switch permanently?" he said, his voice devoid of all humor.

Jensen began to drift to sleep when Ronan shook the bed. "Where can I find Adam? Where's the desomorphine coming from?"

After a long silence, Jensen mumbled, "Detroit."

"Where's Adam? Give me more names. Who else helps you?"

"Rain, something. I don't know. None of us know each other well. Adam keeps it that way. We're just contractors."

Hearing the word *contractors*, Ronan wanted to punch Jensen in the face. *Contractors* made them sound like construction workers, not scumbag drug dealers.

"I'm so...tired—"

Ronan leaned over Jensen again, this time getting so close that he could feel the stale, warm breath pushing from Jensen's lips.

"Adam and the rest of his thug buddies are going down. I'm personally going to see to it."

Jensen turned his head away from Ronan.

"Tell me, damn it! Where is he?"

"A farm—"

"That's a start. A farm where?"

Jensen tried to laugh, but the tube in his throat had already sent in another pulse of air, causing him to cough instead.

"We should've killed you and those people in that car when we had the chance."

Ronan pulled back and looked around the room. The thought of Nick and Melissa being killed incensed him. He leaned forward and slapped Jensen, knocking the trach tube loose from his throat. "One last time. Where's Adam?"

Instead of a small, annoying alarm of beeps, the machine made a loud, piercing squeal that made Ronan want to cover his ears. As he watched Jensen dying before his eyes, a cloud of guilt enveloped Ronan's consciousness. He wasn't a cold-blooded killer. He reached for the trach tube but immediately stopped when he felt the business end of a semi-automatic handgun butt against the back of his skull.

"Back away from him. Now!"

CHAPTER 31

Nick patiently stood in line at the information table in CSC's Assembly Hall.

An older, elegant-looking lady with white hair and silver-rimmed glasses smiled at him.

"Mr. Copeland, registration for the fall semester has already closed, but we'll process your admissions application as soon as we receive your high-school transcripts. Inside your packet you'll find a complete list of programs and majors as well as contact information for all the offices on campus in case you have any questions. Please don't hesitate to contact us if you do," the woman said, smirking. Then she looked behind him, ready to assist the next student.

Ty motioned Nick to move down the table.

"Where'd Mom go?" Nick asked as he shuffled to the next station.

"I sent her to the Coffee Cafe. It's a really neat campus coffee and sandwich shop. I bet you'll visit there often."

"That's cool."

"Come on now. Keep moving."

Ty smiled at Nick and then led him down the table. Nick tapped a foot nervously on the red and white-checkered tile floor. His blue eyes glared at the open space and the various pairs of feet, sliding and stopping at each individual student station.

"The next table is student activities. I met most of my best friends in college through campus organizations and clubs."

Nick hugged the admissions folder close to his chest.

A trim, petite blonde girl extended her hand to him. "I'm Ashley. I'm a student ambassador here at CSC. My major is Music Education. What's your name?"

"Um…my name is…Nick. Nick Copeland."

"He's a bit nervous," Ty said. "But I think Nick is interested in learning more about student clubs and organizations." Ty paused and leaned around to look Nick in the eye. "Right, Nick?"

The young man nodded repeatedly.

"Great! We have student-led clubs, religious and activity clubs, and fraternities and sororities," Ashley said, speaking with a theatrical, patrician warble. "Basically, if there's something you're interested in, we have a club for it. Here's a campus activities list with club names and descriptions."

Nick stared at the paper like it would explode any second.

Ty reached in and snatched it from Ashley. "Thank you for the information. He'll need some time to look it over."

As Nick prepared to move to the left again and pick up a campus parking-permit application, Ashley stopped him.

"Oh, Nick. Alpha Sigma Phi is having a rush party on Saturday at their house on Kanawha Avenue from nine until midnight. This flyer has the directions."

This time Nick tentatively took the paper. "But I'm not really a student yet until spring, maybe," he said. "I'm not sure I can go."

Ashley waved off the comment. "If you've turned in an admissions application and want to go to school here, you're considered a student. I hope you can come."

"He'll be there," Ty interjected, patting Nick on the back.

Nick looked at Ty with a pained expression. "Thank you, Ashley. It was nice meeting you."

They continued down the row of tables until Nick had a CSC folder filled with multicolored flyers about becoming a Falcon. As they walked away from the last table, they saw Melissa standing near the entryway with several white paper cups wedged tightly into a pewter-colored cardboard carrier.

"How'd it go?" she asked sprightly, although the brightness in her tone and face waned as Nick came closer.

"Fine," Nick and Ty chimed in unison.

"I told you this was a bad idea. He's just not ready for college," Melissa said, whispering her reservations to Ty.

"I disagree. He's going to be fine. He'll love college. Trust me."

Nick drifted closer to the door before Ty walked around and cut off the path to the exit. "He even got invited to a rush party Saturday night at Alpha Sigma Phi."

Melissa looked at Ty with a dour expression. "I don't think that's a good idea. I mean…he hasn't been here that long and meeting people for the first time can be intimidating for him. No, I think he'll be better off spending a quiet Saturday evening with me."

Nick looked defeated.

"Nick, hold onto these drinks. It looks like your drink has your initials marked on it." Ty steadied the drink holder and passed it to Nick, who at first didn't take it, but eventually did after setting the folder on the floor.

"Let's talk for a moment," Ty said, leading Melissa away to a corner of the hall. "I think going to a frat party is just what he needs."

Melissa folded her arms and remained indignant. "Well, I'm his mother, and I disagree."

"He needs to meet some kids his own age."

"Please," Melissa guffawed. "Nick's never been one to socialize much with other people."

"That's because you've never encouraged him to do it."

Melissa reared back, her mouth agape. "How dare you speak to me like that? And who are you? You're just some *man* who's living with my brother in some type of relationship that I just don't understand." Melissa rested a finger on each temple and shook her head. "I can't believe we're still here in West Virginia. We need to get back to Florida. We've spoken to the police about what happened at the rest area, and there's no need for us to stay any longer. I came to get Nick and take him home, remember? He'll probably need counseling after all he's been through here."

Ty formed a crease with his lips. "Does Ronan know this?"

"Please. Truth be told, he wanted me gone days ago."

"I disagree there too."

"Don't pretend like you know how I'm feeling or how Nick is feeling."

Ty took in a deep breath. "This isn't about me; it's about Nick. He chose to come to Charleston and find Ronan, and I think he should be able to choose if he wants to attend college or not. The party is only three hours. Let him go and experience it. If he's overwhelmed or unhappy, he doesn't have to enroll here in the spring. But if he likes it, and—"

"He won't. I'm his mother. Nick will hate it."

Ty turned around to find Nick chugging one of the drinks.

Nick noticed Ty and Melissa staring at him, and he immediately stopped drinking. "Can we go now?"

"Yes, sweetie, we can," Melissa replied.

Ty pointed to the door, and they began to head out of the hall.

Melissa reached out and pulled Ty back. Her nails dug into his forearm, making white, spotted marks on the dark skin. "If Nick is harmed in any way from this, I'm holding *you* responsible."

———

"Back off! Now!"

Ronan did as instructed.

The same chubby nurse he'd seen earlier pushed him

aside and rushed to assist a male nurse who was reattaching Jensen's trach tube.

"It was time to check Mr. Williams' vitals when we heard the alarms going off," she said, her voice thick with indignation.

"Get out of here, Ronan!"

The tone of the words and the speed at which they were recited sounded more than familiar. Ronan spun on his heels and hissed, "Shit, Eric! What the fuck?"

Bonamico holstered his pistol, while to the right of him Officer Keenan kept his service weapon pointed directly at Ronan's head.

"Put that thing away, Keenan."

Officer Keenan kept a determined expression as he slowly lowered his Glock. "Sergeant Bonamico, I stepped away just for a few minutes. I didn't know what was going to happen. I swear! He said that you were here to look at security tapes."

"I believe you, Keenan."

The nurses rotated around the bed in long, fluid motions. In a matter of seconds, Jensen had the trach tube reconnected, and the alarms had stopped beeping. The male nurse made sure Jensen was comfortable as the female nurse stormed over to Ronan.

"I'm going to call your superiors," she blurted out, her voice shaking with anger. "I've been working this floor for twenty-five years, and we've had plenty of patients with police protection. In all that time, we've never had a problem. Never! I can't believe this is how our police department acts nowadays. I'm responsible for the wellbeing of this patient, and it doesn't matter if he's a criminal or not."

"That won't be necessary," Bonamico said. "Once our captain gets through with Sergeant McCullough, there won't be any more problems."

He grabbed Ronan by the arm and swung him past Officer Keenan who remained behind to make sure the room was secure. In the hallway Bonamico shoved Ronan in the back, trying to move him along.

"Where do you get off intimidating a witness? If anyone finds out what just happened, the prosecutor's case against him is over."

"If he lives," Ronan said, walking purposefully past the bend in the hallway to the elevator. The thought of Jensen dying in that hospital room gave Ronan great satisfaction.

Ronan slammed the heel of his palm against the elevator panel. "You need to head back to the station and run the name *Adam* through VICAP. Check for aliases and for any known connections that name has with anyone in Detroit. Also, search for crimes in the Detroit area involving desomorphine."

Eric nodded.

"We need to talk about this," Bonamico said, "but later. You know that nurse will probably call the department. If Ashby or Carter find out—"

"To hell with them both. It doesn't matter. Jensen gave me the information I needed."

"You know damn well what you did wasn't right."

Ronan clenched his jaw as Bonamico stared at him with pity. He could almost see the words *you know I'm right* in Bonamico's eyes.

The moan of the elevator car moving up the shaft made the tenuous moment last longer. Ronan reached over and pressed the *down arrow* repeatedly and with more emphasis with each push.

"Come on," Bonamico said from behind. "Don't give me the silent treatment."

"I'm not," Ronan replied harshly. "We're all supposed to be working this case, and that's exactly what I'm doing." He pulled out his cell phone and checked the time. "I can just make it."

"Make what?"

"Make it to the FBI before the office closes for the day."

CHAPTER 32

Ronan hadn't heard from Nick or Melissa since Sean Carter interviewed them. More importantly, he hadn't spoken with Ty, but he figured he would have left a message for him by now on his cell. As Ronan scrolled through the received calls, his face creased with worry. There wasn't even one call from Ty.

He decided to go home and check on things and freshen up. Normally, being fresh was a distant concern during an investigation. But Ronan didn't want to go to the FBI field office looking like he'd just come off a three-day stakeout in a compact car.

Without the approval of his department superiors, Ronan knew he'd be taking a risk by going to the FBI. The Feds didn't appreciate unapproved and unsupervised visits from the local Leos, and he stood the chance of being turned away at the door or laughed all the way back across town. If Bonamico's assessment was correct and the nurse and Officer Keenan did report what had transpired earlier in Jensen's room, Ronan would most likely face a suspension. In that case, he had nothing to lose.

When he pulled into the driveway, it was empty. Opening the garage door, Ronan noticed Ty's car was gone.

He closed the door and walked up the steps, fumbling with his keys before Ty pulled the door open.

"May I help you? Oh! That's right. You're the guy that used to live here but disappeared awhile ago."

Ronan's slate-blue eyes scanned the handsome, dark-skinned man standing before him; his hair combed perfectly, his blue tee shirt and jeans hugging his taut body in all the right spots. *Damn! He looks good!*

"Very funny," Ronan said as he walked past Ty.

Ronan looked around the house. Frequent bursts of noise came from the television in the living room, and Ronan could smell garlic emanating from the kitchen.

"I was making spaghetti before I went to work," Ty said. "I wasn't sure when you'd be home, so I was going to put some in the fridge for later."

"Where are Nick and Melissa?" Ronan asked, placing his duty belt and shield on the table by the door.

"Nick's watching TV, and Melissa went to the grocery store. I needed more tomatoes for the sauce. By the way, you might as well know she's mad at me."

Ronan stopped moving. "Why is she mad at you?"

"I registered Nick for the spring term at Charleston State," Ty began. "While we were there, he was invited to a frat rush party, and I told him he should go. Melissa wasn't happy about that."

Frat party. The words made Ronan cringe and his gut flare. His mind snapped back to what Jensen had said to him at the hospital. The plan was to distribute desomorphine at frat parties.

"Melissa isn't the only one who's mad at you."

"What? Why? Who else is mad at me?"

"Me."

Ronan stomped past Ty and went into the kitchen. A large vat of bubbling sauce simmered on the stove. He stuck a wooden spoon into the sauce and licked it. "Damn, that's awesome, Ty."

As Ronan opened the refrigerator door and pulled out a beer, Ty pushed the door shut. "Why are you mad at me?"

"You had no right to sign Nick up for classes. That should've been Melissa's call."

"Wait…what? Since when did you start taking your sister's side on things?"

"You just don't understand."

Ty stepped back and crossed his arms, the veins in his neck bulging. "No, I really don't understand, Ronan. Why don't you explain it to me."

"I don't have time," he replied as he opened a beer and began chugging the frothy brew.

Incensed, Ty slapped the can from Ronan's hand. It bounced off the edge of the island and landed on the floor, a golden swath spilling across the tile as the can tumbled and swirled.

"Then *make* time! I'm tired of being treated like an afterthought, and I'm sure as hell tired of bending over backwards for people I didn't even know existed and vice versa."

"Ty," Ronan said, pointing a finger. "I don't have time."

As Ronan left the kitchen, an empty beer can pelted him in the back.

"Get back here and talk to me," Ty demanded.

Ronan turned; his eyes filled with rage. "If you were unhappy then you should've said something."

"Oh, right!" Ty spat as he walked to where Ronan stood. "Was I supposed to tell your sister and nephew to leave? Come on, Ronan, give me a break."

"Don't confuse the issues," Ronan barked. "Telling Nick he could go a frat party without talking to Melissa first was just not right. I can see why she's mad."

"God!" Ty replied, exasperated. "You can be so stubborn! Why don't you see anything from my perspective anymore?"

"I'm not going to argue with you. I need to go. I've got a few new leads in the Warner case, and we may be close to getting some answers as to why he was murdered."

"What about getting some answers for us," Ty said. "Is this going to be our new normal? You so wrapped up in a case that I don't see or hear from you? Having Nick and Melissa around is fine, but they aren't you. And it's you I love and need. Every day."

"When's the party?"

Ty ignored Ronan and walked back to the kitchen where he began opening and slamming cabinet drawers.

"Don't fuck with me, Ty!" Ronan shouted. "When and where is the party?"

"It's tonight at Alpha Sigma Phi on Kanawha Avenue, near the campus."

"Thanks."

Ronan collected his duty belt and shield. Hearing only silence now from the kitchen, he opened the front door and slammed it hard behind him.

CHAPTER 33

R onan didn't remember how fast he'd driven on either Interstate 64 or on Virginia Street on his way to the FBI field office. The argument with Ty had left his mind a blur, and the very thought of taking sides with Melissa now after all she'd done ricocheted painfully in his mind. Nevertheless, this time she had every reason to be angry with Ty and with him.

He thought about calling Melissa, but that was the extent of it. Ronan didn't have time. The FBI office would be closing soon, and he wanted enough time to explain his presence, since arriving at the office without an appointment would likely perturb the agents on duty.

Ronan surveyed the square, light-colored brick building on Virginia Street; only an unobtrusive sign on the front door indicated it was a federal building.

Before entering the office, Ronan removed his shield from his belt and dislodged the gun from its holster. Two agents dressed in conservative suits approached him and immediately confiscated the items as soon as he walked through the door.

An agent with a plain, creased face and salt-and-pepper hair asked Ronan for identification. Ronan obeyed and removed his wallet, but the agent snatched it before he had the chance to display his credentials.

As the agent studied Ronan's ID, the other ran a metal detector wand over him and then patted him under the arms. Afterward, he ran his hands along the waist of Ronan's pants, down his legs and across his shoes. The agent, who'd asked for the identification, held Ronan's CPD ID in the air, parallel to his face. He looked and nodded at the younger agent who was bigger and had blond hair and a trimmed auburn goatee.

"Sergeant McCullough, it's highly unusual for a local police officer to come here without prior approval of this office or that of the Chief of Police."

The agent with the goatee spoke with a slight, southern drawl. "I'm Special Agent Chandler, and this is Special Agent Allan."

"Pleased to meet you both," Ronan said, shaking their hands. "I apologize for coming here unannounced, but I need your help."

Ronan waited patiently as the two agents retreated into another room to talk privately. When they returned, Chandler motioned for Ronan to follow and led him into a small meeting room in the middle of the building. Allan momentarily remained behind and asked two other agents to secure the office for the day.

As the three men settled into the black leather office chairs, Chandler got right to the point. "What can we do for you, Sergeant?"

"I'm investigating the murder of a college student named Michael Warner. He's been linked to a drug dealer named Jensen Williams. It appears Jensen was part of a cartel moving desomorphine into the city. It's called krok on the streets."

S.A. Chandler wrote the word down and circled it while S.A. Allan sat back into his chair and rested his open hands on the table. For the next half hour, Ronan detailed everything that had transpired in the last eight days, including the turnpike shootout and the mysterious man who had confronted Ty in the ER.

"We sympathize with the situation, Sergeant. In fact, we're cognizant of the spike in drug-related deaths and arrests in Charleston and its environs."

"Yes, the hospitals, especially Charleston Mercy, are overwhelmed with drug overdoses," Ronan added, thankful that neither agent asked him to verify the source of his information.

"That said," Allan continued. "I fail to see why you think this matter falls within FBI jurisdiction."

"I shot Williams during my pursuit. He survived, and I was able to question him about krok distribution in the greater Charleston area."

"And?" Allan asked.

"The drug is coming out of Detroit, so that makes this case a federal one."

"And how does Warner's murder fit into this scenario?" Chandler asked.

"Warner was a user as well as a dealer. I believe he ran into trouble with his suppliers and was killed."

"You're saying we have a drug war on our hands?"

"It's very likely we do, and the violence is only going to escalate. The members of this cartel are brutal. They aren't afraid of the police or afraid of removing anyone who stands in their way."

Chandler and Allan exchanged glances. S.A. Allan stood up and excused himself from the room while S.A. Chandler reviewed the notes he'd taken; he didn't look up from them until Allan came back into the room with a handful of case files.

"Go ahead. Have a look, Sergeant McCullough," Allan said, pushing a brown file folder into the center of the table. "I trust the information we're about to give you won't leave this room."

"It won't. I guarantee it," Ronan replied.

Allan looked at Chandler and nodded.

S.A. Chandler cleared his throat. "A drug treatment center in Joliet, Illinois went public back in April when one of the doctors reported seeing as many as a dozen users of the drug. When the *Chicago Tribune* ran the story, the DEA Chicago field office wasn't ready to recognize krok as an immediate threat."

S.A. Allan locked his hands together and tapped them on the table. "Concerns that this drug would make its way to the United States have mounted since late 2011."

"Desomorphine isn't new," Chandler added. "Swiss scientists synthesized the drug from morphine back in 1932. It was used as an analgesic until 1981 to alleviate severe pain. Mixtures of chemicals like codeine and hydrochloric acid used to produce desomorphine today cause severe tissue damage. The term *krok* comes from those scaly, green and yellow sores that develop near the injection sites. The drug is cheap to make and once people become addicted, the dealers jack up the price. People will pay anything for it."

"The medical examiner's report on Warner noted similar tissue damage," Ronan stated matter-of-factly.

"The drug is currently being imported from all across the former Soviet Union, and as many as one million people have used it. Despite the Russian government taking some steps to curb the epidemic, including banning websites that explain how to make the opiate, it hasn't helped much. As for the other countries of origin, Interpol is dealing with them," S.A. Allan said.

Ronan was awestruck by the information assaulting him.

"There have also been reported cases of people testing positive for krok in Arizona and Utah. The DEA office in D.C. can give you more information on that. We're collaborating with them, but you know how reticent agencies are to promulgate information."

Ronan leaned forward, almost to the point of falling onto the table. "I appreciate the information, gentlemen, I really do. But how do we stop it?"

"The CPD needs to stop the flow of krok into Charleston—"

"And that will only happen when we crush the cartel importing it," Ronan shot back. The statement was meant to be rhetorical, but it still drew a sharp response from Special Agent Chandler.

"Exactly."

Maybe Arizona and Utah had been test markets for the krok, Ronan thought as he pieced together these startling new facts. He needed to share the information with Ty and the doctors at the hospital, so they'd be prepared for future overdose cases. Carter and Bonamico needed to be briefed as well.

"Will there be anything else, Sergeant?"

Ronan snapped out of his reverie. "Uh, no gentlemen. That will be all. Thank you so much for all your help."

"Good luck to you and to your department," S.A. Allan said politely as he locked the door behind Ronan.

Ronan drove to CPD headquarters like a Le Mans racer. By the time he arrived, the Friday-evening shift had been on duty for nearly an hour. As he approached Bonamico's desk, he glanced at his own desk. It was spotless; all his case files were gone. The only item that remained was the phone.

Ronan turned and headed for the Criminal Investigations Unit. Carter needed to know everything the feds had told him. As he entered the CID unit office, he found Captain Ashby standing in front of a seated Sean Carter. Carter looked disappointed and flustered like he'd just received terrible news.

"Carter, listen we need to talk."

He looked up at Ronan with a far off reflection in his eyes.

"We certainly do," Captain Ashby said, turning back to face Ronan. "And we're going to start with your suspension."

CHAPTER 34

"Ty, you didn't have to drive me down here," Nick said as he pulled on the tag of his new dress shirt before stuffing it back under the collar.

"It's not a problem," Ty replied, flashing a set of straight, gleaming white teeth. "This house can be hard to find because this section of Kanawha doesn't run parallel with the end of the university campus."

Nick lowered his head, feeling his cheeks blush. "I'm still not so sure about all this. Are you sure I'll fit in?"

"This isn't high school, Nick. Nobody cares who you are, what you look like or what you wear. Just go in, be yourself and make some friends."

"Uh, okay. I will."

"Good. Your Mom will pick you up later, and you've got my cell number and the hospital number just in case, right?"

Nick dug into his tan khaki shorts and pulled out a piece of crumpled paper. "Yep. I do."

"Okay." Ty flashed another disarming smile. "Get in there and have fun."

For a moment Nick felt like throwing up as he watched the Jaguar sports sedan slowly pull away. He swallowed hard several times and then turned around and gazed at the two-story Alpha Sigma Phi fraternity house looming before him.

As he tentatively approached the house, Nick noticed clusters of young men and women talking. Some were snuggling and kissing, while others were drinking and smoking. Plumes of cigarette smoke intersected and swirled around the faint yellow porch light that provided just enough light to cast narrow shadows on everyone, accentuating few features. A young man leaned against the faded white siding of the house, near the front door, scrolling through his cell phone. A girl, dressed entirely in black clothes with black hair and black lipstick, stood next to him.

"What's wrong? You lost?" she asked.

Nick stopped as he stepped onto the porch. The comment caught him by surprise. "No, I'm just not sure where to go."

The girl smiled. "If you're looking for the rush party, then you're at the right place."

Nick smiled meekly and glanced around. The man leaning against the wall looked at him for a moment then returned his attention to the phone.

"I'm Raina. This here is Jason."

"Uh…hi. I'm Nick."

"Pleased to meet you, Nick." Raina said as she extended a soft, white hand.

Her skin was wet and clammy.

"What year are you?"

"I'll be a freshman, but I'm not exactly a student yet. At least not until spring, but the person I met at orientation said—"

"Sounds great," Jason said gruffly, still staring at the phone. "Raina, baby, why don't you get me a beer?"

Raina mumbled something under her breath and then said, "Come on, Nick. You can help me."

He nodded and obediently followed the girl.

Inside the frat house, the party was raging. The scene was chaotic and reminded Nick of teenage parties he'd seen on television but was unsure actually existed. The music was loud, but not deafening, and people were kissing and grinding against each other as they danced. In the rear of the living room, young men played pool, oblivious to the frenzy unfolding around them.

Raina reached back and pulled Nick by the hand. Weaving through the mass of tangled bodies, she kept her focus on the kitchen where copious amounts of wine, liquor and beer lined the well-worn Formica countertops.

At the makeshift bar, a thickset young man with a wide, round face stood pouring shots and draining each glass as it was filled.

"Hey, Justin!"

Justin stopped pouring shots and leered at Raina with glistening, lustful eyes.

"I already told you I'm off limits," she said with a disgusted smirk. "Nick, what do you want to drink?"

He looked down, trying to think and channel away the noise that swirled around the room. "I don't drink, not really."

"Damn! There must be something you want. It's hot as fuck in here."

"I'll take a Coke."

Raina flashed a dazzling smile and ordered Nick's Coke, a rum and Coke for herself and a beer for Jason.

Impaired but still able to function, Justin fumbled with the bottles of soda and booze. Eventually, he managed to mix Raina's drink and find Jason a beer and Nick a Coke.

"There," Raina said as she served Nick first.

Surprisingly, the Coke was cold and tasted so crisp and refreshing that Nick nearly swallowed the drink in two gulps.

Raina moved behind the kitchen counter as Jason approached.

He disregarded Nick and looked straight at her. "Everything in place?"

She nodded and then finally turned to Nick, giving him a pitiful look. "I hope you're having fun, but somehow, I doubt it. No worries. The fun will begin soon enough."

Jason curtly shoved a drink, masked in a red plastic cup, into Raina's small hand. With her free hand, she grabbed Nick's arm and led him around the counter. As they walked

Nick caught Raina's sweet, heady scent, which was a stark improvement over the smell of sweat and alcohol overwhelming the crowded, small space.

Nick followed Raina into the living room. The dancing had stopped and people now moved lazily about and whispered to one other in hushed tones. The light Bruno Mars tune that was playing when they came into the house had been replaced by a panicked heavy-metal beat with a deafening base.

"I like you," Raina said as she tossed her arms around Nick's neck, her eyes sliding to the left and right. "I think I want to be with you."

"I'm not sure. I mean…we just met. I don't know you real well."

She pulled back one arm and shook a finger at him. "Stop playing hard to get, little freshman. I can tell you're a freshman. You know how? Because that's what a freshman would say."

Raina let go of Nick and guzzled her drink, throwing the cup onto the floor when she was finished. Then she grabbed his neck again and pulled him closer. Nick noticed small puncture marks on her arms, and the droplets of blood surrounding the holes appeared fresh.

"I love a good party," Raina said under a slight giggle and then kissed him.

Nick immediately pulled away.

Raina reached down and picked up another red, plastic cup from the end table next to the couch. Disregarding its contents or its owner, Raina tossed the cup back and took a generous gulp. "Ah…you're no fun." Raina smacked her lips, belched and giggled again. "Kiss me."

Raina steadied the cup and pulled Nick down again, forcefully, and kissed him deeply, this time poking her tongue deep into his mouth.

He went along with it for a moment and then pushed her away. "Stop it! Please!"

Shock and disappointment rocketed across Raina's pretty face, and she grabbed Nick in retaliation. Instead of kissing his mouth, she bit at the sides of his neck while her hands fumbled with the button and zipper on his shorts. He felt the muscles in his chest tighten, and he pushed her away again, this time with more force.

Raina staggered backward and grabbed the end table for balance. The cup slipped from her hand, and hit Nick's feet; the clear, foamy liquid spilled all over his Nikes and onto the wooden floor.

"Oh, no!" Nick bent down and tried to wipe away the beer. The sickly sweet aroma emanating from his damp shoes made his eyes water. "I'm going to get in so much trouble if Mom knows I've been drinking. Shit! Shit!"

Raina continued giggling as Nick frantically wiped at the alcohol. He paused and smelled his fingers. "Shit! Now my hands smell like booze." He looked up at Raina. "Can you get me a towel?"

She peered down at him. The muscles in her face tightened, and her expression went flat. Then she charged him and smacked him across the face. "Stupid, clumsy freshman!" she screamed. "I didn't want you anyhow!"

A small group of partygoers began to huddle around the scene. Sweating and nervous, Nick panicked and retreated from Raina and went to look for an exit. Once outside, he could call Ty or his Mom and have them come get him.

Passing a small bathroom tucked beneath the vaulted staircase, Nick watched as various party guests sauntered in and out. The smell wafting from the bathroom was horrid, and it made him hold his nose. Inside, he noticed two boys crouched in the corner. The taller boy held a syringe in the air as the smaller boy removed a shoe and sock. Then the taller boy jammed the needle into the webbed flesh between the first two toes.

"Just relax, and let it work. It's going to feel amazing. I loved it!"

The boy leaned back against the wall and closed his eyes. He appeared to be in some type of ecstasy, as the taller boy soothed him.

"Want a hit, man? I've got more."

Nick shook his head and quickly withdrew. So far he'd only met one person who was slightly interested in him and that person had wanted something more. He felt a sick headache forming in the middle of his forehead as he thought about people openly injecting themselves with drugs. Nick had heard such stories about college life, but he didn't want any part of *this* college life.

He weaved around people standing two and three deep in the hallway. Just as he opened the front door, Raina pulled him from behind. She looked different than before. Her face was paler, and her eyes were half-closed.

"You want to get out of here? I think this party is lame."

The question made Nick nearly leap off the floor. "Yes, I do! But not with you. After you slapped me, I don't want to—"

"I'm sorry," she said tersely. "You're really cute, and I thought you wanted to hook up with me. But I think you just want to be friends, and I'm cool with that."

Nick looked puzzled while Raina gazed around the room, trying to take in the sights and sounds one more time before she left. "Can you drive me home?"

"I can't. My…well, my friend Ty dropped me off."

"That's okay," she said, her eyes fluttering. "We can take my car. I'm just in no shape to drive."

"I'm…I'm new to Charleston, and I don't know my way around that well," Nick stammered.

"Don't worry," Raina replied, poking him in the chest with a finger. "I give real good directions."

CHAPTER 35

"Before you start, McCullough, the suspension is my call," Captain Ashby said, the steely resolve evident in his husky voice.

Ronan bit down hard on his lip as Ashby moved past him and closed the door to Sean Carter's office.

"Your theatrics at the hospital this afternoon made quite an impression."

Ronan's slate-blue eyes paled to gray as the captain cocked his head to the side, waiting for him to offer an explanation.

"I did what had to be done."

"Oh, really?" Ashby asked sarcastically. "Detective Carter, why don't you fill in the blanks for Sergeant McCullough, so he understands that what he did can't be undone."

Carter tossed the brown file folder onto his desk and reached for a small notepad lying next to the telephone. "Arrived at CMH Mercy at 1453 hours. Met with Sergeant Bonamico at 1500 hours; questioned Jensen Williams at 1515 hours. ICU nurse Emily Nelson stated, 'Williams went into cardiac arrest at approximately 1600 hours and is now comatose.'"

Ronan leaned against the office door, resting one foot flatly against it. "Can't say that I'm upset at the news."

"Enough!" the captain barked. "Carter isn't finished."

"Emily Nelson," he said, swallowing hard, "also stated, 'Williams had been questioned by Sergeant McCullough prior to Sergeant Bonamico's arrival Mr. Williams' room. Officer Keenan, along with Sergeant Bonamico, had to physically restrain Sergeant McCullough to prevent him from harming Jensen Williams.' Emily Nelson further stated: 'Sergeant McCullough was responsible for detaching Williams' trach tube, which resulted in Williams going into respiratory arrest.'"

Ronan stared straight ahead and remained expressionless.

"Any idea how that happened, McCullough?"

Ronan huffed. "I told you, he was stonewalling me, and I had to get information from him."

"Not that way!" Captain Ashby shouted, pounding his fist on Carter's desk. "We want to nail this bastard and his associates as badly as you do, but we can't use Gestapo tactics to do it!"

"Damn it, Captain! Williams and his crew are moving krok into the city. I witnessed him shooting a state trooper. In fact, I'm the only cop, local or state, who had the balls to pursue Williams and find out what he and his merry band of thugs were up to, and you're damn lucky that I did. You said so yourself. That's why you put me on this case!"

"So! You want a medal now?"

"Captain Ash—"

"If you want to be self-righteous become a politician."

"What was I supposed to do? Williams refused to divulge any information about his cartel's operation. I used what I had to my advantage and pressed him."

Carter arched an eyebrow. "Are you admitting to removing the trach tube?"

"I'm not admitting to anything," Ronan replied. "What I'm saying is we have used similar tactics before when questioning suspects. Since he wasn't in one of our interview rooms, I had to improvise."

"Now the ends justify the means," Carter spat back.

"No! Of course not! But the men behind this desomorphine invasion are ruthless, and we've only got one shot to get them, and Williams is that shot."

"We're supposed to be working together on this case," Carter said, "but as usual, Ronan McCullough decided to go rogue and do things his own way. Why didn't you call Bonamico or me? We would have gone to the hospital with you."

"Because quite frankly, Carter, I don't *like* you. And I don't trust you either."

"Stop it! Both of you," Captain Ashby commanded.

Ronan finally turned and faced the captain. "This pairing was your idea. I was fine working alone."

The captain shook his head. "You're lucky to be working at all. Now I have to try and keep the chief from firing you, which I can guarantee won't be easy. Your years of service and reputation will probably save you this time, McCullough, but it will be the last time. This is going to be a damn PR nightmare for the hospital and for us when the media gets wind of what you did. And the prosecutor's office will want an explanation of how *I* nearly let a potential star witness die. I hope the info you got out of that bastard pans out."

"That's all fine and good, Captain. Suspend me. Whatever. This isn't over."

"Captain," Carter interrupted. "Before you take his weapon and shield, I'd like to hear what McCullough learned."

"Ah," Ronan said, mockingly. "Done with the lectures and ready to get down to business, are we?"

Carter grimaced and hunched his shoulders, preparing for Ronan to leap across the table at any moment.

"Talk," the captain said curtly.

"Williams works for a guy named Adam. I don't have a last name. Neither Adam, nor his associates, had any authorization to take Michael Warner out. Williams seemed pretty adamant about it," Ronan stated matter-of-factly.

Carter scratched his chin. "So what does an average college kid offer a cartel like theirs?"

"I wondered the same thing," Ronan replied, moving away from the door and standing in the center of the office. "Michael Warner gave his dealers and their suppliers access to college kids at CSC through frat parties, socials, study groups, and one on ones."

Captain Ashby pointed at Carter. "Write that down and contact the DEA with the info."

Ronan almost blurted out, *Too late. They already know all about it*, but he didn't. If the captain knew he had spoken to the FBI without his authorization, Ronan would be in deeper shit than he already was. Hell! He'd need a pair of waders.

As Carter took notes, Ronan kept talking. "I think those trucks at the Mahan rest stop were moving the desomorphine."

Carter stopped writing for a moment and looked up. "But the truck Williams was driving was searched. It was empty."

"That's true," Captain Ashby said. "But we never saw what was inside the other trucks. The desomorphine might well have been in them, and who knows where those trucks ended up or where the drugs were distributed."

"You have a point," Carter acquiesced.

"All right then. Carter and Bonamico will follow up. Meanwhile, I need your shield and service weapon," Captain Ashby said, holding out his hand.

"You can't be serious. I'll admit I used enhanced interview techniques, but I wouldn't have let Williams die."

The captain shook off the comment. "I can't be sure of that, and neither can you. Thirty days' suspension pending the outcome of an investigation. You're dismissed."

Ronan stared at Carter, his eyes searching for backup from his so-called partner in the case, but Carter turned away. With a clenched jaw, Ronan tossed his shield and service weapon on Carter's desk.

"This isn't personal—"

"Screw you, Carter, and the horse you rode in on!" Ronan hissed. He flung open the door and stormed out, already planning his next step in the investigation.

CHAPTER 36

Nick followed Raina's directions to her townhouse, goading her every few miles for further directions and constantly asking if they were still going the right way.

"Don't turn too fast," Raina stammered from the passenger seat. "My stomach can't take it."

"Am I getting close?"

"A little farther," she said with a belch. "Turn where you see the sign that says 'Apple Grove' on it."

Nick ran his right hand alongside the Honda's steering wheel, looking for a way to click on the high-beam headlights. He found a switch near the base of the wheel and turned it to the right. The instant blast of bright light fully illuminated the rocky, curving road ahead.

"Keep going. We're almost there."

Ahead, Nick saw the Apple Grove sign where he made a sharp left onto a narrow side road.

"I'm the second townhouse on the right."

He pulled up behind a beige Chevy Cavalier and then stopped and looked at Raina.

"Whew...it's really warm in here," Raina said, briskly fanning herself with one hand and clasping at the door latch with the other.

"If you say so," Nick replied.

He offered to help Raina, but she declined and fumbled with the door latch for several more seconds before rolling out of the car. Weaving and stumbling across the grass, her new Vans sneakers finally made purchase on the walkway in front of her dimly lit townhouse.

"They always say the first step is a doozy," Raina said giggling as she began toppling over.

Nick caught her before she could fall and then steadied her before going any farther.

"My knight in shining armor."

"Be careful," Nick commanded somewhat breathlessly as he tried balancing Raina against him while keeping her feet on the sidewalk.

Giggling and belching, Raina held tightly onto Nick until they were at her front door. "The key is under the mat. Can you open the door for me? I don't think I can keep my hands still enough to get the key in the lock."

Nick opened the door, still holding Raina at his side, and searched the wall until he found the light switch and flipped it on.

"Now that you're home, I really need to get going."

Raina ignored Nick's comment and instead grabbed his hand and pulled him into the kitchen. Walking over to the counter, she picked up her cell phone and snapped a picture of him.

"Is Nick spelled with a *ck* or only a *k*?" she asked, trying to subdue the tremors in her hands as she pushed the phone's tiny keys. "N-I-C...never mind, I got it. Nic Copeland."

Raina tossed the phone back onto the counter and then walked seductively up to where the young man stood. Nervously, he pressed himself up against the wall. She smiled and came closer. Leaning into his neck, Raina's hot breath whispered against his skin; Nick's body swelled in response. Reaching down, she massaged the front of his shorts as she ran her tongue across his throat and up his neck to just below his earlobe.

Nick gasped and pressed forward. Realizing what had happened, his face colored fiercely, and he scrambled for something to say. "I...I really need to go. Thanks for... well...for being with me at the party," he said as he bolted for the door.

"I hope to see you around, little freshman. Next time I'm going to rip off your clothes and fuck you into next month."

Nick slammed the front door and scampered down the sidewalk like a frightened kitten.

CHAPTER 37

Raina woke to a pounding sound and a pulsating pain drumming behind her ears. As she pulled herself up from the couch, the room swirled, and a fierce bout of nausea erupted from the pit of her stomach.

"Nick?" she called out, her voice sounding more like a ragged croak.

The pounding grew louder until Raina realized it was coming from the front door. She took a tentative step but then stopped when she saw her bruised and swollen feet. Bloody, scaly, yellowish green patches had formed between the first and second toes where Jason had injected them with krok earlier that night.

Raina grabbed a tissue and dabbed the bloody wounds. "I'm coming," she yelled.

Stumbling to the door, she rested an open palm against the cool, wooden plank. Thinking Nick was on the other side, Raina took a couple of deep gulps and willed herself not to vomit. Perhaps he'd reconsidered her offer. She always liked to fuck when she was high. It gave her libido that extra little surge it needed to satisfy her partners.

Raina licked her fingers and smoothed down her hair, making sure to flatten any strands that had collected around her eyes. She took another deep breath and opened the door. In the darkness, she realized the person at the door wasn't Nick, but someone else.

"My God, Ben! Where've you been?"

Without a word Ben leapt from the threshold and landed on Raina, knocking her to the floor just inside the foyer. She tried to scream, but he placed a gloved hand over her mouth and pressed with all his might. Raina squirmed and shook like a fish out of water and frantically clawed at the hand. As she felt herself starting to faint, Raina gathered her last bit of strength and dug a fingernail deep into the soft skin next to Ben's eye. He barked and slapped her hard across the face then turned and slammed the door shut. But as he did, Raina managed to scramble to her feet.

She reached for a glass on the coffee table and threw it at him. He ducked, and the glass smashed onto the laminate floor a few feet away. The sound of the ricocheting glass made them both pause. Seizing the opportunity, Raina circled around Ben and ran for the front door. But he lunged at her again, this time knocking her head against the wall. As she struggled to get away, Ben pulled out his Buck knife and thrust it deeply into Raina's back over and over again.

———

Ronan paced restlessly, taking long strides as he crossed the living-room floor to and fro, trying to determine what to do next. Any further involvement on his part in the investigation would have to be done from a distance—and alone. Without support from his colleagues on the force, his investigation might not generate any new information, especially if he pursued the same leads and angles Bonamico and Carter would most likely go after. But Ronan had the information from the FBI agents. He also knew he possessed most of the technical history of the drug and how it came to the United States and made its way to Charleston. The more Ronan thought about his place in this mess, the more he realized one key detail: the police would be on their own to stop this drug before it completely claimed the city.

The phone rang downstairs. Expecting it to be Ty, Ronan answered and was surprised when it was Bonamico.

"Ronan, it's Eric. Dispatch got a 10-32 call from a resident in the Apple Grove neighborhood just south of Elkview—"

"Sorry, Bonamico. I can't help you. I'm suspended."

Bonamico didn't let a beat pass. "I got called in because the investigating officers reported the victim having swollen, scaly skin on her feet."

"Krok?"

"They think so," the detective replied. "I'm on my way to the scene now."

"I appreciate the update. I've got some things I need to take care of, but keep me posted on what happens."

"Ronan, I really think you need to come out here."

"Eric, I appreciate your support and wanting to keep me involved, but there's no guarantee I'm even going to have a job when my suspension is over."

"It's Nick, Ronan," Bonamico said stoically.

A lump formed in Ronan's throat. "What about Nick?"

"Forensic techs found the victim's cell phone. Nick's picture, tagged with his name, was in one of the photo files. The time stamp was earlier tonight."

CHAPTER 38

The neighborhood where the murder victim was discovered was a tenuous one for the Charleston Police Department because it straddled the city limits. Even though Charleston police had jurisdiction, sometimes the Kanawha County Sheriff's Department would intervene if the CPD didn't respond quickly enough to a call.

As he raced past Charleston, with the city skyline in the distance, Ronan wondered about Nick. How and why did the victim have his picture? Was this a girlfriend Ronan knew nothing about? He anxiously dug his cell phone from his pocket and fumbled with the numbers, trying to keep the truck steady in the right lane as he merged onto Interstate 77.

Melissa answered on the first ring. "Ronan, where are you?"

"You first."

"I'm at home."

"Is Nick with you?"

"No. He's still at the party. Why?"

I hope so, Ronan said to himself.

"I want you to stay home."

"Where the hell do you think I'd be going this time of night?"

"I don't want to argue with you. Just listen to me for once."

"Fine."

"I'm on a call, but as soon as I'm done, I'll get Nick from the party. Okay?"

"Is everything all right?"

He held his tongue and lied. "Yes. Everything's all right. I don't have time to explain."

"Anything you say, Ronan," Melissa replied without hesitation.

"Good. I want you to call Ty and tell him I'm headed to a scene."

"I'll call him right away."

"Okay. Thanks."

"Ronan, you seem really tense. Are you sure everything's all right?"

He squeezed the phone tightly in his hand. "Honestly, I don't know, but I hope so. I need to go. Call you later."

Ronan didn't wait for Melissa to reply before hanging up. He didn't know if everything would be all right, especially if Nick and the victim were somehow connected. He thought of several reasons how and why Nick could have made it from the party to the victim's house, but that didn't mean Nick was involved in any crime, let alone a murder. Ronan's leg and back began to throb, and he could feel a blistering headache coming on to join in the fun.

Approaching the Apple Grove subdivision, he pulled off the side of the road and into the gravel parking lot of The Cold Spot, a favorite neighborhood bar. Nobody would bother his truck there, nor would anyone find it suspicious to see a vehicle parked parallel to the side of the road.

Ahead, Ronan saw the swivel and bursts of blue light flickering throughout the neighborhood. About a hundred yards south of the subdivision's entrance, an officer stopped incoming traffic and questioned each driver. As Ronan hobbled slightly down the edge of the road, a CPD squad car sped north, presumably to set up another checkpoint.

Pushing back the thickets of vines and weeds, Ronan eased into the entryway of the subdivision where he came upon two cops whom he didn't recognize. One of the young officers shined a flashlight directly in his face before the other cheerfully acknowledged him.

"Sergeant McCullough. Sergeant Bonamico said you might be here."

Ronan said nothing as he walked past the men and headed toward the command center that had been set up outside the townhouse. Bonamico was talking with a forensic tech but stopped and waved when he saw Ronan.

"I'm glad you're here."

"I appreciate you calling me, especially since this regards Nick."

"The victim's name is Raina Dalton. Twenty-three. A student at CSC. She put up quite a struggle. There's no evidence of a burglary. We found her wallet, ID, computer, television, everything valuable still in the house."

"That eliminates robbery as a motive."

"Right. One of the forensic techs taking her initial walk-through notes noticed Dalton's toes and feet were swollen, and the odor coming from them was the same odor associated with desomorphine."

"That shit smells awful," Ronan said with a grimace.

"You're right about that!"

"I wonder if krok's the reason the girl was killed. Maybe she was making a deal with someone and didn't want to pay the asking price, or maybe she was the one dealing the drug when everything went wrong."

Bonamico stepped back and looked at the row of town-homes along the street. "She very well could've been a dealer. When I pulled up here, I wondered how a college kid could afford such a nice place."

"Carter here yet?"

"He's at another scene, but he'll be here after he's finished there."

"I'd better get on with it. He'll shit bricks if he sees me."

"Come on. We have plenty of time."

As Ronan entered the house, he could see Raina Dalton's lifeless body sprawled

in the far corner of the living room, a pool of blood surrounding her torso. She lay on her stomach with arms stretched out flat and her head angled in an odd position. Wide-open eyes stared at nothing.

"Gentlemen," came a soft voice from behind them. "I see you've met our victim."

Ronan and Bonamico turned to see a beautiful, middle-aged black woman standing before them.

"Dr. Curtis," they said in unison.

Assistant Medical Examiner Dr. Althea Curtis nodded politely and then crouched next to the body to conduct her preliminary inspection.

"All the stab wounds are centered in the midsection of the victim's back and are in close proximity to the heart, lungs and spinal column. COD is most likely sharp-force trauma, but I won't know that, of course, until the autopsy."

"This killing was personal," Bonamico said with little emotion.

"I tend to agree with you, Sergeant," Dr. Curtis replied. "This attack was vicious."

Ronan started to speak, but the words evaporated from his lips when Dr. Curtis lifted Raina Dalton's right hand. Written in blood beneath where her hand had rested were the letters

N I C.

CHAPTER 39

"Jesus! Those letters. N I C." Ronan felt like he'd been punched in the chest.

"What do you think?" Bonamico asked as he circled the corpse, careful not to step into any cast off.

"The letters are dried and so is the satellite spatter from the castoff except for a few skeletonized blood drops," Ronan said. "But the blood pool isn't completely coagulated. The unsub probably used this as his blood source to write the letters."

The sergeant agreed.

Both men moved around the body in sweeping, balletic sidesteps, but for the moment, paying little attention to it.

"There's a blood trail pointing toward the front door," Ronan remarked.

Bonamico glanced at the crimson droplets staining the oak-colored laminate floor. "Except for a couple of drops by the door, the trail ends midway through the living room."

"I imagine at that point the killer decided to wipe his knife clean and tuck it away for safekeeping. The other blood drops probably came from his clothes. You know he had to have been a bloody mess after he butchered this poor girl."

"You right on both those counts. The techs haven't

found any knives except for those in the butcher block in the kitchen, and all those knives have been accounted for and tested," Bonamico replied.

"My God! Nick," Ronan said, looking back at the bloody letters.

"That's why I called. We couldn't figure out exactly what those letters meant at first, but when we found Nick's photo in the victim's cell phone, that's when we thought—"

Ronan's head snapped to the side as he faced his partner. "You certainly don't think Nick did this?"

The sergeant looked around before settling a hard, serious look on Ronan. "No, of course not. But the evidence right now doesn't look good. You know the techs will dust this entire house for prints, and if his are found—"

"Even if Nick's prints are found in here, that doesn't mean he killed Dalton!" Ronan growled. "Look at that blood pool. This girl was bleeding out fast. She wouldn't have had the time or the strength to write perfectly formed letters like these. The unsub positioned her hand over the letters to make us believe Dalton had scrawled them to reveal the name of her attacker. Whoever he is, he's been watching too many movies."

Based on the stunned look on Bonamico's face, Ronan realized he'd nearly been shouting at his friend. "I'm sorry, Eric. I didn't mean to snap at you, but Nick never mentioned knowing anyone named Raina. Shit! He doesn't even know his way around Charleston, let alone know where to meet a girl. And I can't imagine how he could have gotten to Apple Grove on his own."

"There are still plenty of details to figure out."

"If Dalton was involved in this drug cartel, then anyone involved with it could've been her killer. It might be the same unsub who killed Michael Warner."

"And we know it's not Jensen Williams."

"These guys are good—violent and smart," Ronan shot back. He paused momentarily before speaking again. "Ty said more people were recently admitted to the ER showing signs of krok usage."

"So this cartel seems to be successfully dealing the drug to college students and the Mercy pop."

"Correct."

They both stared at the bloody initials.

"So, if the letters mean something other than Nick's name, what is it then?" Bonamico asked hesitantly.

Before Ronan could answer, a chubby man approached them. He ignored Ronan and looked straight at Bonamico. "Sergeant, Dr. Curtis is ready to remove the body."

"Okay, fine."

Ronan stepped away from Bonamico and shuffled past a forensic tech taking photographs. "Did you see this?" he asked, pausing in the foyer.

Bonamico approached Ronan and knelt beside his crouched partner. "Yeah. The evidence marker was already next to it when I came through the door, but I thought a dead girl was more important at the time. There's more in the living room."

Ronan stared down at the blue-colored shape pressed into the light-colored floor. He reached forward and nearly touched it, but jerked back his hand before he could contaminate the evidence. "Is this mud?"

The detective shook his head in the affirmative. "One of the forensic techs said it looks like the mud he encountered last year at a scene over on Hampton Road. It's called Blue Mud, and it's found in several areas of West Virginia. Apparently, the damn stuff is sticky and acts like quick sand. Farmers have lost livestock in it."

"I know mud is thick and creates a mess, but I've never known it to be sticky...or blue. Hell! All of Boston's Back Bay used to be a tidal bay with marshland, but to my knowledge it wasn't anything like that."

"You guys from Boston miss out on all of the fun of us country boys."

Bonamico's attempt to lighten the mood was lost on Ronan.

"Blue, red or white, mud is solid evidence."

Ronan ignored the bad pun and looked at the mud

again. "This was obviously tracked in, but it's impossible to say by whom at this point."

A moment of silence passed between them.

"You do realize that you'll have to confiscate Nick's shoes to see if there's any mud on them, don't you?" Bonamico asked hesitantly.

"I know."

Ronan stood up and crossed his arms. As Bonamico slowly pulled himself upright, Ronan poked him.

"Give me an evidence bag."

"For what?"

"So I can collect a sample of this mud and send it to the state police crime lab to be analyzed. I have a friend there. Pete Linville. Pete owes me a favor or two. I'm sure he'll make processing this evidence a priority."

Ronan held out his hand, but Bonamico shook his head. "I'm not giving you an evidence bag, Ronan."

"Damn it, Eric! Don't fuck with me right now."

Bonamico stepped back. "You've been suspended and prohibited from working on this case or any other. I can't risk the integrity of this investigation, or my job, so you can run some kind of covert operation with evidence from this crime scene."

Ronan sucked in a deep breath, preparing a retort, but Bonamico cut him off. "I know Pete Linville too. I'll take the sample and ask him to put a rush on it."

"Thanks," Ronan said as he looked at his watch. "I need to go before Carter gets here. I can't deal with that asshat right now."

"I hear what you're saying. I'll call you later."

"Okay." Ronan walked out of the townhouse and headed for his truck, his focus now completely on Nick.

CHAPTER 40

Ronan marched back to the truck, unconcerned whether Sean Carter or anyone else saw him leaving the crime scene. As he yanked open the door and flopped into the seat, the blood-soaked images inside Raina Dalton's apartment stained his mind.

The first image that haunted him was the bloody lettering on the floor, possibly indicating Nick was involved in the young woman's death. But the letters could also mean someone else knew Nick had been at the townhouse earlier that night and was trying to frame him for the murder.

Anger and anxiety engulfed Ronan.

The low-hanging moon above splashed slanted beams of light onto the road, which was overshadowed by colored streaks of the strobes of squad car lights. The more Ronan thought about Nick and the trouble facing him, the more anxious he became. Fatigue and stress made thinking clearly and objectively about everything more than challenging. Looking down on his dashboard, he saw two sets of green digits shining under the darkness of the truck cab. One blinked 1:41 a.m. while the other smaller heading indicated the day had changed, and it was now September 1st.

Ronan emerged from the tree-covered canopy that protected the neighborhoods north of Charleston and entered a flat, open stretch of Greenbrier Street. To his right he could see the long, narrow shadow of Capital High School looming in the distance. During the daytime, the campus buildings, set in the middle of a meadow in between two towering expanses of the Appalachian Mountains replete with thick, lush forests, were an idyllic sight. But tonight, the forest seemed one with the mountainside, a tangled, foreboding mass of darkness—the perfect motif for the events of the evening.

As Ronan passed the main entrance to the high school, something caught his eye. Unable to see anything clearly in his review mirror, he swerved to the left, made a U-turn, and collapsed the truck's right side into a narrow shoulder that sloped sharply from the gravel-covered road. Dust from the churned gravel created thin wisps that mixed with the truck's headlights, creating a small, hovering cloud around the vehicle.

Reaching under the seat, he grabbed his Maglite and then exited the truck. As he flashed the strong beam of light across the road, a truck approached from the south side of Greenbrier Street; it sped past, uninterested in the stranger. Taking a deep breath, he strode across the street, holding the flashlight steady. "Charleston Police! Show me your hands."

Ronan instinctively reached toward his duty belt and prepared to draw his Glock, but then realized it was now locked away in the CPD armory. Yet his weapon felt like a phantom limb, its presence still clearly felt at his side.

The figure came into focus.

"Nick?"

Nick rapidly shook his head in the affirmative, trembling as Ronan closed the distance between them. Ronan turned off the flashlight; the moonlight was now the only light surrounding them.

"Uh…hi, Uncle Ronan."

"Jesus! What are you doing out here?"

"Taking a walk."

Ronan scoffed. "Don't get cute with me. I just came from Raina Dalton's house."

Nick instantly tensed. "Uncle Ronan, please don't tell Mom. I met Raina at the

rush party. She was drinking and came onto me. We had a fight, but we made up, and she invited me back to her house and—"

"Whoa! Slow down," Ronan said, placing both hands on Nick's shoulders to stop his rambling. "You were with Raina at the party tonight?

Nick nodded.

"How did you get to her house?"

Ronan could see Nick's eyes darting to the left and right. "Uh—"

"No shit here, Nick. I need the truth, not something you make up as we go."

The boy gave several quick head nods again. "Okay." He explained everything that had happened from the moment he arrived at the party until he left Raina Dalton's townhouse.

"And when did you leave?"

"I don't know, Uncle Ronan. Honestly, I don't. It was late, and I was tired. Raina was drunk or high or something. She made me uncomfortable, so I left."

"Why didn't you call me, or your Mom, or Ty? We would have picked you up. You must've walked five miles down here."

Nick shifted his weight from foot to foot and grimaced each time he looked toward the ground. Ronan switched the flashlight back on and tilted it downward; an angry lump formed in his throat as he looked at Nick's dirty, barren feet.

"Why the hell aren't you wearing any shoes?"

"I got rid of them."

"What? Why? Look at your feet; they're a damn mess!"

"I spilled beer or something on them."

"Something?"

"All right. I spilled beer on them!"

"Why didn't you mention that detail to me earlier?"

Nick ignored the question.

"Talk to me, young man, or you can talk to your mother."

"I tried to wipe off the beer with my hands, but then my hands stunk. I just didn't want you and Mom and Uncle Ty to get mad at me for drinking because I didn't have anything to drink. I swear! Raina was trying to kiss me, and when I backed away she spilled her drink on me."

Ronan wanted to simultaneously hug and furiously shake his nephew. He flashed the light again at Nick and saw the tears welling up in his eyes. Ronan realized if Raina had come onto Nick at the party, there would be witnesses. Depending on what he did and said, however, could make or break him as a murder suspect. Ronan resisted the urge to tell Nick that Raina had been murdered. Instead, his mind ticked to the next important detail.

"Nick. Listen to me. I need those shoes that you were wearing. It's really important, not just to protect your feet, but for something else."

"I...I..."

"I'm waiting. Where are they?"

"I left them at the party."

"Well, let's go and get them."

By the time they returned to the frat house, most of the party guests were gone. Only a few remained, and they were now passed out in various areas of the living room. A couple had made it as far as the upstairs bedrooms.

After half an hour of searching, Nick's shoes were nowhere to be found. Ronan's gut twisted into a painful knot, and he could almost feel his blood pressure rocket into the stratosphere.

"Mom's going to be so mad," Nick whimpered. "Those shoes were practically brand new."

"Come on. I'll take you home," Ronan said to his nephew. *We're fucked*, he said to himself.

CHAPTER 41

Ben returned to the cabin shortly after midnight. He walked straight to the wooden shed and flipped on the dim 40-watt light near the door and examined the dirt covering Adam's grave. Thunder boomed overhead, and he hoped the impending rain would blend the agitated dirt with the harder, firmer dirt that had been baked like clay under the relentless summer sun.

Taking his bloodstained clothes from a plastic bag, he held them up and watched as they twirled in the gusty night breeze. This was one of his favorite shirts and his best pair of Levis, and now thanks to Raina he had to burn them. He grinned when he thought how she had remembered his name, but that wasn't really his name. Ben was the name he used when he infiltrated the cartel, and he'd been an active member of it too until Lorenzo White got sloppy and nearly burned down the entire Smith Street warehouse. The idiot!

The plan had been a simple one from the start: scare Michael Warner into either fulfilling his commitment to push the krok to college students or leave Charleston altogether. But Ben and Lorenzo had never expected an off-duty cop to show up at The Three Minute Warning and change everything. Neither had they anticipated the warehouse security guard to recognize Lorenzo from newspaper pictures and television news reports.

Ben wanted to flee to avoid being captured, but Lorenzo panicked and took the guard hostage. The entire event became a travesty, and when the police showed up, Ben tried to escape down the stairwell. Lorenzo panicked and threatened to burn the warehouse to the ground if Ben left him behind. When he thought he'd been abandoned, Lorenzo lit the doorway on fire using a lighter and paint thinner. The flames scorched Ben's face but he managed to escape and hide, completely avoiding police detection.

Adam never seemed concerned or interested in what happened after Lorenzo was killed. Ben tried contacting him using a burner phone and even tried reaching other members of the cartel, but nobody would respond. To them, Ben was as dead as Lorenzo. Adam even failed to pay Ben the $150,000 fee he'd been promised to come down from Detroit and move the operation into the advanced stages.

Gazing at his bloodstained clothing, Ben's thoughts drifted to Michael Warner. The kid had been killed in a very public place, yet Adam hadn't gotten the message. Instead, the plan proceeded without him. But now Raina was dead, and the rest of the group would soon realize that someone was dismantling the cartel from the inside. Ben would be sure to fill the leadership void left by Adam's disappearance and then claim control of the organization. He even had the perfect pre-fabricated story: *Adam got scared the Charleston Police were getting too close to the operation, and he went into hiding, leaving Ben in control.* The only other person who would know the story was false was Raina, and she wouldn't be speaking to anyone anytime soon.

Ben struck a match, and the fiery orange flames danced in the darkness, instantly engulfing his clothes. Once the flames reached the crewneck of the shirt, he dropped the clothing and let the flames dance and jut away from the cloth and singe the topsoil covering Adam's grave.

The thunder continued as a steady rain began falling. Ben looked up, and the cool droplets splashed against his skin, skin that felt like it was still on fire. Soon the rain would douse the flames, but the clothing was already a pile of ash. No evidence remained of his deed or of Raina's blood.

Ben retreated to the cabin. Inside, he found the binder where Adam kept krok distribution records. Adam had also been keeping newspaper clippings from *The Charleston Gazette*. A news story featuring the CPD and its detectives as well as a story about CMH and its charity fundraising had been cut from the paper. The names *Ronan McCullough* and *Ty Andino* had each been circled in red. Ben had to find a way to distract these two or eliminate them if need be. Then he'd make sure the way was clear to distribute krok all over Charleston, and eventually throughout West Virginia and the rest of Appalachia.

A light knock on the cabin door pulled Ben away from his thoughts. He reached under the cabinet and secured the semi-automatic handgun hidden there. Opening the door slowly, he found Jason framing the entryway; his jacket soaked.

"Expecting Adam," Ben said cryptically. A bolt of lightning flickered in the sky, straining through the forest trees, and then crackled on the ground with a burst of white light that quickly flicked away.

"I didn't expect to see you," Jason replied. "I thought the police had caught you."

"It's good to know I was missed."

"Where's Adam?

"Out," Ben said. "Why are you here?"

"I came for my money. Raina and I pushed a boatload of krok at a frat party tonight. We were going to come out here together, but she left the party with some kid, and I haven't seen her since."

Ben watched Jason shift uncomfortably in the rain. "It's after midnight, and I'm tired and wet. Can I come in or not?"

"Oh, sure. Sure." Ben said, pulling the door back slowly. "As you can see, I don't have any money. Adam didn't tell me anything about it," Ben said as he set the pistol down on the counter.

"I know the money's here, and I'm not leaving until I get it. Plus, I want some krok. I'm crashing pretty hard."

Jason pulled back the rain-soaked hood, dotting the long table with droplets of water. Then he pulled up each sleeve, revealing porous, mutilated flesh on both forearms near the bend of the elbow where he'd been injecting himself with the drug. The smell of the putrid flesh made Ben wince and turn his head.

"It's funny. Adam hasn't mentioned your name in a long time. There's a primary group working here now, and I don't seem to remember it including you," Jason stated matter-of-factly.

Ben walked up to Jason and tapped a meaty hand against his cheek. Jason's grey eyes widened, and the color around the pupils seemed to harden. Ben loved the smell of fear. "So experienced and yet so young in how these operations work. The details are what makes these groups so successful."

"What the hell are you talking about?"

Ben ran the tip of his tongue around his lips. "This whole operation requires a fragile brilliance. A type of brilliance that allows you to think and feel and do things in ways you didn't know you were capable of doing or feeling." Ben paused and picked up the pistol. "The lines become blurred. The drive is money and power and the ability to get away with it all." He held the pistol over his head, waving it around in the air. "This requires brilliance. But when those desires and those feelings mix around an infallible plot that shows some cracks, well then the brilliance that drives the plan suddenly becomes fragile."

Jason shivered. "I still don't know what in the hell you're talking about."

"Just remember that I was involved in this operation from the beginning. I was going to run the distribution of everything. I was here before you even knew what the fuck krok was and how it made you feel like a god."

"Things got sloppy," Jason scoffed. "You guys injured that cop."

"That had nothing to do with it." Ben looked at Jason who seemed to recoil after making the statement. "Lorenzo got sloppy and greedy and forgot the purpose of our business."

"Yeah, but then you took off like a coward," Jason added.

The words resounded in Ben's ears with stinging precision. "Coward? A coward doesn't refuse to follow instructions and then nearly burn to death in doing so," Ben hissed with a sneer.

Jason's face went white.

"A coward doesn't pretend you no longer exist just because a plan didn't go off without a hitch." Ben cocked the pistol and pointed it straight at Jason. "But a coward does come in and make demands of someone without knowing the parameters of the situation. You didn't ask the right questions or the most important one."

Jason backed up against the door. "What do you want?"

"Now the right question has been asked. Adam didn't fix all of the cracks in the plan, and now the brilliance has become fragile," Ben said as he snatched the pistol from the table and calmly fired two shots into Jason's head.

CHAPTER 42

Ty placed the stethoscope above Maxine Taylor's right breast. "Take a deep breath for me, Mrs. Taylor. That's good. Now exhale slowly. Good. Are you still having trouble catching your breath?"

"No, not as much," Maxine said, wiping her forehead with a tissue.

"We'll do an EKG, but I'm fairly certain you didn't have a heart attack. I'd say you experienced a bad bout of gastric reflux from that spicy Creole dinner you ate."

The old woman sat up in bed, silver hair and black dress rumpled from stress. "Oh, I'm sure that I had one. The pain was terrible. Simply terrible! Heart trouble runs in my family, you know."

"Family history is a factor in heart problems, so you did the right thing by coming to the hospital." Ty coiled the stethoscope around his neck.

Maxine grabbed another tissue from the box on the bed. "I'm just so warm."

"It's probably just nerves." Ty collected the other soiled, wadded tissues and dropped then into the trashcan. He patted her on the arm. "Just try and relax, and the cardiologist will be with you in a moment. Dr. Hill is great; you'll really like him."

The old woman dabbed her forehead again with the tissue and then leaned her head back onto the pillow.

Ty stepped out of the exam room and looked at his watch. It read 2:30 a.m. It was almost time for his dinner break. Thinking about food at this time of the morning always made Ty chuckle because most people were sleeping at 2:30, not thinking about food. The ER had been light in terms of patient volume tonight, but each patient had had a myriad of complexities, which made Ty feel like he'd worked a double-shift. Tonight, the hunger pangs and growling from his stomach were overwhelming.

He decided to see if his friend Sarah was ready to eat. But before he could leave the ER, the back doors flung open, and two orderlies scrambled in with a man screaming and clutching his abdomen.

One of the orderlies, Lester Allen, saw Ty and raced over to him. "The patient was sitting quietly in the waiting room when he suddenly began having an attack."

"Any signs of injury or other trauma?"

"Not that we could tell."

Ty ran his hand through his hair and exhaled. "Okay. Put him in Room #7. I'll page Dr. Raskib, and we'll be right there."

Sarah ambled down the hallway with a plastic square dish wrapped in foil. She smiled at Ty who shook his head and pointed to the exam rooms behind her. Sarah nodded understandingly, and patted Ty on the arm as she walked by.

When Ty came into the room, Lester was struggling to help the man back onto the gurney.

"Oh, my God! I'm in so much pain!"

"I know," Lester said through gritted teeth. "You need to lay down, sir, so we can find out what's causing it."

"Please do what the orderly asks," Ty said firmly. "What's your name, sir?"

"Ben…Ben Connors."

"Good. That's a start."

Ty looked down and noticed the man had brought in more than just stomach pains. Clumps of dirt scattered the exam-room floor. As he followed the dirt toward the treatment table, he noticed two muddy clumps partially ground into the tile flooring.

Ben reached down and cradled his stomach, moaning in between small, shallow breaths.

"Lester, please go find Dr. Raskib and ask him to come here as soon as he can. I know he finished up with a tough patient a little while ago, so he may be on break. But get him over here stat."

"Right."

"Oh," Ty added. "Page the custodians and tell them we need to get this dirt and mud cleaned up right away. I don't want anyone slipping on it."

Lester nodded and left the room. As Ty walked closer to Ben, the smell of charred skin wafted faintly from the bed.

"Mr. Connors, can you tell me where the pain is located?"

Ben winced again and began rolling from side to side on the gurney.

"Sir, you need to lie still so I can triage you."

As soon as Dr. Raskib came into the exam room, Ty immediately apprised him of Connors' condition.

"Ty, ask Lester to come back in here. Then administer fifty milligrams of Demerol and two milligrams of Lorazepam to the patient and prepare him for an MRI."

Ben flopped back on the gurney. His small, narrow-set eyes fixed on the ceiling. "What are you giving me?"

"Demerol is for the pain, and Lorazepam is a sedative, Mr. Connors. It will help you calm down," Ty replied as he administered the medication.

"Please, Doc, don't let this nurse go. He's been so nice to me."

"Nurse Andino isn't going anywhere, Mr. Connors. He'll be right here," Dr. Raskib said reassuringly.

"Okay, good. Good."

"Mr. Connors—"

"Please. Please call me Ben."

"Ben, have you had anything to eat today?" Ty asked.

"Yeah. I ate dinner at about ten."

"Good. The Demerol can make you nauseated, but since you've recently eaten, we won't need to give you any Phenergan."

"Okay."

"Have you had any pain, swelling or tenderness in your upper, middle, or lower abdomen before tonight?"

"No. It just started this afternoon. I thought it was heartburn or something, but the pain just got worse."

"Have you felt your abdomen?"

Ben moaned loudly again. "What?"

"Is your abdomen hard? Have you felt it?"

"No," Ben whined. "I've been in too much damn pain to move my arms, much less rub my stomach."

"All right, Ben," Dr. Raskib said. "The medication Nurse Andino just gave you will take effect in a few minutes, and you'll be able to relax a bit."

He cut a sharp look at Ty. "We need to get this exam room cleaned."

"I'm on it, Dr. Raskib," Ty replied. "Lester already paged for the custodians."

The physician nodded as Lester and Sarah entered the exam room. "Mr. Connors, as soon as you're settled and comfortable, we're going to take you for an MRI. That will help us determine the cause of your pain."

"Fine. Fine. Just hurry." Ben groaned loudly again.

He began to relax as Sarah and Lester raised the rails on the gurney and pushed the bed through the narrow doorway and down the hall.

Ty leaned against the wall just outside the exam room. He was dead tired. Glancing at his watch, he realized an hour had passed since he last thought of food. He decided to take his lunch break now before another emergency came pounding through the doors. He turned and headed for the lunchroom, but he didn't get far when an orderly stopped him.

"You've got a call waiting from someone named Melissa."

"Thanks."

Ty walked quickly to the nurses' station, all the while wondering why on earth Melissa would be calling him. It's not like they'd become bosom buddies all of a sudden. He grabbed the phone, and before he could finish his hello, she began talking.

"I'm sorry to call you at work."

"It's okay, Melissa."

Ty could hear the tension in her voice. "It's Nick."

"Is something wrong?"

She began sobbing harder. "Yes, I think so. The police are here. That detective who questioned us..." Her voice was catching in between sobs. "The one who questioned us after the rest-area shooting, it's him, and he brought two police officers with him. I can't get a hold of Ronan, and I don't know what to do."

"Ronan isn't answering his phone?"

"No. He dropped Nick off here at the townhouse after the party, but he didn't come in, and I haven't a clue where he went. Detective Carter wants to take Nick to the station for questioning."

"I want you to call my friend, Braxton Campbell. He's an attorney with the Giatras Law Firm downtown on Capitol Street. His number is in the Rolodex in the living room."

"Okay. I'll call him right away."

Ty looked up and saw Sarah and an orderly bringing Ben Connors back from X-ray and Imaging.

"Hang up and do it right now. Tell Braxton I told you to call and have him meet you and Nick at the police station. Do you understand?"

"Yes. Thank you, Ty."

"You're welcome. Oh, Melissa?"

"Yes."

"Keep trying to get a hold of Ronan."

Melissa sniffed and coughed then hung up.

"Mr. Connors wants to talk to you," Sarah said, returning from the exam room.

Ty furrowed his brow. "Why?"

"I don't know. He just asked me to come find you."

Ty felt his own brand of stomach pain from hunger. He didn't have to honor the request and could instead take a break and eat, but the credo of being a nurse rang in his mind: show care and compassion in how patients are looked after, find the courage to do the right thing, demonstrate commitment, and communicate. Honoring Ben Connors' request certainly fell under the task of doing the right thing.

Ben grinned as Ty entered the exam room.

"Thanks for coming to see me."

"You seem to be doing better."

"Is that Demerol good shit or what?"

Ty noticed the smell of burnt skin once again as he walked closer to the bed. He moved around the dirty floor, which still hadn't been cleaned up, and felt his patience wearing thin.

"Yes, Demerol is a powerful narcotic."

Ben's eyes flickered when he heard those words.

"I just wanted to thank you for being so kind and professional when I was in here flopping around like a lunatic."

Ty pulled up a round stool next to the bed and sat down. "Not a problem. Just doing my job."

"Well, thanks anyhow."

"How'd that happen?"

"Excuse me?"

Ty tapped his cheek with a finger and looked at Ben's face. "The burns."

"Oh, those."

Ty watched Ben sit up straighter in the bed, his face flush with color. "I live on a farm. I was burning some trash on the property, and I tripped trying to add more junk to the pile. It's just a little surface burn." Ben spoke in a leisurely baritone drawl that was part country, part blues.

Ty wondered how Ben could be so cavalier about the burns. They were quite severe and must have been extremely painful. "I can smell it a little bit from across the room."

Ben's face grew more serious. "Sorry."

"Don't be. That smell will persist for a few months. Make sure you stay hydrated and eat plenty of protein. That'll help the skin heal."

"Okay."

"Where's the farm?"

"Jackson County. Say, I've lived here a while, and no offense, but I can tell you're not from around these parts," Ben said, looking Ty up and down.

Ty chuckled and crossed his arms. "I've lived here for a while too, but I'm originally from Hawaii."

Ben clucked his tongue. "That explains the hair and the dark features and all."

Ty felt a bit uncomfortable but continued with the conversation. "I'm told not too many Hawaiians voluntarily move to West Virginia."

"I bet you have one of those funny last names like Samsung or something."

Ty nearly laughed in Ben's face. "No, that's Korean. My last name is Andino, which is Polynesian."

Ben waved a finger at Ty and smiled. "Ah, I see. Not Korean, but not really American either. I gotcha. I've got a friend. Well, she's kind of a friend, not in the way you think. I mean…we're not fucking or anything. Just someone I know. Anyway, she's from West Virginia, a true West Virginian and all of that. Just think if she married you, she could be half an Andino."

Ty knew the Demerol had taken effect, judging by Ben's wandering thoughts and propensity to say exactly what he was thinking. He ignored the rude remark about his ethnicity and gazed at the fleshy finger waving at him. The fingertip was dabbled with blood from small puncture marks, and dirt was embedded under the fingernail. Faint black smudges circled the cuticles.

A young custodian entered the exam room and began sweeping up the small clumps of dirt.

Ben waved a craggy finger at him. "I've been doing some digging on the farm. I had to use a lot of water 'cause it's been so dry lately...at least until today. I'm afraid I got everything a little muddy. Sorry about that."

Dr. Raskib entered the room and nodded at the custodian. "Ty, if the two of you will excuse Mr. Connors and me, we need to go over the results of his MRI."

Ty looked at the physician, who seemed anxious and aggravated, and then turned back to Ben. "Nice to meet you, Mr. Connors."

Ben flopped his head up and down. "Yeah, same to you."

Ty walked back to the nurses' station as the custodian slowly trailed behind him. Ty saw Sarah sitting at the computer. Her foil-covered dish rested beside her.

"Ready for dinner?"

Ty felt his mouth watering at the thought. "Yes, let's go before something else happens."

"That patient was a weird one," Sarah said as she put her lunch into the microwave.

"He was odd, wasn't he?" Ty replied. He laid his arms on the table and rested his head against the cool, hard surface.

Sarah licked her finger and closed the microwave door. "He started mumbling a bunch of crap as we were getting him ready for the MRI."

"Maybe we should send Ben to Behavioral Health after Dr. Raskib finishes with him."

Sarah laughed. "It couldn't hurt."

Lester came into the lunchroom and threw up his arms. "Have either of you seen, Mr. Connors?"

Ty slowly lifted his head from the table. "No. I left him with Dr. Raskib."

"Mr. Connors said he needed to use the bathroom, but he never came back."

Sarah looked at Ty and mouthed the word *weird.*

CHAPTER 43

Ronan drove aimlessly for over an hour, trying to clear his head and put together all the pieces of Raina Dalton's murder puzzle. Finally arriving back to where he started, he pulled the truck off to the side of the road at the bottom of his street. Fearing detection, Ronan silenced the engine and sat in the darkness. Ahead, the blur of blue lights hung low against the spaces between the houses, cars, and trees that dotted the neighborhood. Ronan couldn't ascertain the precise location of the lights, but the area was close to the townhouse.

Perhaps one of the uniforms or forensic techs had reported him being at the Dalton crime scene. Sending officers to the house to remind Ronan of his suspension would be just like Captain Ashby, but that would be a Code-1 situation, which wouldn't require emergency lights.

Ronan saw the lights shift on the horizon as the fluttering blue wave moved to the left and then to the right, and then grow brighter and closer as they followed the curves of the road. He unbuckled his seatbelt and leaned over the emergency brake into the passenger seat and tried to create as much distance between himself and the window. The squad car whisked by, the blue lights faded and darkness enveloped the truck.

As the engine revved back up and started purring, the time on the dashboard clock read 4:04 a.m. Ty's shift wouldn't end until 6:00 a.m., but Ronan worried that something had happened at the house. He called Ty, but his voicemail immediately picked up. Ronan felt the muscles in his neck and back tighten. He slammed on the gas pedal and in a few seconds, he whipped into the driveway.

Ronan thrust open the front door and cautiously scanned the room; nothing seemed out of place. Even though the front entryway was dark, and there were no lights turned on in either of the bedrooms, two small shafts of light, one from the living room and one from the kitchen, provided some illumination in the silent house. The silence made Ronan concerned, but not anxious.

"Nick? Melissa?"

No response.

Ronan went into the living room. Empty. Then he walked into the kitchen. On the small desk against the kitchen wall, Ronan found the phone book. Someone had circled the address of the Charleston Police Department with the words Giatras Law Firm written next to it.

"Shit! Now what?"

He ran a finger over the words and then ripped the page violently from the phone book. The book sailed in the air and skidded across the island before plopping onto the floor. Grabbing the truck keys from his pocket, Ronan headed back into the night.

———

As Ben marched back through the woods, he heard a noise coming from the direction of the shed; his heart pounded hard against his chest. The dirt covering the grave was still firmly packed, and the ground showed no signs of any disturbance. Nevertheless, he wanted to make sure neither man nor beast had discovered the bodies buried beneath. He dug at the earth until he saw his handiwork. Satisfied, he covered the mortal remains of Adam and Jason and then returned to the cabin.

With Adam's notebook in hand, Ben sat down in a rickety wooden rocker and flipped past several *Charleston Gazette* newspaper clippings, which chronicled the spread of drug-related crime in the area, and then studied the account ledger in the back. The remaining krok distributors were listed, as well as their actual contact information and any aliases agreed to between them and Adam. Ben knew they would all expect another payment of cash and drugs soon, and he needed them to believe that Adam was still alive and in charge of distribution before he left the area.

Next to the dealers' contact information, Adam had checked off each person he considered an obstacle to the operation and who needed to be eliminated. With Jason and Raina now dead, the circle of subordinates had been shattered. Jensen Williams may or may not recover from his injuries, but Ben would be gone and in control of the operation before Jensen realized it.

Ben had been able to successfully infiltrate the emergency room, and he now had more information about the nurse who had chased Jason. He knew what the nurse looked like, and soon he'd know where he lived. After all, how many Ty Andinos could there be in Charleston, West Virginia?

He tore a page of paper from the binder and on it wrote *Ty Andino*, underlined the name and added details he'd learned from his fake emergency visit to Charleston Mercy. The ruse had been worth the risk. Ben had gotten what he needed and that information would result in the death of Ty Andino.

CHAPTER 44

t's always darkest before the dawn. That was Ronan's guiding principle for each night shift he worked. Often, the dark night sky would look like it was ready to crush anyone beneath it, but there was always the clarity that it held in its invisible hands.

Those dark clouds now seemed to hang low to the skyline, pressing tightly against the valley in which Charleston rested and the Kanawha River ran through. As Ronan merged onto the Virginia Street exit, the sky pushed together, and a sudden flash of lightning struck. A moment later, a rumble of thunder—resembling the growl of a hungry animal—followed.

Tires squealed as Ronan pulled into a parking space and then stomped on the brakes, bringing the truck to a jarring stop. He charged up the ramp at the back of the Charleston Police Department headquarters and through the rear door. Hopefully, his covert entry would go unnoticed. The last thing he needed was for someone to report to Captain Ashby that he'd been spotted on department property.

Inside, the pinging and ringing of cell and desk phones, coupled with the scuffing of feet across the floor from cops and suspects alike, gave the room an active hum. Ronan weaved in between several of the desks and went straight into the Criminal Investigations Division.

When he turned left past Sean Carter's office and reached the first interview room, Ronan saw Nick sitting at the metal desk, shoulders slumped, the swipe of low-hanging hair falling over his brow. Small translucent splotches of liquid dotted the desk, which Ronan assumed were tears… or sweat. Nick looked scared and miserable, and he trembled each time Carter circled the table.

Melissa stood in the room next door, looking through the two-way mirror, anxiously watching the proceedings. Eric Bonamico stood beside her, his head resting on an arm that he'd draped over the top of the mirror. Suddenly, he heard a noise behind him.

"Ronan, you can't be here."

"The hell I can't." Ronan looked into the interview room and then back at Bonamico, who had a pleading look in his eyes. "This your idea?"

"Ronan, you know that—"

"Cut the bullshit, Eric! You don't have to cover for Carter."

Melissa stepped away from the glass and dropped her head. "Ronan."

Ronan pointed at Melissa. "Just a second." He turned back to Bonamico, his face a twisted mass of anger. "Nick shouldn't be talking to Carter without a lawyer present. Did anyone tell him that?"

Bonamico cast a long look into the interview room. "Melissa said one was on the way."

"Ronan! Enough! Stop it!" Melissa turned around; her red-rimmed eyes filled with tears as she covered her lips with a few fingers and began sobbing. "Nick's so scared, and I don't know what to do."

Ronan approached his sister and wrapped his arms around her. Melissa resisted the embrace at first but then let herself fall into Ronan's broad chest. Her sobbing grew heavy and deep as Ronan peered at Bonamico.

"I want to see Nick," Ronan whispered.

"No. I can't let that happen. You're not even supposed to be in the building."

As Ronan tightened his grip around Melissa, he listened intently to the questions being asked by Sean Carter. Carter now had a folder on his desk and was pointing to it. Nick hovered over it as Carter kept telling him to take another look at Raina Dalton's photo because that was all that was left of her.

Melissa pushed Ronan back slightly. Her fair skin seemed weathered, and the veins in her neck pulsed with each deep breath she took.

"I called Ty after I couldn't reach you."

"I'm sorry. I was out for a bit, and I didn't have a signal."

Melissa sniffed and wiped a tear from her cheek. "Ty gave me the name of a friend of his who's an attorney. Somebody named Braxton Campbell. Ty said he could help Nick."

A large man dressed in a white shirt, blue tie, blue blazer, and grey slacks came bursting into the room. He marched right up to the mirror, paying little attention to Ronan and Melissa. After a moment, he spun on his heels and glared at Bonamico.

"Braxton Campbell, legal counsel for Nick Copeland. Stop the questions right now, Sergeant! I want to speak with my client. This interview is over."

Bonamico wringed his hands and then politely said "Excuse me," before going into the interview room. He cut off the line of questioning, which made Carter instantly bolt up.

"Nick's lawyer is here."

Carter made a face and picked up the case file and then leaned back down near Nick. "We're not done yet, son," he hissed, making Nick shiver again as another two tears dropped into the others that had now dried on the table.

Braxton Campbell looked at Ronan and shook hands with him and Melissa. He had a powerful handshake that mimicked his booming voice.

"I was expecting to see Mr. Andino down here since he referred me."

"He's working. His shift ends at six a.m.," Ronan said, careful not to add many more details.

Campbell arched an eyebrow at Ronan before looking into the interview room. "I'll find out what's going on. Don't worry."

When Carter came out of the room, his eyes widened at seeing Ronan standing before him. Before anything could be said, Campbell filled the space between the two men.

"I want to have a moment alone with my client." Campbell looked at Melissa with a stalwart expression. "Mrs. Copeland, please join me."

Carter stepped aside and extended a hand, demonstrating a modicum of courtesy, and allowed them into the interview room.

Bonamico raised a hand. "Before you say anything, I didn't know Ronan was coming."

"Get out of here, McCullough," Carter spat, exasperated that Ronan had the gall to be there at all.

"Nice to see you too, Carter."

Carter tugged at the rolled-up sleeves of his blue dress shirt and began buttoning the cuff. "You can't help. You're suspended and off the investigation."

"My nephew is in there. It doesn't matter who I am or what my role is in anything."

Carter unrolled the other sleeve and buttoned the cuff. "Bonamico, what about the party on Kanawha Avenue?"

Ronan clenched his jaw and remained silent.

"The scene was cleared. Forensic techs found a few unused syringes, but no drugs."

Ronan walked over to Bonamico and stared at his friend and partner. "How many syringes?"

"Don't answer that," Carter ordered, pointing a finger at Bonamico. "McCullough's no longer on the case."

Ronan shook off the remark. "If there were syringes at this party, I can guarantee you that somebody was pushing krok."

"How's Nick connected to this party?" Bonamico asked.

Carter sighed and loosened the knot on his tie. "Eyewitnesses said he was with Dalton at the party, but they had a fight and didn't stay long after that. They did leave together. Now I've said enough, and you need to leave, McCullough."

"Carter, please. I need to know why Nick is involved in this. He hasn't lived here but for a few days. If he met this Dalton girl at that party, then I'm sure what happened to her, however awful, didn't involve him. He wouldn't even know how to get himself out to Elk—" Ronan slapped his lips shut.

Carter's normally boyish looks hardened, and the creases in his face were more pronounced. "Leave now, or I'll call the captain and have you escorted out."

Ronan set his jaw. "Fine. You want to make this about policy and procedure, be my guest. But your staff had better question every witness at that party, and you'd better make sure the forensic techs have combed every square inch and collected every piece of probative evidence before accusing Nick of anything. If not, I'll have Mr. Campbell slap a lawsuit on you and the department for defamation."

Ronan could feel the detective's hot breath on his face.

"Get out! Now!"

Carter was playing a psychological game of chess with Ronan, and Nick was the pawn. He knew Ronan would show up at the police station once he found out Nick had been taken in for questioning. At least Bonamico hadn't told Carter about the visit to Raina Dalton's townhouse, which still gave Ronan an edge. But if Ronan had any idea that he could work on the periphery of the investigation, Carter had stymied those thoughts when he made it quite clear that Ronan was to stay away.

Ronan stood on the front steps of the station house, the early-morning rain cascading down upon the city, cleaning the grimy buildings and gritty streets. The rain rolled off him in sheets, sending a shiver through his body. As the doors to the police station opened, Ronan turned around, the rain blurring his vision. Two shadows grew larger, and

Braxton Campbell emerged from the shadows first, holding a large umbrella over both him and Melissa. Melissa stared ahead, eyes vacant and unblinking.

"What happened in there, counselor?"

"Nick's been arrested for murder."

CHAPTER 45

"Can I get you anything?" Ronan asked, as he headed to the kitchen for a beer.

Braxton Campbell shook his head back and forth then looked at Melissa, whose smeared makeup and eyeliner had run down her cheeks and dripped into her open palms.

"No, thank you."

"Melissa?"

She shook her head but didn't look up.

Campbell smoothed his tie against his shirt and waited for Ronan to return.

"As I said, the bail has been set at $100,000. In light of Nick's age and lack of criminal history, it was fairly easy to negotiate a lower-than-normal bail for this type of crime."

"Criminal history." Melissa repeated the words as if she were in a trance and then turned away as tears began to flow again.

Campbell turned his attention to Ronan as he sat down on the couch next to Melissa.

"Until bail is satisfied, Nick's being held at the South Central Regional Jail. I have an appointment to meet with him at one p.m."

Melissa stood up. Again, refusing to make eye contact with anyone in the room. "I need to call Bruce. He can help with the bail," she mumbled, wiping the tears from her cheeks. "My God! What is he going to think about all of this?"

Ronan pulled his aching body from the couch and reached out to Melissa, but she sidestepped him and headed for the guest room.

Sensing bewilderment, Campbell held up a hand. "It's okay, Sergeant. She needs some time. She's been through a lot."

Ronan remained standing until he heard the guest-room door slam. He looked down at Campbell who looked away for a moment before motioning for him to have a seat.

"I don't understand it. My nephew isn't a murderer, Mr. Campbell. I mean, you've spoken with him. He's shy and really lacks self-confidence. He's been staying with us for several days now, and he was just starting to feel comfortable here and with himself. I think he was excited about starting college at Charleston State in the spring."

Campbell scooted to the edge of the couch and folded his hands together. "I understand, and I'm going to do everything I can for him. But Nick's photo is in Raina Dalton's cell phone, and it's time stamped shortly before her death. Plus, the police found two fingerprints belonging to Nick in the living room.."

Ronan clenched a fist and slammed it hard against his palm. "What about a murder weapon or a fucking motive?"

"Neither the detectives, nor the forensic techs have found the knife yet. They're currently searching the woods around Apple Grove, as well as the woods along Greenbrier Street. As for a motive—"

"I don't think Nick would even know how to hold a knife," Ronan said, ignoring Campbell's remarks.

"I get the same impression."

Ronan fell back into the couch. "What do we do?"

"Well, first off we need to post bail and get Nick out of South Central and get him home."

Ronan agreed.

"Sergeant McCullough, Detective Carter seems quite resolute in solving this case, and I also get the sense he isn't going to stop until he sees everyone remotely involved arrested and prosecuted."

Ronan ran a finger around the open hole in the beer bottle and then took a large swig. "Good luck with that."

"He told me you two were working together on the case at one time. May I ask what happened?"

Ronan closed his eyes and took another drink of beer. "I got a little aggressive during an interview." He opened his eyes to find Campbell staring at him in astonishment. "If I continue my involvement in this case, Nick won't be the only member of this family who'll need legal counsel."

Campbell considered Ronan's statement.

"Are you sure you don't want one, counselor?" Ronan asked, raising the beer bottle to his lips. "It tastes damn good first thing in the morning."

"No, thank you," Campbell replied with an arched eyebrow.

"Don't give me that look. The beginning of your day is the end of my night."

The front door opened and Ty, with his loping gait, entered the room.

"Braxton," Ty said, shaking his friend's hand. "Where's Nick?"

"In custody, I'm afraid."

The sight of Ty and the tone of his voice made Ronan want to scream in relief. He bolted up from the couch and took a step toward Ty, ready to embrace him but caught himself and withdrew.

"Sorry I'm late. I came home as soon as I could."

Campbell watched as Ty sat next to Ronan. "I got the impression that Sergeant McCullough lived here."

"No, this is my home."

Ronan elbowed Ty in the ribs. "Actually, we're best friends. We first met at Mercy and then several times again when more than one of Charleston's finest citizens ended up there after getting in trouble. Right, Ty?"

Ty swallowed hard and looked at Campbell. He could tell his friend wasn't buying the story. "That's right. Ronan watches the house sometimes when I work back-to-back shifts…gets the newspaper, the mail…that type of thing."

So why is McCullough's sister and nephew staying here, Campbell thought. The attorney cleared his throat, stood up and extended his hand to Ty. "Thank you, Ty, for recommending me to the family. Why don't you all try to get some sleep? I'm going to meet with Nick at one o'clock, but let me know when you have the bail money, and we'll get him released sooner if possible."

Melissa came out of the bedroom as Campbell left. She had changed into a cream-colored nightgown and had removed her makeup.

"Did Mr. Campbell just leave?"

"He did," Ty replied, giving Melissa a slight hug.

"I'm so scared and worried about Nick."

Melissa began crying again. Ty looked back at Ronan who approached them and rested a hand on his sister's shoulder.

"Were you able to talk to Bruce?"

Melissa broke the embrace with Ty and for the first time locked eyes with Ronan. "I did. He's going to the bank, and he'll put the money in my account as soon as our branch opens."

"I don't want you to worry about Braxton's legal fees. I'll take care of that. The important thing is that Nick is okay, and we get him home," Ty said, trying his best to comfort the distraught woman.

Melissa tossed up her hands. "I don't even know where that is or what that means anymore."

The comment brought a heavy silence to the room.

"I'm sorry," she said. "I didn't mean that."

"It's okay," Ronan said. "I think we all need to get some rest." He motioned to Ty.

"I agree. We can't help Nick if we're exhausted."

Ty looked at Ronan with a sad, pleading look. Ronan had no answers, but he remained certain that Nick didn't kill Raina Dalton, nor did he have anything to do with the drugs.

CHAPTER 46

Ronan clasped both hands behind his head as Ty slid close to him, draping an arm across his chest.

"I didn't sleep much," Ronan said as he stared at the bedroom ceiling.

"I know," Ty said, curling a leg around his lover. "I felt you tossing and turning."

"All I can think about is Nick sitting in a jail cell for nothing more than meeting a girl at a party."

"But she wasn't an ordinary girl, was she?"

"No, she wasn't. Obviously, Dalton was a drug addict who Nick apparently met at the frat party." Ronan could feel the muscles in his chest tighten and his heart thump harder. "But all that aside, how can Carter seriously think Nick killed her?"

"Shh, shh," Ty said, stroking Ronan's chest with his fingertips. "I don't know, but there's no sense in getting upset over it until we know more."

Ronan huffed.

"Getting upset won't change anything that's happened, and it won't help Nick."

Ronan pulled a hand from behind his head and began running his fingers along the smooth slope of Ty's shoulders. "I'm not giving up on him or this case."

Ty craned his neck up and settled a hard look on Ronan. "Don't keep pushing your luck by interfering in the investigation. You're suspended, and if you keep meddling, you might just be fired."

Ronan paused for a moment. Telling Ty about being at Raina Dalton's crime scene might infuriate him, but he wanted to be honest.

"I'm well past the meddling stage, Ty."

Ty stopped caressing Ronan's chest and pulled himself up. Rolling over on his stomach, he rested his chin on his hand. His face was expressionless. "I can't wait to hear this."

Ronan grinned for a moment and then said, "Eric asked me to the Raina Dalton crime scene."

"Ronan."

"I know, I shouldn't have gone, and I know I took a big risk in doing so, but I'm glad I did. The letters N I C were written in blood on the floor. Eric thinks after the killer stabbed Dalton, he left, not realizing she was alive. It could be Dalton knew she was dying and was trying to identify her killer or someone was trying to frame Nick."

"God! That's awful," Ty said, his voice dry and quiet. "That poor girl. Alone and knowing death is coming, and all she could do was write a message in her blood." His voice trailed off.

"It's a gruesome way to die."

"Did anyone see you there?"

Ronan scratched the stubble on his chin. "Yeah, but I don't think the news of my suspension has reached everyone quite yet. Besides, the uniforms and techs were all preoccupied with the crime scene, and I don't think anyone gave me a second thought."

He waited for Ty to say something else, but when he didn't Ronan placed the edge of an index finger against Ty's lips. "Don't worry, I didn't stay much longer after that."

A silence enveloped them as Ty rested his head on Ronan's chest.

"Do Eric or Carter think what happened to that girl is connected to everything else?"

"I'm not sure."

"What do you think?"

"When the people in this cartel strike, it's brutal, violent and often used to send a message. Dalton's murder was consistent with the cartel's MO."

"I don't think Nick is capable of doing something like that," Ty remarked.

Ronan grimaced. "Neither do I. Nick couldn't hurt anyone, let alone a girl he'd only known for a few hours. But getting Sean Carter to believe that is going to be tough."

Ty kissed Ronan on the cheek. "Braxton is an excellent attorney. He'll do whatever it takes to help Nick out of this situation."

Ronan looked lovingly into Ty's eyes. He adored how Ty was always so optimistic and always believed that everything would be okay for everyone in the end. He pulled Ty close and kissed him passionately.

"As much as I enjoyed that, we need to get ready for the arraignment."

Ty pushed off the bed and glanced at the clock. "It's one-thirty. We'd better get ready."

Ronan groaned and pulled himself up. The pain in his leg had subsided, but his body ached all over, and he was exhausted. As he tried to walk around the bed and head for the shower, the muscles in his body didn't want to cooperate. The lethargy frustrated him.

While Ty disappeared into the bathroom, Ronan went looking for his cell phone. He rummaged through the clothes pile on the floor at the foot of the bed. At the base of the pile, he found his phone; it had slipped out of his pants pocket. He tossed it onto the dresser and then picked up Ty's scrubs in his burly hand. He ambled into the bathroom to find Ty already in the shower, lathered in soap and his golden skin glistening under the light overhead.

"I found your scrubs from last night. Do you want Betsy to wash them?"

"No. They're an old pair. I was going to throw them away."

"Okay." As Ronan turned to throw the scrubs into the wastebasket, he dropped the pants. When he retrieved them, he noticed the mud spatter near the hem of the pant legs. "Did you go rolling around in the mud yesterday?"

"Me? Mud? You've got to be kidding!"

"Then where'd you get mud on your scrub pants?"

"Probably from that farmer who came in near the end of shift. His boots and clothes were covered in it. It was really weird. The guy was agitated and complaining of stomach pain, but after his exam and MRI, he bolted."

Ronan clenched the scrubs in a tight fist.

Ty emerged from the bathroom, his body glistening. "Shower's free. Your turn," he said, smiling.

"I need to run an errand before the arraignment."

Ty cocked his head. "Ronan," he said pleadingly.

"I'll be there in time. I just need to do this."

Before Ty could object, Ronan went over and kissed him.

"I'll be there in time. Promise."

Ty draped the wet towel over a shoulder. "And just where are you going, and why do you need my scrub pants?"

CHAPTER 47

Ronan stood in front of the Apple Grove townhouse and flicked the yellow police tape that crisscrossed the door, the scrub pants held tightly in his right hand.

"Are we going in or not?"

"Damn it, Ronan! I don't know. Besides, don't you ever sleep?"

Ronan turned around to find his partner running a hand through his dark hair. He knew Eric was thinking hard because the tiny vein near the bottom of his hairline pulsed every time he set his jaw.

"Of course we're going in, or we wouldn't be standing here."

Bonamico placed his hands on his hips. The Sergeant's shield clipped on his belt sent faint rays of light dancing onto the doorframe as he shifted his weight uncomfortably in the midday sunlight.

Ronan looked down at the shield for a moment, determined to get his own back somehow.

"And we're here because of mud on Ty's scrubs? I don't see the connection," Bonamico said, a bit perturbed.

Ronan went back to flicking the yellow ribbon and

staring intently at the words, POLICE LINE: DO NOT CROSS. Those words never mattered to him much before, but now they took on a special meaning because he wasn't a cop anymore—at least temporarily.

"I don't know if there's anything to it, but I just need to compare something."

Bonamico stepped closer to Ronan. "There's a problem. Remember? You're not supposed to be here, no matter what your suspicions might be. You realize I had to make up a lame excuse to keep Carter from coming with me. Luckily, he bought it. By the way, shouldn't you be at the courthouse now?"

Ronan looked seriously at his partner. He knew Bonamico was having a crisis of conscience and should never have allowed him to come to the crime scene yesterday, let alone again today. Ronan also knew he had put both their jobs on the line.

"Eric, I know the risks you're taking, and I appreciate it, but this will only take a minute. I don't know if this is anything more than a gut reaction, but I want to be sure."

Bonamico looked at the door and then down at the ground. He tapped his foot nervously on the concrete. "All right. You've got ten minutes and not a second more."

Ronan nodded as Bonamico reached up and tugged one side of the yellow tape away from the doorframe. He opened the door slowly, and they quickly stepped inside. The narrow living room seemed darker now. Despite the fact that a legion of cops, techs, and emergency personnel was no longer rummaging through the house, a sick pang of death pinched at Ronan's gut. It was the same feeling he always got each time he entered a homicide scene.

In trying to make sense of what happened to someone, often every variable was connected to another. The way furniture was positioned in a home; who was in the home at the time of the crime; determining how the victim died, and when and by what means, often made all the other elements of a crime scene seem incidental at first. However, the totality of the scene, which included all of the fringe details and evidence, gave Ronan the clues he needed to solve the crime.

He took a deep breath and crossed the little threshold; just beyond, the muddy impression was still perfectly preserved.

"Unfold this."

Bonamico took the scrub pants and held the garment out in front of him as if examining a potential purchase.

"By the way, the M.E. said Dalton wasn't a first-time krok user."

"Why am I not surprised? Is Williams still in a coma?" Ronan asked, changing the subject as he stared at the floor.

"Yeah. There's some faint brain activity, but the doctors don't know if he'll wake up."

"Now hold the pants next to the mud and give me your flashlight and magnifying glass."

Bonamico sighed, and held the scrubs against the floor, close to the evidence. Ronan pushed back the pant leg, making sure the cloth didn't come into contact with the muddy impression.

"Ty said this mud came from the farmer he treated last night in the ER. It looks like the same color and consistency as the mud on the floor here. But before you say it, I know the lab will have to confirm it."

"At least you hope."

"But if both samples of mud are identical, it would allow for probable cause that someone other than Nick could have committed the murder. We need to get these pants to Pete immediately."

"Okay. I'll rally the cavalry. Now we need to go. We've both been here far too long."

Bonamico led them through the front door, peering out into the neighborhood to make sure nobody was watching the house or paying attention to anyone leaving it. Then he hurried to his unmarked Crown Victoria, which he'd parked away from the townhouse to avoid notice.

Ronan rapped on the driver's window.

"Yeah?" Bonamico asked as the electric window rolled down with a hum.

"Thanks, Eric. I mean it. For everything."

"I know." Bonamico winked at Ronan and drove away with a huge grin on his face.

CHAPTER 48

en stood like a mercenary, at ease among the troops seated around him in a circle on the soft grass.

"I don't know where Adam's gone or what's happened, but he's left me in charge." Ben looked down at the bag resting on the ground next to him. "But I've got the next payment from the boys in Detroit. We're going to follow the same plan as before just as if Adam were still here giving the orders. Is that understood?"

A dozen sets of cruel eyes peered at Ben from beneath hooded sweatshirts.

"I've also got some fresh krok for you. Remember now. Keep yourselves covered, especially the injection spots. The minute someone sees your skin, they're going to be on to you."

Leroy sat near the back of the circle, leaning against the base of an oak tree. "Where'd Jason and Raina go?"

Ben glared at him.

Leroy met him glare for glare.

Leroy was tall and wiry and had the physique and temperament of a flat piece of steel. He bobbed his head back in a taunting manner, wanting Ben to explain their absence.

"I don't know," Ben replied. "They're both on CPD radar now, so I assume they've headed to Canada and will stay there until things have settled down."

"So how do we know Adam left you in charge?" Leroy asked, this time leaning forward and hardening his stare.

The other men in the circle looked at each other and nodded, before settling all eyes on Ben again.

"You don't," Ben replied, looking at each man individually before glancing back at Leroy. "But I'm the only one that's got access to the bank accounts and, more importantly, the krok. So, if you motherfuckers want paid and want the drug, then you're stuck with me."

Ben knew the men would buy the lie. Adam had always paid well for their work. He also made sure to hire criminals who were looking at their third strikes and who didn't ask too many questions and were easily swayed. He waited for the men to refocus their attention on him before continuing.

"I understand from talking with some of you that the krok is now in Fairmont, Parkersburg and Morgantown. Everything's going according to plan at Fairmont State and West Virginia University too. The plan here is the same: start at the colleges; get the kids hooked and desperate, and then spread out into the cities and suburbs. The Charleston Police and the hospitals are scrambling to keep up with us, so we can now focus on a more stable supply line."

The men nodded their heads, and Leroy, who'd been staring at his hands, agreed.

"All right. You've got your money, and boxes of krok are in front of the cabin. You all have your assignments. Leroy, I want you to lead a team to Charlotte. The cartel is going to get things started there. We're being paid in cash, all large bills. Make sure those shits don't cheat us."

Leroy looked up for a moment, held a stare with Ben, and then nodded.

Ben enjoyed being in command. He was born to it. He had the respect and fear of his troops. He knew he could continue the ruse of Adam being away to conduct business elsewhere, as well as Jason and Raina going into hiding, as long as necessary. In time, these idiots would forget all about them.

"The Charlotte group heads out in the morning," Ben said. "As for the rest of you, you get started tonight. Any questions?"

The circle of men stared at each other and then rose one at a time.

"And remember. No communication with one another until the drops are made. We don't want any loose lips sinking our krok ships," Ben said with a mean laugh.

The men scurried away, heading for the cabin behind them. Leroy was the last to leave. Before he disappeared, Ben called out to him.

Leroy stopped and slowly turned around. His face was twisted and tight, and he shuffled back to Ben with slumped shoulders, walking like a man on his way to death row.

"I need you to help me with a job tonight."

Leroy crossed his arms. "I'd like to get some sleep, man, especially since I've got to go to Charlotte in the morning."

"Would twenty-five grand in cash change your mind?"

"Maybe."

"Good. I've got a little problem we need to take care of."

Leroy made a face. "I don't get it. You just said everything was going as planned and—"

"I know what I just said," Ben replied in an agitated tone that made Leroy narrow his brow. "There's a nurse at Mercy that's getting a little too close to what we're doing, and he may have ties to a cop."

"So you want to off him?"

Ben winked. "I prefer to call it *playing it long.* Determine your opposition and then eliminate them one by one."

Leroy looked around, hearing the men breaking open the sealed boxes and hoisting them onto dollies for transport.

"Is Adam fine with this?"

Ben tilted his chin lower and looked at Leroy through the tops of his eyes. "Don't worry what Adam would want.

If taking someone out keeps everything moving, he won't mind. So, you in?"

The underling waited for a moment. "Yeah. I'll do it."

"Good. Let's go inside, and we'll get ready."

———

Men clad in suits scurried about the narrow hallway outside the courtrooms, flipping through files and cradling cell phones in between their necks and ears, trying to balance the physical information with the verbal information coming through the phones.

Even though the building was equipped with closed circuit television, duress alarms, metal detectors, X-ray machines, controlled accesses, and alarmed doors, being in the courthouse made Ronan feel uncomfortable, especially now that he was on the other side of the badge.

He'd sped from Raina Dalton's townhouse in Apple Grove and parked in front of a fire hydrant by the courthouse steps, his still-intact CPD sticker on the truck's windshield. Despite his best efforts to arrive on time, the preliminary hearing was already underway.

Ronan weaved through several fast-moving attorneys and prosecutors, charged up the hallway and looked through the small glass square in the courtroom door.

Braxton Campbell stood on the left side of the courtroom, and Nick, dressed in a dark suit with his head down and the swipe of blond hair bunched up on the back of his head, stood next to him. To the right of Nick stood a tall man, making hand gestures in the air. Ty and Melissa sat behind Campbell and Nick, Ty cradling Melissa with an arm.

The pudgy, bearded judged looked at both sides of the room and mouthed instructions to each side and then raised and slammed his gavel onto the sounding block. The preliminary hearing was over.

Campbell patted Nick on the back as the bailiff slowly approached. Nick flinched, then stood up and looked straight ahead as the judge left the bench. Nick continued staring straight ahead as the bailiff led him back to lockup.

The Assistant County Prosecutor quickly stuffed his notes and folders into his briefcase and prepared to depart for other trials.

Melissa leaned heavily into Ty.

Ronan walked back across the corridor and leaned against the wall. The courtroom doors swung open, and Melissa and Ty emerged first. "It'll be okay. You'll see," he said, rubbing her shoulder as they walked toward the courtroom exit.

Melissa was dabbing her eyes with a tissue as Ty led her across the hallway. Suddenly, she pulled away from him and threw herself into Ronan's arms, which caused his back to press farther up against the wall. He embraced her lightly and silently mouthed, *What happened?*

"Everything went as expected," Campbell said, resting his briefcase on the floor.

"Define 'as expected,'" Ronan demanded.

Campbell looked down at Melissa who moved away from Ronan when he broke the embrace. She leaned against the wall next to him and waited for the attorney to continue.

"The judge has determined there's probable cause to believe Nick committed the murder."

Ronan let out a groan. "That's not good news, counselor."

"Let him finish," Ty said.

Campbell cut a quick look at Ty and blinked hard, seemingly glad that someone wanted the information and then continued. "The judge considers Nick a flight risk, so he'll remain in custody until the trial since…" he said, tossing a furtive glance at Melissa, "…his family has means and resides out of state. The fact Nick has no criminal history didn't work in his favor as I would have thought. I'm sorry."

"But there must be some way to get Nick released."

"I'm afraid not," Campbell said. "Now we need to prepare for trial."

Melissa sniffed twice and stuck the soiled tissue under

her nose. "You'll stay with Nick and us through all of this, won't you?"

"He will," Ronan said.

A panicked expression washed across Melissa's face, and her eyes filled with tears, crested and then rolled down her cheeks. Nick's situation finally began to hit her full bore. "But this means Nick can't come home."

Ronan grimaced and deferred to Campbell who agreed. "That's correct, Mrs. Copeland."

Ty stepped closer to Melissa. "There's nothing we can do right now except wait."

"Ty's right," Campbell said. "Right now, you've all been through a tough stretch. Go home and rest. Nick will need all of you in top shape as this ordeal progresses. I'll be in touch as soon as I know more."

The attorney flashed a sympathetic smile as Ronan slipped his arm inside Melissa's and led her away. "Where did you park?"

"Somewhere," she said. "I don't know. In a parking garage somewhere. I was too upset to pay any attention."

"We parked in the garage near the annex," Ty said, trailing behind them. "It's not too far away."

Braxton Campbell called out to them. "Sergeant. Ty. May I have a word?"

Ronan walked around Melissa and pressed both hands against her shoulders, looking down at her. "At the end of the hallway, there's a snack bar. Get us something to drink, and we'll be right there." Ronan dug into his pocket and pulled out a wad of cash. "Here's some money, but don't leave until Ty and I get there, okay?"

Melissa raised her head enough to mumble, "All right."

Ronan and Ty exchanged glances and then walked back to Campbell, who hadn't moved.

"I want you to know I don't think it's a slam dunk for the prosecution. The fingerprints from the house and the cell-phone picture are circumstantial evidence at best, and even if Nick was in Raina Dalton's townhouse, the police have no concrete evidence that he's the one who killed her. Besides, he had no motive. A little tiff at a frat party is not grounds for murder! Nick's a good kid, and he's never been in any trouble. The jury will have to take that into consideration. Besides, no murder weapon was found, and there's no DNA evidence that links Nick to the crime."

"What about the bloody letters on the floor?" Ronan asked.

"Who knows? Maybe Raina thought Nick was still in the townhouse when she was attacked and thought he did it. Maybe the killer saw Nick leave the townhouse and wanted to frame him for the murder."

Ronan blinked. "Sergeant Bonamico told me about a couple of muddy impressions on the townhouse floor. Perhaps they can be connected to Dalton's killer. This evidence needs to be introduced the court." Ronan begged without giving himself away.

"All evidence will be presented at discovery."

"But," Ty interjected. "Raina Dalton was a krok user, right? Maybe she was a dealer too and made some enemies during the course of business."

"Exactly," Campbell said. "All of this will definitely help us at trial. The more doubt that can be placed on the prosecution's argument the better our chances. I just wanted to share this information with the two of you. Nick has been awfully silent through this whole thing, and Melissa is still having trouble processing it all."

Ty extended a hand to Campbell. "Thanks again for everything."

Ronan stared at the handshake for a moment. "Yes. Thank you so much."

As Campbell and Ronan went to shake hands, the heavy clomping of feet echoed in the hallway. Ronan turned around to find Sean Carter and two uniformed officers marching toward them.

"I hope you aren't busy this afternoon, counselor," Ronan said. "It looks like I'll need your services after all."

CHAPTER 49

"We're really going to do this here?" Ronan asked, causing Sean Carter's eyes to flutter with indignation.

"You're damn right we're going to do it here. The Professional Standards Division is prepared to fire you for misconduct. We've been ordered to retain you."

Ty touched Ronan on the arm. "What's going on?"

"My friend here isn't happy about something." Ronan flashed an impish grin at Carter that made the detective stand on his toes and lean forward.

"Captain Ashby wants to see you."

"Tell him I can't."

Carter flinched at the statement.

"I'm suspended. Remember? Plus, I'm in the middle of a family crisis at the moment."

"What's this about?" Campbell said, moving into the tight, open space between the two men. "Detective, this is really not—"

"With all due respect, sir, this issue has nothing to do with you," Carter said authoritatively.

Ronan looked at the three men who seemed ready to pounce and drag him out of the courthouse. The officer flanked to the left of Carter was Officer Keenan. Keenan looked pale and drawn as he waited for instructions.

"No need for a scene or handcuffs. I'm going," Ronan responded calmly.

"Ronan!"

Ronan looked back at Ty. "Take Melissa home. I'll be there in a little while."

Campbell put a hand on Ronan's shoulder. "Call me if you need anything."

People moving through the courthouse stopped and watched intently. Carter moved alongside to the left of Ronan while Officer Keenan walked alongside Ronan on the right. The third cop trailed behind. Ronan felt like he was under arrest; he'd occupied the same space as Carter many times when escorting a suspect. The walk didn't bother Ronan as much as the person leading it did.

Ronan sensed Sean Carter's amusement about the situation, judging by the odd little hop he had in each step and the fact he paraded Ronan down the middle of the courthouse hallway. As they reached the snack bar, Ronan looked over at Melissa; she refused to look back. Ty gazed at Ronan as he comforted Melissa, a probing query filling his dark eyes.

The men exited the courthouse just as the WSAZ news van pulled up in front of the building. A whippet-thin young woman and her cameraman fanned away from the vehicle, carrying a camera and microphone.

"Let's move before we have to make a comment."

"Don't say anything," Ronan added. "Just say, 'no comment.'"

"Shut up," Carter said with a biting edge to his words. "I'm in charge here."

The men managed to get Ronan into the backseat of Carter's car and drive away before the reporter could get the camera set and the microphone ready.

———

Carter pulled his Crown Vic into the loading zone behind the police station and got out of the car first. Keenan didn't move until the other officer stepped out and opened the rear door.

"I don't have to be escorted like a prisoner, Keenan," Ronan said, making eye contact with the young officer. "I'm not going to run away."

Keenan didn't respond, but took a generous step to the left, allowing a courteous distance between them.

As they approached the entrance, Captain Ashby filled the doorframe, resting an arm against it. Small specks of sweat dappled the crease in the blue dress shirt that cut deep into his armpit. He didn't make eye contact with Ronan as Carter and Officer Keenan escorted him into the room.

"Have a seat," Carter said, motioning for Ronan to occupy the empty chair in front of the captain's desk.

Ronan plopped into the seat as Ashby sat down behind his desk.

A few moments passed when Ronan flinched and leaned closer. "What's this all about? Is someone going to say something?"

"We're waiting for Kathy Parks from PSD to get here," Carter said. The pinched tone of Carter's voice couldn't hide the excitement that piqued the words as they were spoken. Ronan knew Carter was enjoying every second of the situation.

As if by cue Kathy Parks whisked into the room, muttering a breathy, "Sorry I'm late," before she pulled another chair from across the room and sat down. She opened the cover of a sleek binder and began scribbling words onto a yellow legal pad.

Ronan had always liked Kathy Parks. She had a reputation for being someone who was firm, but fair, and a true believer in the rules of criminal procedure. Everyone respected her, although her partners sometimes found her unflagging attention to the exact letter of the law a bit taxing.

When Parks was diagnosed with breast cancer, the

fatigue and sickness that accompanied the chemotherapy kept her off the beat for nearly a year. It was the recommendation of the chief and the Charleston Police Department brass that if and when she returned to work, she'd be the new director of the Professional Standards Division, which was responsible for investigating officer misconduct. At her appointment reception, Parks told several people, including Ronan, that she would always consider herself a beat cop first and a PSD officer second.

She looked briefly at Ronan and then checked her watch. Parks' piercing dark green eyes and blood red lips commanded attention when she spoke.

"All right, Captain. Let's begin."

Ronan could hear Carter rubbing his hands together in anticipation.

"Since this is a personnel matter regarding Detective Sergeant McCullough, I would appreciate it if Detective Carter would leave the proceedings."

Ronan turned around and flashed another grin at Carter. Stunned by the request, Carter glared at Parks. She made another note on the legal pad then furrowed her brow, causing the freckle on the side of her forehead to dip and slide.

Captain Ashby leaned back in the chair and loosened the thick knot of his red tie. "Fine. Get going, Carter."

"But, Captain—"

"Thank you, Detective. If we need you, we know where to find you."

Ronan watched as an indignant Sean Carter, stunned by the dismissal, flinched and flopped like a spoiled child being told *no*. As he departed the room, the captain got out of his chair and closed the door.

"Ronan, I just don't know what to say or what I can do for you at this point."

He watched the captain march around the perimeter of the room and slide in behind the desk before deferring to Parks.

"I understand you've been working independently on the Raina Dalton murder investigation," she stated.

"Says who?"

"Sergeant Bonamico."

Ronan huffed. "That's impossible."

"Actually, Sergeant Bonamico didn't say anything per se," Parks replied, her lips now pressed tightly against her face. "But the video camera in his Crown Victoria recorded the trip to Apple Grove and both of you coming out of the townhouse and walking up to the vehicle."

Ronan sat back and let the mashed and somewhat flat stuffing of the chair absorb his weight. "Fine. I was there with Sergeant Bonamico. You know damn well my nephew was connected to Dalton's murder, so forgive me for getting involved."

Captain Ashby clasped both hands together and leaned over the desk. "I'm sorry about that. I truly am. But damn it, Ronan, suspension means you don't work!" Captain Ashby dropped his voice to a mere whisper. "I'm trying to save your ass and career, but you're not making it easy for me."

"It's my understanding the suspension was initiated because of hostile action toward Jensen Williams, a suspect in an officer involved shooting, which came on the heels of you breaking into a closed-and-barricaded rest area on the West Virginia Turnpike. Is that correct?"

"There's nothing suspicious about it," Ronan scoffed. "Williams nearly killed a state trooper and would've killed me if someone hadn't gotten him first."

Parks arched an eyebrow. "I take it we don't know who shot Mr. Williams."

Ronan jutted a thumb in the direction of Captain Ashby. "I don't know. I'm out of the loop."

The captain's frozen stare on Ronan melted momentarily as he addressed Parks. "No. We have no suspects at this time."

Parks penned more notes. "Sergeant McCullough, why do you continue to violate the terms of your suspension?"

"Because the case is active and open, and no one else is

doing a damn thing about it! What's going on in this town is something no one has ever experienced. There's a drug called desomorphine. It's known as krok on the streets, and it's rapidly infiltrating our communities and neighborhoods with devastating results. Jensen Williams, Lorenzo White and Michael Warner were all involved with it. Dalton's killer may be involved with it as well and…" Ronan stopped when Parks' expression became tenser, and Captain Ashby sat back in the chair, drumming his stomach with two thumbs.

Parks nodded and Ronan collected himself and reset.

"These men, whomever they are, are not afraid of the law. We stand a good chance of losing control of Charleston. Someone is systematically pumping drugs into this city and then slowly exterminating the people who brought it here in the first place."

Parks cleared her throat. "That still doesn't give you the right to go into a suspect's hospital room and threaten to suffocate him unless he talks. The man clearly wasn't in any condition to speak with you or to anyone else."

"The sonofabitch should've thought about that before he shot a state trooper."

"Ronan," Captain Ashby said. "Easy."

Parks repositioned herself in the seat. Even though she was only 5'6", her commanding presence made her seem taller than her diminutive frame indicated.

"Okay," she said before clipping the cap back on her pen and closing the folder. "I have all I need here."

"That's it?" Ronan asked incredulously.

"Yes."

"I don't understand. I barely got a chance to say anything."

Parks looked at Ronan with a steely resolve. "I heard all I needed to, Sergeant. I've been looking into this matter since you were suspended. Hearing your side of things is the final step in the process."

Ronan stood up and raked a hand through his short-cropped hair. "I admit I've made some mistakes, but I wanted to catch the criminals intent on destroying our city and its citizens. Whether or not the victims were drug dealers, we can't have cartel enforcers carrying out executions. This situation started with Michael Warner. There are far too many disparate pieces in an unsolved puzzle, but I'm sure desomorphine is the missing piece that makes the picture complete."

Parks stood up and smoothed her uniform with one hand. She looked at the captain. "I'll be in touch. Good day, gentlemen."

Before Ronan could say another word, Parks left the room. Ashby saw her out then perched himself on the corner of his desk.

"Come on, Cap...you know I'm a good cop."

"I know it," Ashby said, looking past Ronan at the partially open door. "I'm not sure it matters though."

The words slammed hard against Ronan's chest. "What do you mean?"

"I think because Parks was a cop first, she knows the pressures of the job. Everything you described, we all know it. We feel the same sense of urgency to catch these bastards as you."

"Then—"

"But," the captain said, holding up a finger, "if we don't follow procedures and maintain standards, then the line between us and them gets blurred and nothing good can come from that."

Ronan wanted to argue more but resisted. "So, what now?"

"Parks will probably recommend your suspension be longer than thirty days and, no doubt, will require you to seek counseling, which I will agree with in order to save your job."

Ronan let out a long breath of relief. "Thank you."

"But it may not be enough. The chief has the final say here, and it's not just what happened that concerns him. Bonamico should never have granted you access to the Dalton crime scene, and *you* shouldn't have asked him in the first place. You've placed your partner in a compromised position. Parks has already interviewed him, and he's likely facing a suspension as well."

Ronan thought about Eric's family, which was something his partner valued more than his own life. The suspension could be with pay or without pay, and if he was suddenly without the paltry income the city paid, it would place the entire family in a very difficult situation.

"Why were you there?"

"I have my reasons."

"Now's not the time to play coy with me, McCullough."

"I wanted to re-examine the muddy impressions on the floor of the townhouse."

Ronan had expected a gesture of disapproval, but Ashby remained still. "Keep going."

"Since my suspension, I've been looking into a report of a suspicious patient in the emergency room at Mercy."

This time Ashby's disapproval came in the form of slumped shoulders. "Not another incident at the hospital."

"Hear me out."

The captain pressed both palms against his expansive forehead and gazed back on Ronan.

"I'm friends with one of the nurses in the ER. A couple of days ago, he contacted me about a mysterious patient who came into the hospital."

Captain Ashby reaffirmed his position at the end of the desk, intently listening to the half-truth.

"The man had mud on his clothes; said he was a farmer or something. I examined the mud on Ty's scrubs, and it's the same type of mud found at the crime scene."

"And your point?"

"The point is this mud is called 'blue mud,' and it's indigenous to only certain areas of the country."

"That doesn't prove anything."

Ronan leaned back again in the chair. "Ty told me the man in the ER fled once the doctor wanted to discuss the results of his MRI."

"I imagine people leave all the time to avoid paying the bill."

"True, but this was the second time a suspicious man fled the ER after encountering my friend."

The light in the captain's eyes flickered. "Ty Andino. Both men talked to him and both men then fled?"

"Yes. The man Ty treated said he'd been digging in the mud out on his farm, and that's why his boots and clothes were so dirty. When I was at the crime scene the first time, I saw a blue-colored muddy impression in the foyer. It wasn't enough to be a partial shoeprint, but I did think it was odd though that there was mud in the house since the front yard had already dried out since the last rainstorm."

Captain Ashby stopped Ronan with an open palm. "Wait a minute. The *first* time you were at the crime scene? For God's sake, Ronan!"

"Forget about that, Captain." Ronan paused a moment to let Ashby regain focus. "The mud at the Dalton crime scene and the mud on Ty's scrubs look like a perfect match."

"That's speculative at best. Anyone could have tracked that mud into the crime scene."

"But it's the best lead we have. Eric's taking the mud sample and scrubs to the crime lab for analysis. I realize my theory is a long shot, but it may be the only chance I have to save my nephew."

"The connection is loose at best, but we can explore it. I'll send Sean Carter over to Mercy to talk with Mr. Andino."

"Thanks, Captain."

Ashby slid off his desk and said, "Get out of here. We can't discuss this case because you've been suspended, Detective McCullough."

"Ah, right."

"By the way, Chief Toler also knows you spoke to the feds."

CHAPTER 50

Autumn Road featured a cul-de-sac of homes and a paved turn circle for parking. Ben considered parking his car in between some of the others but assumed everyone in the circle would know each other and which car belonged to which home.

Instead, he parked at the intersection of Autumn and Loma, past the cul-de-sac of homes on the end of Autumn Road. There was an untouched area of trees and high grass that clung close to the road at the head of Loma, and Ben thought it would be the perfect place to leave his car without drawing the attention of neighbors.

The faded blue overalls Ben found at the local thrift store in Ripley were too small, and the fabric was itchy. When he tried on the outfit, the coarse, thick material rubbed against the puss-filled abscesses on his legs where he'd repeatedly shot up with krok. Ben covered the skin with gauze and bandages, but the material still made both legs itch and burn. The navy blue hat he bought would hide much of his face, and the worn DirectTV patch on his shirt-sleeve provided an aura of authenticity.

If anyone in the neighborhood stopped or questioned Ben, he would default into his planned story: he was a DirectTV installer canvassing the neighborhood, assessing the number of current company customers and looking for potential new ones.

Ben liked the neighborhood. It seemed quiet, and nearby Kanawha State Forest gave the homes, situated on large lots, a country-estate kind of feel. Both deciduous and evergreen trees hung high and low around the well-kept homes. Ben could see a variety of songbirds fluttering about, and he imagined plenty of other wildlife too like deer, raccoons, possums, rabbits, and squirrels.

Near the end of Autumn Road, he came across the townhouse belonging to Ty Andino. Ben located the address online, and luckily for him, Ty was the only *Andino* listed on Anywho.com. Leroy had already been to the house earlier in the day and had scoped out its access points and security system. Ben had managed to find Leroy another discarded uniform at the thrift store, although this one was a powder blue, button-down shirt with two holes just below the first button. Leroy had worn Ben's hat, passing himself off as a West Virginia American Water Company employee investigating customer complaints of low water pressure.

Ben scaled the sloped yard and moved to the side of the townhouse, pretending to look for satellite installation points. Leroy had left a crowbar and a black duffel bag under a hibiscus bush near the heating and air-conditioning unit of the home. Ben wouldn't risk dragging the bag with him, but Leroy could justify those tools as part of the equipment required to assess water lines.

Ben reached down and picked up the bag and crowbar. Cautiously, he looked around, making sure nobody was passing by the house or watching it. He eyed the rear window. Taking a deep breath, he gripped the crowbar tightly and started to sling the curved metal end toward the glass when suddenly the window opened.

Startled, Ben let the crowbar slip from his hand and slap against the brick wall. As he fumbled with the zipper on the bag, trying to grab a gun, Leroy's face appeared in the open space.

"What the fuck are you doing?" Leroy asked.

"Fuck you!" Ben hissed, trying to regain his composure. "I didn't know you were inside. You scared the shit out of me."

Leroy smiled and bobbed his head. "I've already *cased* the place."

"Good. Now let me inside before somebody sees us."

———

Ronan left CPD headquarters unsure of himself and more irritated than ever. Not knowing what Kathy Parks would say in her report made his stomach churn and his head thump. Maybe he shouldn't worry too much, at least for now. He may lose his job, but a longer suspension was also on the table. Ronan decided to concentrate on the latter possibility.

Unfortunately, the concerns didn't end there. Captain Ashby had learned of Ronan's visit to the FBI and because of policy had reported the visit to Chief Toler. Special Agents Chandler and Allen had promised total discretion, as long as Ronan never acknowledged the visit. Ronan denied meeting with the agents at first, but when the department inquired about the FBI assisting in the krok cartel investigation, a secretary in their office brought up Ronan's name. She swore to Captain Ashby and the chief that she thought the local police were already working with the agents in the Charleston field office.

Ronan had been sloppy and didn't check to see if anyone aside from Chandler and Allen was in the office during his meeting. Now the FBI considered Ronan a rogue cop, and that compromised the overall trust and cooperation between the two agencies.

Exhausted, both mentally and physically, Ronan was ready to go home. He could've requested a patrol officer to take him, but he was in no mood to be in the company of anyone from the CPD. The only thing he wanted now was a shower and some sleep, hopefully doing both activities with Ty. Ronan also wanted to visit Nick and console Melissa, but the words from Braxton Campbell resonated deeply: *Nick will need all of us*. But Ronan couldn't help Nick if he was physically and emotionally spent.

The taxi smelled musty, and the lack of air-conditioning made him claustrophobic. Thankfully, the ride was short, and Ronan was home before his discomfort could turn into a full-blown anxiety attack. He dug into his front pants pocket and handed the fare to the cab driver. The swarthy man of indeterminate origin ripped the money from Ronan's hand and then dumped a few crumpled bills and a couple of worn coins into his hand.

As Ronan headed up the walkway, he could see Ty's slender, curvy shadow in the illuminated window upstairs. Ronan's heart skipped a beat. He was glad to be home. Taking his eyes off his waiting lover, he stopped briefly to pick up the morning newspaper. When he looked to the window again, Ronan saw another shadow appear behind the first. Suddenly, both shadows rocked back and forth, arms flailing and heads bobbing. Ice-cold panic engulfed Ronan's heart as both shadows disappeared.

CHAPTER 51

onan anxiously reached for his cell phone, but it wasn't in his pocket and neither were his keys. "Shit!" He immediately ran back to the cab and shouted to the startled drive, "Call 911. Now!"

The unkempt, slovenly driver mumbled a couple of incomprehensible words and slowly looked around the seats and floorboards, lacking any sense of urgency. Ronan reached through the open window and grabbed a tuft of the man's greasy hair.

"I'm a cop! Call 911 now and tell them to hurry!"

The frightened man yanked a cell phone from the glove compartment and drove away as Ronan raced to the townhouse. His legs churned out of control so quickly that he nearly fell onto the sidewalk, but he regained his balance by resting a hand on the small, stone wall that ran along the front of the property. Instinctively, he reached for his missing weapon and let out a loud curse to the heavens for another one of life's injustices.

Ronan leaned against the front door and could hear low groans coming from the foyer. He took a couple of steps back and then rammed the door with his full weight. The door buckled slightly but didn't open. Three more times

Ronan slammed into the door, putting every bit of energy he had into each charge.

Finally, the door crashed open. Shocked, Leroy stood up, a plastic syringe in his large, dirty hand. Ty lay on his side at Leroy's feet; blood dotting his white tee shirt and gray shorts. Ronan didn't wait for Leroy to recover and viciously charged, knocking them both to the polished hardwood floor.

Leroy jabbed at Ronan's neck, but Ronan saw the syringe coming and slapped it away. As Leroy followed the rolling syringe, Ronan leveled a devastating punch to his nose. The cartilage cracked like a dried twig, and he screamed in pain as blood gushed from both his nostrils. Before Leroy could make another sound, Ronan leveled another punch against his jaw, slapping his head to the right.

From the corner of his eye, Ronan gazed at Ty's motionless body. The synapses in his brain fired like gunshots but his body was paralyzed. Unsure of what was in the syringe, Ronan was unsure of how to help Ty.

Leroy seized on Ronan's indecisiveness and grasped the syringe. He stood up to strike again, but Ronan pounced on the intruder before he could move a muscle. A meaty forearm slid around Leroy's throat, and his breath caught in his lungs as his windpipe began to collapse.

"Who are you?" Ronan demanded as he squeezed tighter.

A hideous gurgling noise rattled in Leroy's throat.

"You're pushing krok, aren't you, you sonofabitch? Did you kill Michael Warner and Raina Dalton?"

With his last bit of strength, Leroy wriggled from Ronan's chokehold and bit down fiercely on his arm, breaking the skin. Ronan reeled and staggered backward, pulling his attacker with him. Both men crashed to the floor once more. As Ronan scrambled to get up, Leroy got to his feet first and kicked him in the ribs. A blinding right cross followed. Ronan buckled but then got to his feet and landed two heavy blows into Leroy's gut. Leroy bent over and sucked in a couple of shallow breaths as Ronan stood staggering before him. Eying a decorative plate on the wall shelf, Leroy grabbed it and smashed it over Ronan's head, sending fragments of glass cascading around them.

Streams of blood erupted from the gash on Ronan's forehead and streamed down his face. At first he thought pieces of the plate had damaged his eyesight. Dazed and weak, he saw Leroy standing close enough to touch, but the once solid image of the man was now misshapen and hazy.

Ronan wiped away the blood and frantically punched at Leroy with tightly clenched fists but managed to hit only air.

Leroy cackled sadistically, taunting the detective. "You fight about as well as a little bitch, copper. I've seen people strung out on krok put up a better fight."

Ronan heard the words, but they didn't penetrate his jumbled thoughts. The rivers of blood continued coursing down both cheeks, coming to a point at his chin as he staggered about, punching vainly at his elusive target.

Leroy retreated further into the house as Ronan strained to focus. Even though Leroy remained a blurred, shifting shadow, Ronan managed to dodge the needle plunging at him from every angle. The last forceful swipe of the syringe sliced the air and swooshed by Ronan. After a few more seconds, the blurring eased, and he could see Leroy, who now stood mere inches from him, clutching the syringe and preparing to strike once again.

Leroy made one final cut through the air, but Ronan swerved to the right and stepped around him. This time he placed a hand on each side of his attacker's face and sank his nails into the blotched skin, snapping the man's head in the opposite direction with all the force he could muster.

The bones in Leroy's neck shattered like porcelain, and the crackle of crushing bones ricocheted throughout the quiet room. Leroy collapsed silently onto the floor.

Ronan reached down and placed two fingers across the man's carotid artery. A faint beat. Unseeing eyes, once pulsing with energy and rage, stared at the ceiling. Two shallow breaths escaped Leroy's lips before his chest contracted one last time.

Ronan pried the syringe from the dead man's hand then raced to Ty's side.

"Oh, God, Ty! Come on, wake up!"

Ronan repeatedly checked for a pulse until he found a stronger, more vibrant beat. Gently, he stroked Ty's face, speaking softly but firmly between each tender touch.

"Come on, Ty. Stay with me. Damn it! Where are the damn cops?"

Each minute seemed like an hour as Ronan waited for help, but finally he could hear the faint sound of sirens creeping up from the valley. It would still be several minutes before the police arrived, so he went back and checked on Ty again. This time Ty's lips moved a bit, and there was a slight tremor in his fingers. Unsure if the movements were death throes or life returning to his body, Ronan whispered close to his lover's ear. "Please, Ty. Please be okay. I love you. I don't want to lose you."

Ronan pulled Ty into his arms and cradled him close. As his mind finally cleared, his thoughts instantly turned to Melissa. She'd come home with Ty! He released Ty and laid him gently back on the floor, stood up and then crept into the living room. Seeing nothing he slipped into the kitchen. Only the soft glow from the streetlights illuminated the otherwise darkened room. He grabbed the large French knife from the butcher block and made his way around the center island where he found Melissa.

Ronan's head was still spinning. Everything around Melissa was a gray blur, but he could see she'd been tied to a chair with a long, white cord. Her arms were pinned behind her back, and her feet were knotted together with the cord and tied to the legs of the chair. A dark cloth was stuffed in her mouth.

"Melissa."

She panted, mumbling as Ronan dropped the knife and raced toward her.

"It's okay. The cops are on their way."

With trembling fingers Ronan tugged at the cloth.

"Ronan, there's someone else!" Melissa screamed as the last bit of material was pulled away.

Something sharp pierced his neck, and then a terrifying, black shroud enveloped the dim light.

CHAPTER 52

Ronan coughed, and his eyes fluttered open. He could barely breathe. The nylon diamond braid cord bit sharply into his arms and legs, and the fatigue was overwhelming. But in this painful haze, he felt as if he were floating. Thick black tree branches swirled overhead, and stars glinted between the leafy stalks. It was like a very odd dream had invaded his waking consciousness.

Without warning the movement stopped, but the pain in his limbs continued. The shadowy trees that had been blazing past his vision were now still, frozen in a frame with the moon overhead.

"I never thought dragging someone would be so fucking hard."

The person speaking sounded like a man, although Ronan couldn't be sure. He tried desperately to process everything that had recently happened. He remembered a man standing over Ty clutching a syringe, and then Melissa being restrained and gagged. Yet putting those events in order with details was difficult. He had no sense of how much time had passed or where he was at the moment.

"It won't be long now, Sergeant. In just a few minutes, it'll all be over, at least for you anyway."

Ronan squinted and saw the man fumbling with the

cords that wrapped him up like a rodeo calf. He tried reaching out, but his hands were cusped together. Ronan knew he had to focus and concentrate in order to find out where he was and what might be happening to him. The problem was focusing. As he tried to organize his scattered thoughts, the fleeting moments of lucidity were followed by great chunks of nothingness. *Ty. Melissa. An intruder. A fight.*

He rolled his neck to the left. The long-legged man bent forward at the waist and pulled on the cord. The nylon braid dug deeper into Ronan's skin.

"There. All secured. It's time to take a little swim," Ben said with a cruel grin. Ronan's police training finally kicked in. The steps of assessing the situation, determining who was involved, and the circumstances of the situation rocketed through his brain with perfect clarity like he was a newly graduated cadet. Ronan dropped his gaze and noted the man's black sweatpants. He'd seen those pants before. They were the same pants Michael Warner was wearing on that stifling summer evening outside the Corner Diner.

"We'll be at the pond any minute now."

For a moment Ronan managed to sort through the cobbled pieces of disparate thought. "Krok...krok..." The words escaped between shallow breaths.

The man stood back and briefly regarded Ronan then said, "No. I injected you with succinylcholine. Krok won't do you any good now."

The succinylcholine had been the one part of the plan that had been executed perfectly. Once the viscous liquid started coursing through Ronan's veins, all Ben had to do was wait for the paralysis to set in.

Succinylcholine. Ronan didn't recognize the word, and the enunciation of the syllables seemed dreamlike. But Ronan knew whatever was coursing through his blood wasn't any dream; it was a nightmare.

He tried kicking and flailing his tethered legs and arms again, but his limbs felt heavy and disproportionate. Ronan could feel the cord slacken a bit, allowing him some degree of movement. But Ben saw him move ever so slightly and jammed the toe of his boot deep into Ronan's thigh in response.

"Stop moving!"

Ronan tensed every muscle, frantically trying to loosen the cord even further. He had to escape.

"I said stop moving!" Ben shouted as he struck Ronan in the face with the butt of his pistol. Then he placed the cold, steel barrel against Ronan's temple and cocked the hammer. Oddly, the cold steel felt good against his face.

Ben resumed dragging Ronan across the ground like a wounded animal. Ronan tried to refocus on the situation. This time, the dragging didn't go on for long before Ben stopped again and knelt beside him.

"Soon you'll be at the bottom of Farmer Mitchell's muddy, little pond and nobody will ever find you."

"Fuck you!" came the blistering response.

"Easy, Sergeant," Ben said, pulling Ronan into an upright position.

A pulsing thud pounded inside Ronan's head. Shaking off the sensation, he tried letting the features of the scene fill in. A flat, broad expansive landscape appeared before him. The woods were dark and uninviting, but Ronan could see a large, placid pool just beyond from where he sat. The silvery beams of moonlight glistening off the smooth surface made the watery grave seem almost inviting.

"I wouldn't want to send you swimming without the right equipment," Ben said with a laugh.

"So, you're going to drown me. How original."

"Unoriginal maybe, but highly effective all the same. Just as effective as snapping someone's neck," Ben said, dropping the cinderblock and heavy chain onto the ground. "Adam noted you were wily and tough."

Ronan registered the names.

"If by some miracle someone does find your body, I'll be long gone."

Ben spun two ends of chain through the large openings in the middle of the block. As he pulled the chain through the holes, it grabbed his pants leg, making the material ride up over his ankle. Even in the moonlight, the familiar swollen, puss-filled, mutilated skin of a krok user was more than visible.

"How long have you been using?" Ronan asked. He wanted to keep Ben talking. Anything to stall him.

Ben stopped and arched an eyebrow at Ronan. The moonlight struck the side of his face just at the right angle, revealing the charred flesh.

"Long enough to know it makes me feel like a god besides making me a shitload of money. The fine citizens of Charleston seem to like it too." The same sinister grin from earlier reappeared.

"That's quite a drug."

Ben clamped a padlock onto the chain, connecting the two ends, and then tested its strength. "The good thing about Charleston is it gives us three good highways to take the drug north, south, east, and west. Once krok infiltrates a city, it's too late. By the time you cops figure out what's going on, we're already gone."

"But you're still here, and so am I," Ronan replied, eliciting a dismissive gesture from Ben. "I've been onto you since the beginning. I'm the one who found Michael Warner before he died. I followed your men to the rest area on the turnpike. I saw the trucks being emptied and moved."

"Actually," Ben countered, with a slightly deeper pitch in his voice, "someone else saw that too, and it just happened to be your sister and nephew. I'm proud to say they've both been dealt with, and viciously I may add."

"You kill everyone who gets in your way, don't you?" Ronan asked as he tried to remain upright.

Ben stood up and smacked his hands together, knocking off the caked-on dirt. "Loose ends need to be dealt with," he replied matter-of-factly.

"So, Warner, Dalton and White were nothing more than 'loose ends'?"

Ben looked at the stars as if seeking an answer from the heavens. "Raina and Michael were just stupid kids who got in too deep. It happens, but they were expendable. You know, I was the one in the warehouse with White that night."

Ronan blinked hard, but said nothing.

"When the cops showed up, that crazy bastard wanted to burn the entire building to the ground and kill everyone in it. The dumb fuck started torching the stairwells before I got out, and this is what happened in the process," Ben said, pointing to his face.

Ronan tried to say something else but was cut off.

"Adam made sure all the loose ends were tied up. Even Raina. What a fucking, stupid idea to shoot a state trooper! And never mind that idiot Jensen."

"Speaking of people being 'taken care of,'" Ronan said. "I can't say I wish Jensen well."

"Jensen will be dead soon enough, and now that Adam's dead, I'm in charge of everything. Once we get it into Appalachia, we're going to spread south and west from Detroit and soon we'll control every drug route in this country. We spread the krok; get people hooked, and then sit back and watch the money roll in."

Ronan flinched as Ben knelt down and pushed the cinderblock toward him.

Keep talking, Ronan thought. *If I make it out of here alive, I've got enough names and information to help shut down this entire operation.*

"It always comes down to money, doesn't it?"

"Never underestimate the power of money, my man, or the power of addiction."

Ronan tried to free himself once again from the braided bonds securing his hands and feet.

"Stop moving!"

Ben wrapped the chain around Ronan's ankles twice and then tied into a knot. The snap of the lock echoed like a gunshot through the quiet woods. He tugged on the chain around Ronan's chest and then at the point where it wrapped around the cinderblock. "Good. Both ends nice and tight and ready to go."

"Where are we going?"

"*We* aren't going anywhere," Ben replied calmly.

Ronan looked up just as Ben slammed the pistol butt into his face once again, and this time he toppled to the ground with a heavy thud.

"Don't worry, Sergeant. It will be a long, slow death, and you'll have plenty of time to say your prayers."

Ronan bit down hard on his lip and willed the pain away.

"This pond here is for cattle, but it's pretty low right now. The soil looks dry, don't it? But it's really all mud just below the crusty surface. It's blue mud. Ever heard of it? Funny stuff, blue mud. It's just like quicksand."

Ronan's heart slammed into his throat when he heard the words *blue mud*. "Thanks for the geology lesson, you fucking prick," he hissed defiantly.

Ben dragged Ronan and the chained cinderblock closer to the water's edge then stopped and slapped Ronan again. Ronan snapped his head around quickly and spit a bloody wad of saliva at Ben, which landed on the charred flesh.

The sinister grin reappeared as he wiped the spit from his damaged skin. "Now don't try and fight it. The more you struggle, the faster you'll sink."

Ben grunted and then hoisted the cinderblock over his head and heaved it into the pond. The block plopped into the muddy goo, and Ronan helplessly followed.

CHAPTER 53

"Mr. Andino has contusions of the neck and face and a possible concussion, but his vitals are within normal parameters," the paramedic said as she scanned Ty's eyes with her penlight.

Ty looked up at Eric Bonamico and tilted his head to the side. "I'm fine."

Bonamico crossed is arms over his broad chest. "Why are medical personnel always the worst patients?"

Ty grimaced as the light crossed back and forth once again. "I thought you said I was fine."

The woman looked at Ty with an earnest expression and said, "Just making sure."

As he waited for Dr. Curtis to arrive, Detective Carter consulted with the other officers and crime-scene personnel that had flooded the house.

After the dazzling, colored specs of light had disappeared from his eyes, Ty could see Carter kneeling beside a body that was most certainly dead. He stood up and struggled to maintain his balance. Bonamico leaned closer and offered his shoulder for support.

"Thanks."

"Don't mention it."

Officer Mack led a pale and frightened Melissa into the

foyer. She didn't look up, but her slouched shoulders and trembling steps said more than any words.

Mack searched the room and headed for his superior officer. "Sergeant, I've taken Mrs. Copeland's statement."

Gauze bandages encircled Melissa's wrists and ankles; a Band-Aid covered the small cut on her forehead. Seeing Ty, she broke away from the officer and hobbled into Ty's open arms.

"Shh, it's okay. It's over now."

Ty looked pleadingly back at Bonamico, but all the sergeant could do was nod. The silence that passed between them let him know that things were far from over.

"I'd like to have Mrs. Copeland examined for head trauma," the paramedic announced.

Bonamico and Ty exchanged glances. Looking at the battered woman, they both concurred.

"I'll have Officer Mack stay with you, Mrs. Copeland. The exam should take just a few minutes," the paramedic offered reassuringly.

Melissa's pained expression waned a bit as the paramedic motioned for her to sit down in a living-room chair.

Ty let a fragile Melissa move away before speaking again. "Any word on Ronan?"

Bonamico shook his head. "Nothing yet, but the paper we found in the dead man's pocket had directions from Ripley to here. That gives us a good starting point for our search."

Ty raked his slender hand through his thick, dark hair. "I can't believe this is happening."

Bonamico scanned the room quickly and noted Carter's preoccupation with the body lying on the floor then settled an inquisitive look on Ty.

"Are you sure there's nothing else you remember?"

Ty closed both eyes and shook his head. When he opened them again, he found Bonamico's eyes searching his for some hint of what had happened to Ronan.

"No, I don't think so. Melissa and I had just come from

the courthouse. Seeing Nick taken away in handcuffs was a jarring moment for her. It was for all of us."

Bonamico nodded understandingly.

"When we came home, Melissa went into the kitchen to make some coffee, and I went upstairs to change. The next thing I know, someone jumped me from behind and tossed me down the stairs."

Ty looked in the direction of the stairs and saw a forensic tech positioning a camera at odd angles and snapping several pictures.

"I heard Melissa scream from the living room, and when I got there I saw someone standing next to her. I couldn't get a good look at him, but it was definitely a man, and he was saying something to her. I heard another man's voice too. After that they were gone."

"Did the intruders call one another by name?"

"I heard the name Lee or Roy or something like that."

Bonamico let a beat pass. "And you're sure Ronan was here at some point?"

"Yes. I can remember hearing his voice. I tried speaking and opening my eyes, but it was like I couldn't get my body to do what I wanted. Ronan was trying to wake me, but then his voice faded. But I know it was Ronan. I felt his hands on my skin. I know that touch…" Ty snapped his mouth shut. "I'm sorry. I need to be more careful. The concussion must be lowering my inhibitions."

"Don't worry. Nobody here knows anything. I'll make sure of that."

Ty felt relieved. "Thank you, Eric. I know Ronan is in enough trouble with the department right now. If they knew he was gay—"

"Like I said, they won't." Bonamico patted Ty on the arm.

"When is Lee, Roy or Leroy over there going to be taken out of my house?"

The detective tapped his foot as he thought. "Soon. Speaking of the name, don't worry about not knowing exactly what it was. No identification was found on him, and it's probably just an alias anyway. Thugs like him often assign themselves nicknames, especially in the drug trade, and they use them like code. As for the other guy, he left nothing behind other than an unconscious woman."

Ty grimaced. "You think this guy was a drug dealer?"

"The body has all the telltale characteristics of krok use. If he wasn't dealing, he was at least using."

Ty sighed. "I know those characteristics well. We've seen plenty of patients present with them at the hospital over the last few weeks."

"What we don't know is if Leroy was an enforcer for someone higher up in the drug cartel, or if he was sent here to deal with Ronan but found you and Melissa instead."

Carter swooped into the conversation and bumped purposely into Bonamico. "It seems Leroy suffered a broken neck. If Ronan did it, he did a damn good job."

Bonamico glared at the presumptuous detective.

"I'm going to send some guys over to Ripley to see if we can find McCullough," Carter stated. Ty sensed the conversation needed to continue in private, so he stepped away. As he did, Carter grabbed his arm.

"I have a few more questions for you, Mr. Andino."

"Instead of questioning me, you should be out looking for Ronan."

"As soon as we process everything here, we will. Trust me."

"And when will that be?" Ty asked, jerking his arm away.

"I need to figure out something first," Carter replied as he opened a notepad and clicked his pen. "Sergeant McCullough investigated the suspicious man who you chased from the ER at Charleston Mercy a week or so ago. Now there's another incident, and Sergeant McCullough, according to your statement, was here as well. I'm trying to figure out the connection between the two of you, and why is it that whenever events happen in this investigation, the two of you are both involved."

Ty didn't like the tone or direction of the question.

"Ronan and I are friends, Detective Carter. But I don't imagine you can relate to something like that, can you?"

Carter's eyes darkened and sharpened. He closed the notepad as Ty looked at Bonamico, who was grinning like a Cheshire Cat.

"That still doesn't answer my question, Mr. Andino."

"Will there be anything else?"

"Actually, yes."

Ty felt the muscles in his face tighten with anxiety. "What else then?"

Carter quickly looked around the room, drinking in the luxurious setting.

"Is there something more to your relationship with Detective McCullough than you're telling me?"

"As I said before, Ronan and I are friends. His sister and nephew are staying with me, and he asked me to go the preliminary hearing with them today."

Carter didn't seem impressed with the answer, but he stopped his questioning.

Bonamico coughed as he looked at his watch.

"Do you need to be somewhere more important than this particular crime scene, Sergeant Bonamico? You seem awfully impatient."

"I've got something else I need to investigate involved with this case."

"Like what?"

"I don't know yet."

Carter huffed. "Were you planning on sharing any of it with me?"

"Like I said, I don't know if there's anything to it. If so, then yes."

Ty took the spat between the two detectives as an opportunity to leave and slipped back across the room to Melissa. He felt uncomfortable walking away from Carter, whom he believed already had a theory in mind to answer the questions he'd asked. Ty wanted to make sure he didn't provide any additional details that would make Carter even more suspicious about his relationship with Ronan. If the detective knew he and Ronan were lovers, then Ronan's career would be all but finished.

Melissa sat alone, a faded orange towel draped across her shoulders. Stoically, she sat staring at the floor with a look that was both dazed and distant.

Ty knelt down in front of her and sweetly asked, "How are you feeling?"

"Sore," she replied but without making eye contact. "Have they found Ronan?"

Ty looked back to the detectives who were locked in a hushed conversation. "Not yet, but the police have a good lead."

Melissa began trembling. "I can't…I can't lose any more of my family. I've already lost my son, and now my brother—"

"Hey," Ty said, reaching up to cup Melissa's face and bring her eyes over to meet his gaze. "We'll find Ronan. And we're going to do whatever it takes to make sure Nick is back with us soon. Okay? But we have to think positively about everything. Ronan and Nick would expect that from us."

The tears that almost spilled over the rims of Melissa's eyes held steady. "I know. It's just so hard."

Bonamico tapped Ty's shoulder. "Can we talk for a minute?"

"I'll be right back, Melissa."

Bonamico lead Ty to a small space near the front door that was void of any people or noise. "I got a text message from a friend at the state-police crime lab in South Charleston."

"So."

Bonamico looked around and then leaned in closer. "Ronan had a theory that the person who killed Raina Dalton framed Nick for the murder."

Ty's eyes widened with excitement. "That's great news."

"It may be," Bonamico replied. "But it all hinges on the mud we recovered at the crime scene, the same mud as on your scrubs."

"Are you saying I treated a killer?"

Bonamico quirked an eyebrow and then looked at his watch again. "I need to go. The search for Ronan will be starting any minute now. I'll let you know as soon as I hear something."

"Thanks. I appreciate that," Ty said to the detective. *Dear God, let Ronan be all right,* he said to himself.

CHAPTER 54

Ronan bounced hard against the rough embankment near the edge of the pond before being dragged into the shadowy mire. Ben's words pinged around in his brain like an out-of-control pinball, crashing against memories and matter. He remembered how he got here, but he didn't know *why* he was here.

Ben lurked on the pond's shore, both hands stuffed into his pants pockets, admiring his handiwork. He rocked back and forth comfortably on the heels of his feet, and Ronan knew he was enjoying the moment.

As the cinderblock sunk lower, Ronan felt his right leg jerk downward. Frantically, he lifted his cord-bound arms into the air, trying to keep some part of himself from being drawn deeper into the sticky abyss. The mud felt cool and thick, and Ronan was surprised it only rose to his waist. Another heavy tug yanked at his leg. The mud was now at his stomach.

Ben let out a sinister laugh. "It'll be over soon. Just relax."

Ronan struggled, but the mud pulled him deeper with each movement.

Pacing back and forth across the pond's edge, Ben was

becoming anxious about how long it was taking Ronan to die.

Sweat poured into Ronan's eyes, making his vision blur, and he desperately tried to focus. His heart raced faster, and his breathing matched the pace of each beat. Ronan feared he would faint, so he closed his eyes and willed himself to relax despite the opposition of every fiber in his being. When his breathing had slowed somewhat, he opened his eyes. In the distance, a sliver of moonlight illuminated the long root of a fallen oak tree that jutted out from the edge of the bank. Squinting, he tried judging the distance between himself and the bank. But as he leaned his body forward, he was pulled deeper into the mud. Ronan couldn't calculate how close he was to the bank, but he could tell the root was long and round and could possibly hold his weight, as well as the weight of the cinderblock and chain.

A searing burst of pain coursed through Ronan's body as the chain dug into his leg, the result of gravity and physics working in unison with the vortex of the viscous substance. His shriek momentarily stopped Ben's pacing, but the man only stared as if to question the reason for the outburst.

Realizing his time was running out, Ronan knew he had only one chance to free himself. After the pain had subsided somewhat, he turned a foot, and it felt as if the chain had slackened. Had the cinderblock severed the chains in its downward journey? He couldn't tell, but somehow Ronan knew he'd been relinquished from his metal bonds.

He took a deep breath and tightened every muscle in his legs and lower body. Silently counting to three, Ronan released the tension, and propelled himself forward. Reaching out as far as he could, the muscles straining against bone as they were pushed to their finite limits, Ronan snared the root with his still-fettered hands. He pulled himself hard against the mud, which continued to pull him lower. After one final thrust, Ronan loosened himself from the sludge.

"I don't think so," Ben sneered. He pulled a gun from

the waistband of his jeans and fired into the air twice before lowering the barrel directly at Ronan's head.

"Kill me quickly or watch me suffer."

"Either way you're dead."

"Not true. You could've put a bullet in me at any point. It's more fun to watch me suffer, isn't it?"

Ronan called Ben's bluff, and it worked. Ben tossed the gun to the ground, but picked up his leg and slammed the heel of the boot against the root.

"Back to suffering."

The stomping increased in force and frequency. Ronan began panting, taking several deep breaths as he tried to regain stamina and focus. Ben's boot crushed mercilessly down on Ronan's fingers. Between each agonizing blow, Ronan tried moving his hands around different parts of the root, but Ben's relentless torture found purchase with each stomp on Ronan's battered flesh and bone.

As he stomped harder and faster, cackling sadistically at the game he created, more of his boot dangled above the pond. Again and again Ben slammed the heel of his boot against Ronan's hand, causing Ronan to recoil in pain. The sudden movement caught Ben off guard, and Ronan took advantage of the fleeting respite. He let loose the root and grabbed Ben's foot. Ben lost his balance, but as he fell his elbow slammed into the side of Ronan's head. But Ronan was ferocious and wouldn't loosen his grip. With a fierce growl, he reached up and pulled Ben into the muddy pond.

Ben flailed and thrashed as he clawed at the mud in a frantic attempt to right himself. He wiped at the mud covering his eyes and searched for Ronan's position. Ben flopped forward, using swim-like strokes, but the movements made him sink faster. Ronan quickly closed the distance between them, but Ben rose up and swung at him. Ronan dodged the blow, and Ben fell back into the mud, gasping and struggling to gain balance and traction. He rolled onto one side. Ronan struck hard and fast with a punch into Ben's gut, knocking the wind from his tormentor. As Ben gasped for air, Ronan wrapped his shackled hands around his throat.

———

Bonamico waited on the small concrete porch outside the West Virginia State Police Crime Lab in South Charleston. The metal emergency door opened, and Pete Linville peered out cautiously. The detective flashed a smile and his police shield. Linville nodded and beckoned Bonamico inside.

"Hurry. You shouldn't be here after normal business hours."

The detective nearly tripped on the waifish criminalist's long, white coat as they stepped into the crime lab.

"I examined the evidence."

One of the main traits Bonamico liked most about Linville is that he was all business all the time. Not much for small talk, he preferred as little human interaction as possible. Not because he didn't like people, but because it cut into his lab time.

Linville led Bonamico through a swinging glass door and into a cinderblock room full of lab tables overflowing with microscopes and computers. A state-of-the-art mass spectrometer, the jewel of the lab, sat prominently on the main table in the middle of the room.

"What's the good news?"

"I examined the mud from your crime scene and compared it to the mud on the scrubs."

"And?"

"It's blue mud, which is a deep-sea sediment of fine silt and clay. It derives its name from the bluish color caused by organic material and iron sulfide. The samples match right down to the particulate debris. I can even tell you what area of the county the mud came from. I've got my report in the file here," Linville said as he nodded toward a manila file folder in the center of the lab table.

A burst of energy rushed through Bonamico. "You're

amazing! Thanks!" The detective grabbed the report and dashed from the lab.

CHAPTER 55

Ben's hands frantically clawed at the chain, but they repeatedly slipped from the muddy links. Ronan pulled the chain tighter until a gasp escaped Ben's lips, and his body grew slack. His anger and strength spent, Ronan gratefully released the chain that once bound him and now bound Ben for all eternity.

"Rot in hell!" Ronan spat as he turned his back on Ben and waded to the shore.

Just as Ronan reached the edge of the pond, a muddy hand grabbed him by the throat and yanked him back into the mire. Ronan struggled to stay upright as he wildly punched at the man he thought dead. Bodies twisted and bobbed, sinking together into the darkness. Only their heads remained above the surface now, but Ronan knew the pond wasn't that much deeper. He could feel the sole of his boot scrape against the chain coiled below.

Thrusting his boot into the unseen depths, he tried to grab the chain with his foot. Again and again, the metal links wound around his boot only to slip away as the chain was dragged downward. Ronan's leg cramped from exhaustion, but he continued. Finally, he wound the chain around his foot twice and carefully pulled it up until it was only inches away from his anxious hands. With a deep breath

Ronan plunged into the mud and grabbed the chain. He popped back to the surface, his body completely covered in the blue goo, and slung the chain around Ben's neck once more.

Ben squirmed from side to side, desperately trying to suck in one last breath before his trachea collapsed beneath the weight and force of the metal noose.

"Die, you sonofabitch," Ronan shouted, leaning back with all of his might. Again Ben's

body went limp, but Ronan waited for any further sound or movement. After what seemed like a lifetime, he let the chain slip from his hand, and Ben slowly disappeared into the mud.

———

"Unit 3. Come in, Unit 3. Officer Howard, what is your location?" came the no-nonsense voice across the radio.

The young deputy smiled as he heard the lovely voice. His wife had just gotten the dispatch job, and this was her first call.

"I've just finished my coffee and donuts," Patrick Howard replied. "Over."

"Please be advised, Officer Howard, breakfast will be served at 0700 hours. Over."

"10-4. Returning to headquarters now."

"Copy that, Unit 3."

Howard replaced the radio handset in its cradle and slowly pulled his squad car out of the small convenience store's parking lot and headed toward Madison. The sun was just peaking over the horizon, and he was more than ready for his shift to end at 0600. Route 17 was still fairly quiet, and Howard enjoyed this time of the morning even more now that Carolyn would be waiting for him. The honeymoon phase was still in full swing since their wedding in early June.

As he concentrated on the road ahead, Howard saw a figure emerge from the woods that paralleled the road. The figure stumbled and weaved, and the young officer sighed. "Great! A 10-39!"

Pulling closer to the pedestrian, he was startled to see the man covered in what appeared to be blue-colored mud. Howard hit his siren. A whoop, whoop—accompanied by flashing red and blue lights—sounded, breaking the early-morning silence.

Ronan instantly stopped, turned around and then collapsed to the ground.

CHAPTER 56

Ronan sat back in the plush chair. He'd never been inside a suite at the Charleston Town Center Marriott before, but his first impressions were positive. The room was large and spacious with plenty of room for sleeping, working and living. An in-suite kitchen with a sink, dishware and utensils, stove, pots and pans, microwave, and fridge completed the room. Since his arrival, Ronan had happily helped himself to the complimentary candy bars, chips and nuts, as well as the soda and beer, both kept to a frosty-cold temperature in the mini-bar next to the 52-inch flat-screen TV.

He wiggled his toes against the plush carpeting. The velvety texture felt good, and helped him forget his injured ankles, which were now heavily bandaged and taped just like his wrists. A soft thumping sound came from the suite's front door, and Ronan padded across the room and answered without looking through the keyhole.

"Hey! Hungry yet?" Ty asked, the smile on his face as bright as the summer day outside.

"Nope. Not really. I've been snacking," Ronan replied with a grin as he opened the door.

Ty looked at the candy wrappers wadded up in Ronan's burly hand. "You're nothing but a big kid."

"What? I have a sweet tooth. And speaking of sweet," Ronan said as he pulled Ty into his powerful embrace. "I think I could use a little of your sugar."

Ty blushed.

Ronan dropped the candy wrappers and cupped Ty's face with both hands and kissed him with all the love he had in his heart. He couldn't imagine a life without this man. "I'm so happy just to be with you."

Ty stroked the top of Ronan's hands with his own. "Me too. How are you feeling?"

Ronan grimaced a bit as he walked back to the chair and sat down with a grunt. "Sore. I feel like all of the muscles in my body were ripped out, stomped on and then shoved back inside me with a bulldozer."

"That good?"

"I can't complain though. My medical care has been excellent, and the pain meds are great."

When another knock came at the door, Ty answered it. "Oh, my God! Ronan, look!"

Ronan pressed both hands into the seat of the chair and strained to pull himself up. By the time he steadied himself, Melissa had flung her arms around his broad shoulders and was hugging him tightly.

"Oh, Ronan. I've been so worried. I'm so glad you're okay."

"A little worse for wear, but I'm going to be fine."

Melissa stepped back, and Ronan wiped away a trickling tear from her cheek with his thumb. She looked exhausted; deep, dark rings ran beneath her eyes, and her face was drawn, but she still looked better than the last time he'd seen her—chained to a chair like a wild animal.

"Tell Bruce thanks for the accommodations."

A faint smile crossed her face. "I told him we were going to enjoy ourselves while the house was cleaned and repaired from the…" Her voice trailed off as she looked away.

Ronan lifted her chin with a finger to meet his gaze. "It's okay. It's over now."

"Uncle Ronan!"

"Nick, uh…how, I mean…" Ronan said as he spun toward the sound of his nephew's voice.

Nick and Braxton Campbell ambled into the living room with huge smiles on both their faces.

"I presented the evidence to the judge this morning. Nick was released from custody shortly thereafter," Campbell said matter-of-factly.

"I don't understand…"

"It was Eric," Ty said, resting a hand on Ronan's chest.

"Ty's right," Campbell confirmed. "Sergeant Bonamico pursued your hunch, Ronan. It turns out you were right. The mud at the crime scene was a match to the mud on Ty's scrubs, and both samples were identical to the blue mud from the pond where Connors died. Oh, and we found Connors' car keys. They were in his pocket. Too bad they hadn't been left in his truck—you could have saved yourself that long trek through the woods."

"You're right about that," Ronan said, looking at his bandaged ankles. "But, hey, I'll survive. The main thing is Raina Dalton's murder has been solved. We got justice for Michael Warner, and we know that Connors paid the price for their deaths."

"Indeed. Well, if you'll excuse me, I have a meeting with a new client in about an hour from now."

As Campbell prepared to leave, Ronan called out to him. Melissa walked alongside her brother as he approached the attorney.

"I can't thank you enough for helping my family."

"My pleasure," he replied with a wink.

Melissa pulled Campbell down by the neck and kissed him on the cheek. "Thank you for helping my son."

Campbell grinned and turned to leave the room but encountered Bonamico on the way in as he was on the way out.

"Am I too late for the happy reunion?"

This time it was Eric who was intercepted with a hug, this one by Ronan. "Thanks, man. For everything."

The detective held the half-hug for a moment and then

slapped Ronan on the back. "Don't mention it. You'd do the same for me."

"Damn right."

"I need to speak with you privately."

"Sure," Ronan replied and led Bonamico to the bedroom.

Ty, Nick and Melissa watched as the two men disappeared from view.

"What's up?" Ronan asked as he sat down on the king-size bed.

"CPD and the feds raided the Mitchell property earlier this afternoon. Cadaver dogs found two bodies buried in a shallow grave behind a shed near the cabin. No IDs and no weapons were found."

"Doesn't surprise me."

"The good news is folders with cargo manifests and krok-shipment schedules, along with the supply points in Detroit, were found in the cabin. We have the whole enchilada, Ronan. Names, aliases, bank accounts—everything! Apparently, the head honcho of the cartel is a guy named Dominic Purcell. The feds arrested him a few hours ago at his summer home in Tawas," Bonamico said, but then his smile quickly turned to a frown.

"Why so glum, chum? That's great news."

"But," Bonamico replied with a slight catch in his voice.

"But what?"

"Connors' prints were run for an official ID. They had a hit in AFIS."

"And?"

"The prints belong to a career criminal named Paul Bennington. He's part of middle-management in the Midwest drug cartel."

"So, Connors had an alias."

"There were two blood types found at the Dalton crime scene. Obviously, one belonged

to Raina Dalton, but the other didn't belong to Bennington."

Ronan frantically processed the information. "If it

wasn't Ben Connors'...I mean Paul Bennington's blood, I wonder whose blood it was."

"I haven't a clue, but I'm thinking the bloody letters were a calling card."

"Could it have been Purcell? Maybe his alias is Nic. Short for Dominic. He could have been with Bennington when the killing went down and took the knife from him to dispose of it and was cut in the process."

"That's a good theory."

"But Purcell's in federal custody, so his DNA should be on file. What's the problem?"

"Apparently, Purcell and his attorney traded clothes during their meeting with one another today. When officers went to return Purcell to his cage, they found Alex Booth instead. Purcell's vanished."

"Vanished?"

"Like a fragile, brilliant thought, my friend."

A LOOK AT:

DOUBLE-CROSSED

From the award-winning author of Fragile Brilliance comes another gripping Ronan McCullough mystery.

Recovering from the emotional and physical damage of his last case, Ronan McCullough is trying to put his life back together. But when a federal agent's charred remains surface, linked to a professor's encrypted money laundering scheme, Ronan becomes embroiled in a high-stakes game of life and death with someone who is willing to kill everyone that knows anything about the encryption codes.

Ronan soon uncovers several dark secrets and learns that nobody is being honest with him, including the people he trusts the most. When the encryption codes are stolen and Ronan learns their real purpose, he finds himself in a race to stop a plan that will make it nearly impossible to stop the funding of dangerous crimes.

How will Ronan succeed when the main suspects is a set of numbers? Dive into this heart-pounding thriller today and experience the adrenaline-fueled ride of Double-Crossed.

AVAILABLE AUGUST 2024

ACKNOWLEDGMENTS

I wanted to write this type of a novel for a long time. The plot and the characters drifted into and out of my consciousness for a while, before taking a firm hold in my thoughts a few years ago. As I wavered back and forth with the decision, several people encouraged me along the way and helped convince me that this book was worth writing.

I am thankful for the support of my family, who always encourage me to write the stories I want to tell. My friends and fellow writers in the Patchwork Writers Group have also been instrumental in keeping me motivated to finish the book, especially when life-issues crept into my writing and revising time.

The support and encouragement of several writing mentors was also invaluable during writing this book and through every other writing experience I've ever undertaken, so to Amanda Eyre Ward, Skip Horack, Jim Grimsley, Bob Johnson, Young Smith, Julie Hensley, Nancy Jensen, Derek Nikitas, and John Herrick, I want to express my sincere gratitude for your teaching and your friendship.

Brian Tucker, Jesse Wooten, Travis Roman, John Banner, Lindsay Frantz, and Joey-Lee Campbell provided lots of laughs, good vibes, and friendly conversation and visits when I needed a "brain break" to refocus my energy. Also, Carter Taylor Seaton, John Patrick Grace, Laura Tracey Bentley, Marie Manilla, Sandy Tritt, Sheila Redling, and Chip Gue listened to me just talk about whatever was on my mind as this book progressed.

Countless hours of attention and assistance were provided by my friend and editor Brette O'Connell. Her experience and knowledge as a former police forensic investigator taught me so much about the forensic processes of police investigation and her attention to detail led to the completion and accuracy of the book. Thanks to Mike Valentino for helping me with more writing guidance on this book than I could ever repay, and thanks to my uncle, Scott Perry, a cop in Atlanta whose experiences in law enforcement found their way into the book, in some form or another.

Also, I want to thank the various law-enforcement officers who shared with me their stories about working in law enforcement. These brave men and women go through more physical and psychological stress everyday than most people realize. Several of the police officers and their stories were the inspiration for some of the characters and events in the novel and I appreciate their time and openness in sharing their stories with me.

I owe a great deal of thanks to the public-information officers and their staffs at several West Virginia state government agencies, including: The West Virginia Parkways Authority, the West Virginia Board of Education, Kanawha County Schools, the West Virginia Division of Tourism, the West Virginia Department of Agriculture, and the West Virginia State Police. The information provided to me from these departments helped ensure that the settings in the book were correct and accurate. Also, thanks goes to journalist Joshua Miller, whose articles and research on krokodil helped me understand the dangerous and lethal drug

Finally, a special thanks goes out to you, the reader. Time and money are precious items in our society today. If you spent money and time on this book, I appreciate it so much. Your efforts are not taken for granted.

ABOUT THE AUTHOR

Eliot Parker is a graduate of the Bluegrass Writers Studio at Eastern Kentucky University with a M.F.A. in Creative Writing and a graduate of Murray State University with a Doctorate in English. Hw teaches writing that the University of Mississippi.

He is the author of five thriller novels and a collection of short stories. His short story collection Snapshots won the 2021 Pencraft and Feathered Quill Book Awards for outstanding short story anthology. His thriller novel Fragile Brilliance was a finalist for the Southern Book Prize in Thriller Writing.

His other works have been Amazon #1 bestsellers and have earned the honor of being named "Best Books to Discover" by Kirkus Magazine. Eliot has received the West Virginia Literary Merit Award for his works and was inducted into the inaugural class of the West Virginia Literary Recognition Hall of Fame for outstanding contributions to West Virginia and Appalachian Literature.

www.ingramcontent.com/pod-product-compliance
Lightning Source LLC
Chambersburg PA
CBHW011757010726
47497CB00013B/3247